P9-DGP-491

The

Sword-Edged Blonde

The
Sword-Edged
Blonde

Alex Bledsoe

TOR®
fantasy

A TOM DOHERTY ASSOCIATES BOOK
NEW YORK

NOTE: If you purchased this book without a cover, you should be aware
that this book is stolen property. It was reported as "unsold and destroyed"
to the publisher, and neither the author nor the publisher has received any
payment for this "stripped book."

This is a work of fiction. All of the characters, organizations, and events
portrayed in this novel are either products of the author's imagination or are
used fictitiously.

THE SWORD-EDGED BLONDE

Copyright © 2007 by Alex Bledsoe

Originally published in 2007 by Night Shade Books.

All rights reserved.

A Tor Book
Published by Tom Doherty Associates, LLC
175 Fifth Avenue
New York, NY 10010

www.tor-forge.com

Tor® is a registered trademark of Tom Doherty Associates, LLC.

ISBN 978-0-7653-6203-2

First Tor Edition: July 2009

Printed in the United States of America

0 9 8 7 6 5 4 3 2 1

For Tia Sisk

A long time ago in the swampy west end of Tennessee, an awkward teenage boy wanted to impress the hot new teacher and hoped this story would do it. He never got the nerve to show it to her then; he hopes she likes it now.

SPECIAL THANKS TO:

The ever-helpful:

My wife, Valette, Jake, and Charlie

My mom, Grace

Marlene Stringer, the best and most patient agent

Jason (no Shatner!) Williams, the editor who got it

The ever-faithful:

Virginia Alexander

Lisa Marie Brodsky

Jo Carol and Jim Crisp

Thomas Kopp

Lisa Krupa

Lucy Mogensen

Mary Ann Sabo

Christi Underdown

Sarah Vermillion

The past and present members of Moon's Inkwell

The
Sword-Edged
Blonde

ONE

Spring came down hard that year. And I do mean hard, like the fist of some drunken pike poker with too much fury and not enough ale, whose wife just left him for some wandering minstrel and whose commanding officer absconded with his pay. The thunderstorms alone would be talked about for years, and the floods that followed erased whole towns along the Gusay River. Nature, as always, had the last word.

I worked in a small town in Muscodia back then, out of an office above a dockside tavern. Located on the Gusay midway between the capital city of Sevlow and the border town Pema, Neceda was a place you stopped when you weren't in a hurry, for a drink, dinner or quick companionship. Only about three hundred people lived there, but at any one time the transients tended to double that population. The money that flowed into town didn't stay there, though, so Neceda always looked rundown and disreputable. It was a good place for someone like me, a private sword jockey with a talent for discretion, to quietly ply his trade. Clients liked coming to a small town where they could pass unrecognized. Some days were lucrative, most were not, but it all evened out at the end.

The flood and its aftermath had essentially shut Neceda down, and that had created a crisis of conscience among the population. Suddenly a bunch of bottom-feeding strangers had to act like an actual community, and it was amusing to watch people interact who normally wouldn't: whores and moon priestesses did laundry together, blacksmiths and cardsharps repaired buildings, soldiers and beggars rounded up stray animals and children. I helped sandbag the tavern below, and we'd gotten off pretty light; except for the smell, there wasn't much damage, which said more about the place than the flood. The river was now mostly back within its banks, and soon would subside enough for normal transportation to resume. Then Neceda would be back to its old rapacious self.

My "office" consisted of two rooms in the attic over the kitchen, one always open with a bench against the wall in case anyone decided they needed to wait. I kept the inner office locked, but there was really no reason for it; it merely gave an illusion of confidentiality, which on most days was enough.

That illusion was definitely enough for the well-worn emissary from King Felix of Balaton now seated across from me explaining his master's needs. I wasn't surprised that the king himself hadn't come, but at first it amused me that he'd trusted this tired old man with something of, shall we say, such surpassing delicacy. Still, as he related the situation, I understood why he'd been chosen. The very thought of describing the way Princess Lila had gone off to be a girl-toy for a bunch of randy border raiders left him too embarrassed to even meet my eyes. Any other man might've been too tempted to make bad jokes, but not this one. He'd been trusted with a job, and he was going to carry it out as best he could.

"So as you can see, Mr. LaCrosse, the princess could not possibly have had any intention of, ahem, joining these young men, so she must have been taken against her will. A noble daughter of the house of Balaton would never simply take up with vermin of this sort." He took a long pull on the drink I'd poured from my office bottle.

Behind my desk, I kept my face neutral and said nothing. Nervous people hate silence, so I knew eventually he'd start talking again. In the meantime, I studied him: about sixty, thin and frail-looking, but with traces of a much larger, stronger man left in the set of his jaw and the way he sat up sharply each time he caught himself slumping. A soldier once, maybe even a high-ranking officer, now reduced to an errand boy.

I took pity on him and broke the silence. "So what did the guys in the pointy hats have to say about it?" I asked.

"I beg your pardon?"

"The king's wizards." I'd only known two or three kings who didn't rely on wizards for decisions. Some couldn't put on their royal slippers without checking the stars' alignment, and rumor claimed that our own King Archibald, the ruler of Muscodia, had one who read the pattern of mucus in his handkerchief each time he sneezed. I'd heard that King Felix kept three wizards and a moon priestess on retainer for emergencies, and the disappearance of the princess certainly qualified. "They're supposed to see the future. Didn't they see it coming?"

"They claim," he said without looking at me, "that the future is murky at this time, and beyond their power to envision."

"Convenient."

"Yes. Their failure is one reason I've been sent to hire you." He shifted nervously in his chair. "We've had no demands for ransom, nor any threats if royal policy isn't changed, so I don't believe it was a politically motivated crime. Still, King Felix doesn't wish word to get out that his family is so, uhm . . . easily swayed, whether by force or, uh, conversion. You can understand that, can't you?"

"Would be kind of hard to hold your head up around all the other kings," I agreed. If he caught my sarcasm, he didn't mention it.

He finally raised his eyes to mine and said, "Then I hope I—I mean, *we*—can trust your discretion on this."

"The royal 'we'?" I asked, and this time the irony stuck.

"This is a serious matter, Mr. LaCrosse." His voice grew stronger now that he wasn't talking about the exploits of sex-crazed fifteen-year-old princesses. "I was told that you understood these things, and could be trusted."

"Yeah?" I leaned back and laced my fingers together over my stomach, which seemed larger than the last time I'd done so. "Who by?"

"Commander Bernard Teller of the Civil Security Force of Boscobel."

I smiled. "So Bernie made commander, huh?" Bernie was no-nonsense, tough as nails and way too honest to ever get promoted so high. If he had, then things in Boscobel had changed for the better. "Well, did he also tell you I get twenty-five gold pieces a day, plus expenses?"

He produced a small pouch that jingled distinctively. "I have been instructed to give you 200 gold pieces now, with another 200 upon successful completion of the job."

I leaned over and took the pouch, which was too heavy not to be genuine. "Let's be clear on exactly what constitutes 'successful completion.'"

"The return of the princess to her father."

"Intact?" I pressed. We both knew what I meant.

"In any condition. He just wants her back before anyone finds out about this."

I opened the pouch and took out fifty of the small gold coins, then pushed the bag back across my desk to him. "I don't need the whole amount now, just enough for a couple of days' travel to the border to look for these guys you say she ran off with. Pay me the balance when she's back in her own canopied bed."

He looked at me oddly for a moment, but didn't argue. As he stood, I asked suddenly, "So tell me—why'd she leave?"

"I beg your pardon?"

"Princess Lila. There must've been a reason. Spoiled rich girls don't usually go to that much trouble to get away from home."

"As I told you—"

"You told me she ran off to get laid by some rough boys. In my experience, rich girls don't have much trouble with that, and they don't throw away their meal tickets just for a night of slap-and-tickle. So why'd she leave?"

"The princess is . . . headstrong. As was her late

mother." He seemed to feel that this was enough explanation.

"Do you have a picture? I'd hate to show up with the wrong girl."

The old man produced a small engraved image of a dark-haired, dark-eyed beauty. She wore a low-cut court gown that revealed her assets quite nicely; her liabilities were less obvious. She had a pronounced, sharp nose that gave her an earthy air at odds with her finery. "Kids these days," I said, and pocketed the picture.

After the old man had gone, I swung my chair around and looked out the window toward the river. The odor of drying mud and dead fish filled the air. It would take several normal rains to get all the crap off the streets, and in the meantime the thought of a little time away from home, even if it meant tangling with border raiders, seemed like a good idea.

I studied the girl's picture. This missing princess could be one of two types. The first kind, protected and sheltered from the harsh realities of the world, retained their childhood innocence throughout their lives, and were unconditionally honest, kind and loving no matter what the world threw at them. I'd known at least one princess like that.

The other kind, much more common, grew up spoiled, selfish and arrogant. Where I needed to look for this one depended on which type she was.

I knew King Felix's elderly messenger hadn't told me everything; clients like him never do. But I suspected the pieces of the truth were there in the information he'd given, and I'd have the whole trip downriver to put them together. It was another reason I didn't take all his money; I'd agreed to find the girl, and I would, but I wasn't ready to promise what would happen after that.

I opened the sword cabinet and took out my old Fireblade Warrior three-footer, the one with the narrow dagger hidden in the hilt. I had bigger swords, but this one wouldn't attract attention and, since I'd filed the distinctive Fireblade monogram off the blade, it looked a lot more fragile and decrepit than it actually was. I slipped it into the shoulder scabbard and strapped it across my back, outside my jacket.

I grabbed the basics for a short overnight trip and threw them into a saddlebag. I put five pieces of gold in my pocket and the remainder in the hollow heel of my right boot. Then I locked up the inner office and went downstairs.

Angelina looked up from washing the mugs. It was just after lunch, so there were only a couple of men drinking, and neither of them seemed to require much of her attention. Angelina was not young, although she was beautiful in a way that only grew stronger the more time you spent with her. She could've done much better for herself than owning this ratty tavern where she endured the occasional gropes and rudeness in return for respectable tips. I knew she was hiding out from something, but it was none of my business. We all have secrets.

Callie, her teenage waitress, stood at the end of the bar carefully arranging a small ring of pebbles around a tiny metal cup. When she finished that, she cautiously measured powder into it. She kept referring to a scrap of vellum covered in red lettering beside it. Her lips moved as she read.

"What are you doing?" I asked. Callie was a beautiful

girl, but I'd seen elderly glowworms that were brighter.

"A spell for no more rain," she said as she worked. "I'm tired of cleaning the mud out from between my toes every night."

"A spell?" I repeated. "So are you studying to be a moon priestess now, Callie?"

"No, but I got this from one. It only cost me three pieces of gold, too."

"Bought spells aren't worth the blood they're written in," Angelina said disdainfully.

Callie looked up, annoyed. "Yeah, well, I bought it to stop the rain, and it hasn't rained since."

"So a teenage barmaid can now control the weather," Angelina snorted. "What will they think of next?"

"Everyone knows you're bitter, Angie, but it gets tired after a while," Callie snapped. "*I'm* trying to make a difference in the world, not just bitch about it."

Angelina wasn't impressed. "Make a difference at the corner booth, why don't you? Those plates won't collect themselves. Oh, unless you bought a spell for that, too. Maybe I'm paying you too much, if you can throw money around like that."

Callie's eyes filled with tears. "Angie, you're just mean," she said. She gathered her little spell and stomped off into the kitchen.

I looked at Angelina. "That *was* mean."

For an instant regret flashed in her eyes, then they hardened over. "I don't need waitresses who still believe in magic. Their religion should be tips and serving customers."

"You don't believe in magic?"

She snorted. "And you do?"

"I believe in possibility."

"Name one magical thing you've ever seen."

"Why, you in the firelight, Angel."

She barked a laugh at me, then turned back to washing. "So, are you going out of town?" she asked.

"Yeah. Should be back day after tomorrow at the latest."

"Have something to do with that old rattletrap who came down a little while ago?"

"Where you from, Angel?"

She grinned and winked over her shoulder. "Right. No questions, no lies. Well, watch yourself. You're ugly enough without more scars."

"And you be nicer to Callie. A lot of people come in here just to watch her bend over and pick things up."

TWO

The streets of Neceda swarmed with activity. Women and children cleaned the walls of the buildings, while men worked to level out the mud in the road so it would dry faster. A few wagons braved the terrain, but most of them ended up stuck, and the horses clearly understood the futility of working too hard to get free. I crossed the road on a plank, and as I walked down the opposite side a voice said, "Excuse me, sir, can you help a poor stranded pilgrim of Eludo?"

I turned. A beggar stood, hand out, under the eave of an apothecary shop. He was middle-aged, with long gray hair in two braids down his shoulders and a neat pointed beard on his chin. His cheeks were smooth. He wore an old cloak tattered at the edges, and his feet were wrapped in rags. On a long chain around his neck hung the symbol of the Eludo religion, a two-headed owl. I said, "You're not poor. You're not stranded. And you're no pilgrim of Eludo."

He blinked in surprise, sputtered a moment and then began, "Sir, I promise you—"

I held up my hand. "You had a shave this morning. That couldn't have been cheap with the town in this shape. All the barbers are busy tending the sick and mopping out their shops. If you've got gold to waste on personal grooming, then you probably can afford passage out of town, and you're only stranded because everyone else is. And Eludo pilgrims, as a rule, don't worry about either shaving or moving; they believe their all-seeing owl god will provide. So now I have a question for you: Why would a wealthy man be begging on the street like this?"

He'd grown progressively paler as I spoke, and now was bone-white. "I have no idea what you mean," he stammered.

"Let me tell you what you don't have any idea about," I said. I grabbed his cloak, jerked him close and used the snarl that once made a young crossbowman wet his pants. "You got the money to afford that expensive shave by finding out who in town would donate to an Eludo pilgrim. When you identified those folks, your pals down the street or around the corner would watch for your signal, follow the mark until the right moment and then induce them to give an even bigger donation, probably at knife-point. That's your trade, pal, and I understand that, but I don't care how thick the mud is, you better get your ass out of town before I see you again. Understand?"

He nodded, rapidly and emphatically. He'd retained bladder control, but I still felt I'd made an impression. I let him go.

Something sent a tingle up my spine. I looked behind me in time to see a man duck inside a butcher shop. I got an impression of someone young and well-dressed, which was as out of place in Neceda as a spider on a fairy cake. The first obvious thought was that it was the phony pilgrim's partner, but I didn't get the same grubby sense from him. I considered investigating, but it would take time, and I might just be paranoid to think he was watching me. Maybe he just wondered why I was slapping around a pilgrim of Eludo.

My feet *splock-splock*ed over the mud as I went down an alley and emerged along the dockside road. A big empty flatboat sat moored at the end of one pier, awaiting a cargo commission. Extra lines tied it to the dock, since the current was still raging. Most boats, I knew, wouldn't even attempt the river at this level.

A barrel-chested, dark-skinned man sat on a chair next to one of the pylons, puffing on a pipe and watching the water. He looked up as I approached.

"Eddie LaCrosse, the town's favorite blade-basher. Here to enjoy the lovely spring breeze?"

"I need a ride, Sharky," I said, and draped my saddlebags across the dock's rail. "Down to Pema. No cargo, just me."

"That's not really worth my trouble, is it?" Sharky said. He gestured toward his boat. "Your ass is big, but it ain't so big it needs a cargo boat. Go down and wait for the ferry like everyone else."

"The ferry won't run with the river this high."

"And you think my boat will? With just a single passenger?"

"I think it will because you're the best pilot in town, and you and me both know there's not any cargo to be had. I got three gold pieces with your name on 'em to prove it." I jingled my pocket for emphasis.

That got his attention, as well as the eye of a shifty character shoveling mud from the back of a nearby house. I turned and faced him, and he quickly returned to his task. Most of the lowlifes in town knew me, and while they certainly didn't tremble at my name, they had enough sense not to try anything in broad daylight, especially when I had Sharky as back-up.

"Keep wavin' that money around, somebody's likely to wave back with something sharper," Sharky said.

"So come on, just a quick run down to Pema. You don't even have to wait on me, I'll rent a horse for the trip back."

"Why don't you just *buy* a horse like everyone else?"

"Then I'd be deprived of your charming company."

"Huh." But he stood and gestured mock-grandly for me to step aboard the barge. I took a seat on one of the stools nailed to the deck and usually reserved for the crew.

"Wait a minute," he said, and stepped off the boat. I watched the tan-colored, opaque river as it slid by, its passage marked by foam and debris. When I turned, Sharky was leading two horses onto the boat, along with a sleepy-eyed boy of about ten.

"You need them?" I said.

"That's exactly what I asked him," the boy yawned.

"Not you, Kenny. Them." I despised horses, which was why I didn't own one.

"Have you *looked* at the river?" Sharky said. "Yes, I need them, and I need this worthless manure pile . . . " He smacked Kenny on the back of his head, not brutally but almost with affection. ". . . to guide them while I steer the boat. I ain't poling this thing back upstream against this current." Horses and mules were common sights when the Gusay was at its normal depth, hauling flatboats upstream along the riverfront roads. Sharky dropped two long coils of rope beside me that would be used to tie the horses to the boat. "You're getting a bargain here at any price; don't give me a hard time."

"Fine," I said, making no effort to hide my disgust. I caught the eye of one of the horses, a jet-black mare with two white socks. She regarded me with cool contempt, something all horses held for me.

Well, not all. I suddenly recalled one horse, in a forest a long time ago, who had a completely different look in her eye. I hadn't thought about that horse in years, or about the woman in the cottage I met soon after. I shook my head and made myself return to the present, and the task at hand.

Sharky cast off the ropes and shoved the flatboat away from the dock. The water, as thick as syrup with mud and debris, carried us slowly into the middle of the stream. When the current finally caught us it nearly knocked me off my seat. The horses, old hands at this, adjusted their balance with a minimum of hoof-clopping. Kenny curled up like a cat and went back to sleep.

"Can't promise you a smooth ride," Sharky said, "so be ready for anything. And I hope you can swim."

"Can you?" I asked, bracing myself as best I could.

"Hell, no," he cackled. "That's why I won't let my boat sink. But it also means I can't rescue your sorry ass if you fall off."

Sharky stood at the rudder, and Neceda receded in our wake. I thought I glimpsed the same young, well-dressed man suddenly appear at the foot of the dock, then turn and rush away. But I hadn't really seen him clearly before, so I couldn't say for sure it was him now. Maybe it was just some guy needing his corn shipped to market.

I took the engraving from my pocket and tried to memorize it; I didn't think I'd have time to hold it next to the face of every ready-to-go girl I'd meet. I looked into her eyes, and tried to get inside her head.

Fifteen was awfully young to jump the wall and run off, especially for a princess of the House of Balaton. What *would* induce her to do such a thing? Despite her palace isolation, I couldn't believe the girl in this picture would be susceptible to such naive daydreams. And even accepting the engraver's artistic liberties, there was real intelligence in the rueful set of her smile, the way her eyes didn't have that popped-open blankness of so many royal children. She had to know that most border raiders were not romantic ruffians, that they'd have her bent over the nearest fence rail at the first opportunity and most likely leave her dead in a ditch soon after.

"Who's the doll?" Sharky asked from behind me.

"Runaway," I said, and put the picture away. "Daddy wants her back."

"Never figured you for a baby-sitter."

"Never figured you for a busybody."

He clutched his heart in mock-offense. "Oh, you wound me, Eddie." Then he scowled at something on the bank. "But if I wasn't a busybody, I wouldn't have noticed *that*."

I followed his discreet little nod with an equally surreptitious glance. A lone rider traveled the towing road that ran parallel to the river. He was far enough back that I couldn't see his face, but his demeanor told me it was the same man who'd watched us at the dock. "Following us?" I said.

"Yep. With the river this high, I can't ride the main current, and we ain't exactly makin' record time. He could've passed us a while back if he wanted."

"You owe anybody money?" I asked.

"Sure. But nobody who's that desperate to get it."

There was no way to lose our new shadow, so I simply put him aside until we reached the border. I returned my thoughts to the emotions of a beautiful spoiled fifteen-year-old, pondering what could make her run away like that. I pulled out one of the coins and idly turned it in my fingers. Like most money, it had the king's profile on one side, and I perused it to get insight into the kind of father King Felix might be. Was he so strict his daughter fled his discipline? Or so perverted she ran from his embrace?

His proud, piggish face gave me no answers. But suddenly a new thought struck me: maybe I was looking at it backwards. I took the drawing from my pocket and held it up beside the coin. Had I stumbled onto something crucial in this father-daughter relationship? What if she hadn't run *away* at all?

WE ARRIVED AT Pema in the dark and docked at the torch-lit wharf only long enough for me to disembark. Sharky immediately moved his horses off the boat for the trip back to Neceda. It took three solid kicks to awaken Kenny, who sleepily went to his duties. Sharky had made enough money off me that he'd still turn a nice profit, so I didn't feel too bad about putting him to so much trouble and making him return to Neceda in the dark.

In contrast to Neceda, Pema was a jumping little burg that had escaped almost all flood damage behind its solid levee. Situated on the line between Muscodia and Balaton, its border-town vibe attracted people the way dogs drew fleas. Folks shipping goods up or down the river had to stop here to get their papers authorized, and legal travelers had to go through the security checkpoints for both countries. The town itself was wide open, and everything was for sale. That is, once you got through customs.

Balaton understood the old adage that good fences made good neighbors, and if you were caught without properly authorized papers, you could be executed on the spot. I was willing to risk a lot for the amount of gold King Felix provided, but not my head. I'd go through the official channels.

Unfortunately, at this time of night only one of the ten customs gates was open, creating a total bottleneck of people who'd arrived on passenger boats. These low-riding craft, all delayed by the flood, had arrived at the same time instead of on the normal staggered schedule. The passenger line extended down the hill to the docks, and I got there just ahead of a whole boatload of imported Fechinian well-diggers. They were herded into line by a pair of big, scarred foremen who liberally applied a sharp sword poke when one of the Fechinians acted up. I was behind a family from Ocento who appeared to be veteran travelers; between the three of them they had four bags and a wooden box slung beneath a carrying pole.

"Bowie, will you be still?" the Ocentian woman said as she fumbled for her traveling papers. The toddler squirmed in her arms like a minnow avoiding a fish-hook and whined at a pitch that could probably be heard back in Neceda. She shrugged apologetically at the rest of us. "I'm sorry, he just went through his purifying ritual and it's got him all jumpy."

Considering that the standard Ocentian "purifying" ritual involved male genital mutilation, I didn't wonder. I noticed the father had the sad, haunted look I'd seen on other men from Ocento, and he made no move to help his wife. She clearly carried the mace and shield in the family.

Once their pass was stamped, they moved with the precision of a military operation. The husband picked up three of the four bags and one end of the pole, and his wife got the other end and the remaining bag. Bowie crawled up onto his mother's shoulders like a trained monkey, and started yanking on her hair with a happy giggle. She did not react.

At last it was my turn. The little gate was manned by a fat woman with way too much face paint, and hair that towered higher than the plume on a Dromelier cavalry helmet. A bored guard stood behind her, one hand on the hilt of his sword.

"And where are you from, friend?" the woman asked me. Her tone belied the friendliness of her words.

"Neceda. Up the river."

She propped her chin on one meaty palm. "I hear the flooding was pretty bad there."

"Bad enough."

She looked me over skeptically. I kept my face neutral. "And what brings you here?" she sighed, bored.

"I'm looking for a wife, and I hear the best place to meet one is right at the border."

She started to smile, then couldn't decide if I'd insulted her or not. "What the hell does that mean?"

"It means I'm too damned tired to barter with you," I said in a low voice. "Tell me how much you want, and I'll pay it and we can all get on with our lives."

"Are you offering to bribe me?" she demanded, her voice loud with false outrage. The Fechinians behind me began to murmur, and the customs guard looked up, suddenly interested at the possibility of action.

I just looked at her. She was only the latest in a lengthy roll of corrupt minor officials I'd encountered, and I'd learned long ago that the best thing to threaten them with was a break in the routine that would mean more work and uncomfortable explanations. Finally she scratched her forehead with two fingers, and I put two coins down when I bent to sign my pass. She stamped it with a wax seal, palming the money in the same motion. "This is good for three days. If the sun rises on the fourth day and finds you here, you'll be subject to arrest and immediate death by hanging."

"If I'm still here in four days, I'll hang *myself*," I said, and pushed through the narrow opening past the guard. He tried to trip me, but instead I locked his ankle with my own and threw him off-balance. He didn't fall, but he stumbled back into the fat woman who snapped in annoyance, "Harry, will you watch it, please? My *hair*."

THREE

Pema was what Neceda would be if King Archibald gave a rat's ass about anything beyond his castle walls and let real businessmen flourish. People and wagons traveled in unbroken lines in both directions on the cobblestoned main street. Every other building seemed to be a tavern, and most of those were also whorehouses; these would attract the newcomers, and if that didn't hold them, the gaming houses waited a little further down the street. Past them, though, would be the real rough part of town, home to the folks who made their living off the weary and unguarded travelers and knew how to slip across the border without niceties like travel papers. If they were in town, this was where I'd find my princess-snatching border thugs. If they weren't, a little money might grease someone's memory about where they could be found.

I appeared suitably bad-assed with my sword and general scruff, so I had not bothered with a disguise. I tossed my saddlebags over my shoulder and kept my eyes resolutely ahead. I knew what a real potential victim looked like, so I didn't look like one unless I meant to.

I passed an alley, and caught a peripheral glimpse of a mugging in progress. I considered aiding the victim, but he slammed one of the tough guys against the wall, and I heard the *snick* sound of a knife, followed by the wet gurgle of a cut throat. He whirled on the other mugger, dagger ready. He seemed to have it under control.

I'd gone half a block before I had the odd feeling that I knew the mugging victim from somewhere. I backtracked, but by then the whole encounter was over, and the alley was empty except for the sprawled body of one of the attackers.

The edge of town, and the businesses that catered to its denizens, was the first place to start looking for the kind of cocky border raiders who might kidnap a princess. I checked three disreputable and dangerous taverns before I reached a low-roofed building with only the words *RUM* and *GIRLS* painted on its sign. A pair of torches blazed on poles just outside the entrance. A dozen horses stood tied to the hitching posts, and from the size of their shitpiles, some of them had been there awhile. All had worn saddles and tack, but they'd been modified and personalized the way you do when you want to show off.

This rum joint had one big main room, with a small kitchen and stock area blocked off in the back. A bar ran the length of the wall to my left, and about ten small tables filled the open floor space. A bunch of those tables had been pulled together in the back corner, and were occupied by the owners of the horses. The hanging oil lamps along that stretch of the wall had been extinguished, creating a pool of relative darkness; I couldn't see them, but I knew at least some of them would check me out as soon as I walked through the door.

I let my shoulders slump and my gut stick out (easier to do the older I got) so I would appear no more than a poor weary traveler anxious for a drink and maybe a quick roll with one of the working girls. I shuffled to the bar and took an empty stool on the end. It wasn't the best vantage place, since it kept my back to the door, but if I'd chosen a better one, I might've given myself away. If I squinted, I had a pretty good view of the room in the long, smoke-stained mirror.

I counted ten big rough-looking hard boys in need of haircuts and shaves. They were armed with swords and knives, including some big two-hander blades that, if their wielders could actually lift them, would slice through a cow. A quick count of the empty mugs on the tables told me they'd been drinking a while, and that might take the edge off their skill. I wasn't going to bet on it, though.

"What'll you have, pal?" the bartender asked. Tattoos ran down his arms and his right eyelid drooped.

"Cheapest rum you got," I said, sounding like I'd been on the road for weeks. "I'm on a tight budget."

"Cheapest I got'll take off varnish," he said.

I shrugged. I had no intention of drinking it anyway. "Challenges make you a better person." He nodded and went to pour the drink.

I checked out the women milling around the tough guys. Like bars, bar whores tended to be the same everywhere. If they were under twenty-five, they still had that little hint of hope that some shining knight would rescue them from their life of degradation and despair. Over that age, they were either resigned to their fate, or they actually enjoyed the job and thus were always the happiest people in the room.

Five ladies sought the attention of the men in the corner. Three of them were not young enough to be my missing princess. The fourth had a bit too much flesh spilling over her bodice.

The last one sat demurely next to a big man who, in the dimness, looked familiar. I put it down as a trick of the firelight; although it wasn't impossible, the chances that I really knew the guy were pretty slim.

The bartender brought my drink, and I nonchalantly turned to survey the room, the way any traveler would. The demure girl's face wasn't any clearer from this angle, but she had the right kind of hair and looked about the right age to be my missing princess. Travelers from Gurius, Balaton's capital, might stop in here; it was pretty ballsy of these guys to bring their prisoner into a bar where she might be recognized, even dressed like a farm girl come to town.

At that moment the girl raised her head and said something to the man next to her. Damn if it wasn't her all right, Princess Lila of the Royal House of Balaton. She looked only slightly the worse for wear, although some kinds of wear wouldn't show. The man turned to answer her, and suddenly I knew why he had looked familiar, and why the princess had run away.

Lila stood and walked a bit unsteadily toward the door that led to the outhouses, clearly unused to whatever she'd been drinking. The man watched her the whole way.

I guess I wasn't as smooth as I thought, because the bartender suddenly appeared and cleared his throat. "Wouldn't stare at Ryan's girl if I was you," he said.

"If he don't want people to look, he shouldn't bring her to town," I said gruffly. I made myself take a sip of my drink for effect, and immediately wished I hadn't. It burned all the way down.

"I'll make sure they put that on your headstone," the bartender said, and walked away.

I gave the princess time to get settled on her throne, then threw down the rest of the drink and got to my feet. I hoped no one saw how red my face turned from the rum; I couldn't drink like a young man anymore.

I went out the same door, and in the moonlight saw four outhouses in a row at the end of a narrow stone walkway. Three of them were unoccupied; I threw open the door to the fourth.

Lila looked up sharply from her seat, and her eyes widened in surprise when she realized I was a man. One eye didn't widen as much as the other, due to the puffy, fading bruise around it. I said, "So this is the real story behind the 'Princess and the Pea.' "

"Who the hell are you?" she cried. She tried to pull down her skirt without standing. Then, more in control, she said, "There's three empty ones, you know."

"No, I'm in the right spot, Lila."

She froze, and glared at me. "I'm not going back," she said through her teeth.

"Yeah, I figured you'd say that." I wearily scratched my beard. "So who gave you the shiner?"

"Who do you think?" she muttered. "Would you mind turning around so I can get decent?"

"I didn't get to be this old turning my back on people. You just go ahead, I promise I won't enjoy it." And I didn't. Battered children don't do a thing for me.

While she adjusted her pantaloons and skirts I said, "So I guess we have a dilemma."

"I'm *not* going back," she repeated. The bruise around

her eye looked about three weeks old, right around the time she disappeared. "You can kill me, but you can't take me back to that place."

I hadn't quite made up my mind how to proceed, but there was no need for her to know that. "I've already taken some of their money."

She reached for a pouch at her waist. "I can pay you twice what they did—"

"Doesn't work that way." I took her chin gently and turned her face toward the light. "So who gave you the eye, really?"

"My father," she spat, and twisted out of my grasp.

"Which one?"

Before she could answer, my luck ran out. The tavern door behind me burst open, and the man who'd sat next to Lila strode out, followed by three other big, slightly drunk guys. I reached over my shoulder and grabbed the handle of my sword; I twisted the hilt, and the knife sprang into my hand. In the same moment I jerked Lila in front of me and put the point of the dagger to her throat. I backed into the outhouse.

"I'm sure you guys know the drill," I said to the man in front. "There's no way you can get me before I cut her throat, so don't even try. Swords and knives on the ground."

The four men complied at once; as professionals, they knew I was right. To Lila, who was very still in my arms, I said, "You didn't answer my question. Which one popped you in the eye?"

"That asshole who thought I was his daughter," she hissed.

"*Not* me," the man in front, who the bartender called Ryan, added helpfully. He smiled coldly beneath the distinctive nose that was identical to Lila's. She looked nothing at all like King Felix.

"That why you ran away?" I asked the girl, although my eyes stayed on the men.

"No, it was because I didn't get a pony for my birthday," she snapped. "Yes, it's why I left. The bastard never let me forget I wasn't his real child, and after he hit me I agreed with him."

"And you took her in?" I said to Lila's true father.

Ryan shrugged. "She's my daughter. Her mother wasn't always the queen."

I nodded, sighed and released Lila. Another job well done; I couldn't return her to her abusive royal household, and she certainly seemed in no danger here. She leaped into Ryan's arms. I slipped the knife back into the sword hilt, twisted it so it locked and then crossed my arms. "So that's that."

"Not quite," Ryan said. "You know where she is."

"Yeah," I agreed. "But I don't *care*."

"That's not much of a guarantee. Lila, go tell everybody to come out here." He gently guided her to one side; the men behind him took her and passed her out of the way back toward the tavern. The last I saw of her was a triumphant, murderous gleam in her eye as she went inside.

Now the outhouse seemed a *lot* smaller. None of us had weapons in our hands, but I was seriously outnumbered. "You realize this isn't necessary," I said. "I really *don't* care."

"Bet he got a fat fee for this," one of the other men said.

"Bet he's got it on him," another agreed.

Oboy. I started calculating the distance between

us, deciding whom to go for first, what parts of their bodies to aim at and what my last words were going to be.

"Whoa!" a new voice said. "It's a whole pissin' convention!"

A young guy with short, neat hair and clothes far too stylish for Pema stood in the tavern door. "Damn, fellas, I don't know if I can wait through this line. I gotta whiz like a racehorse."

"Use one of the others," Ryan said. "Or a damn tree. This is a private conversation."

The young guy frowned and took in the five of us. "That a fact?"

"It's a fact," Ryan said.

"Okay, okay, I get the hint." He turned his back to us and undid his pants, apparently intending to piss right there in the yard. When nothing happened immediately, the young man looked up sheepishly. "I think my trouser snake's got a little stage fright. You guys mind not lookin' at me?"

"Oh, for God's sake," Ryan said in exasperation, and for a moment all their attention was off me. I took the chance.

I kicked Ryan in the balls as hard as I could, the effect helped by the little metal toe cap inside my soft-looking boot. As he fell I grabbed the two men directly behind him by the hair and slammed their heads together. The *thonk* was satisfyingly loud, and they dropped like bags of wet sand.

Piss-boy, who'd been faking drunk, grabbed the last man and dispatched him with three quick blows in a style I instantly recognized. When he looked up from the crumpled form, I had my sword out and at the hollow of his throat. "Hey, buddy, I was just tryin' to help," he said nervously.

"Fasten your pants and tell me who the hell you are." This was the well-dressed man I'd seen in Neceda, and the mugging victim I'd passed earlier, waylaid as he shadowed me.

He didn't flinch, and his eyes held mine. "We've got about a minute before the princess brings the cavalry," he said without the country accent. "Just accept that I'm on your side. We can discuss why that is, later."

He had a point, so I sheathed the sword and followed him around the building to the row of tied horses. "You'll need a horse, too," he said as he leaped onto his animal.

I untied the one nearest the end. It was a big mare, and she regarded me with the same disdain I got from all females. I put my foot in the stirrup, then stopped. "My saddlebags are still in there."

"Get some new ones," he said as he expertly turned his horse toward the road.

"I need what's *in* them. I don't want to end up dangling from a gallows tree."

The young man scowled. "Mount up and wait here." He slid from his saddle and went in through the front door. When he ran back out a moment later, six of Ryan's men were right behind him. He gave a sharp whistle, tossed my bags at me and yelled, "*Go!*"

I kicked the horse hard, and she lurched forward into a ragged trot. In a moment the young man was beside me on his own mount.

"Mike Anders," he said, and actually offered me his hand.

"Eddie LaCrosse," I said. "But I figure you know that."

He glanced behind us. The rest of Ryan's gang had mounted up and wheeled into the street as a unit. They quickly closed the distance between us. "I think we need to get out of town," he said.

"No," I answered. "Follow me."

The big mare didn't protest as we rode into the crowds just past the docks. Here we could barely move, but neither could our pursuers. Still, we stood out plainly against the mostly pedestrian traffic. People bounced off my uncertain mount like logs shooting down the swollen river. Some of our pursuers dismounted and shoved through the crowd toward us, but their progress on foot was no faster.

"We've gotta ditch the horses," I said, and led us toward an alley.

"I don't *think* so," Anders protested. "Do you have any idea how long it took me to train this big guy?"

I didn't have time to argue. I led us between two buildings and onto the next street, which was just as crowded. Worse, these people weren't moving, but instead stood watching an open-air burlesque act. I saw the first pair of pursuers reach the far end of the alley. We were stuck, and if they started drawing swords in this crowd, innocent people would get hurt.

"Okay, now I'm open to suggestions," I said over the show's music and cheering.

Calmly, Anders pulled a small pouch from his saddlebag. He drew his crossbow, tied the pouch to the tip of the bolt and fired it at the pursuers. I was impressed; he shot one-handed, on a horse being jostled on all sides, and still managed to part the hair of the closest pursuer as he ran toward us. The bolt stuck hard in the wooden side of a refuse barrel, and the impact tore open the pouch. I heard the distinctive tinkle of coins hitting the ground.

The two men at the head of the gang immediately skidded to a stop, turned and ran toward the money. The men behind them converged on it at the same time, as did a bunch of bystanders.

"Damn, how much money was that?" I asked.

"Enough to keep them busy. Now you follow me for a while."

He cut his horse in front of me and edged along between the crowd and the buildings. His mount was pretty impressive, picking carefully over fallen drunks and uncertain muddy spots, until the crowd began to thin and we reached the edge of town. The road became a highway that stretched north in the darkness. We continued on until we were far enough away we'd get plenty of warning if anyone pursued us. Then we stopped to let our horses rest a bit.

"Thanks," I said.

"Just doing my job," he modestly replied.

"Want to tell me exactly what that job is?"

He reached for something inside his jacket. Instantly I had my sword out and at his throat again. "Slow, buddy," I warned. "No hurry now."

"Okay, okay," he said easily. With two fingers, he withdrew a tightly rolled parchment, sealed with wax. "I'm just the messenger."

I recognized the seal, and blood pounded in my ears as I broke it. I turned so that the glow from town gave me enough light to read. The message was short and, like all the best messages, left the reader with only one course of action. I rolled it up and stuck it in my bags. "I ought to say no," I told the young soldier.

"He said you wouldn't," Anders replied with an easy grin.

"What else did he tell you?"

"That I could trust you. And not to lie to you."

I nodded. "Good advice. So why did you follow me for so long without saying something?"

"I tried to find you in Neceda, but you left just as I got there. I saw you coming out of that tavern where your office is, actually, but didn't know it was you until I talked to the barmaid."

"Did she rat me out right away?"

"Sure. After I gave her five gold pieces and my best smile. *And* she lied about which way you went, but after she described you I knew I'd seen you and which way you'd really gone. I followed you to the river, but by then you were on the boat. I figured I'd keep following you and wait for a chance to talk privately." He shrugged. "Things kept getting in my way, though."

"Like those muggers?"

"Amateurs," he snorted. "If they'd known when to quit, they'd still be alive."

My full reaction to the message hadn't hit me yet. "I guess we should get started, then." I gestured toward the moonlit road ahead. "Lead on, then, Mr. Anders."

"Sir Michael," he corrected with another grin. "But you can call me Mike."

We headed away from Pema toward a place a hundred miles away, and for me, twenty years back in time.

FOUR

⟜

We crossed the Gusay, which put us back in Muscodia, and headed north. We traveled the length of Casselward and, at last, entered Arentia in the middle of the night.

The Hornfisher River had been unaffected by the rains to the south. We used a small raft hidden beneath a well-built camouflaged shed that was also stocked with many other things a secret agent like Sir Mike might need.

All kings and queens employed people like him, and they all denied it publicly. But power wasn't a gift for life, and to hang onto it, sometimes nasty things needed to be done. The best men (and often women) for these jobs never looked the part, and Anders certainly didn't. He laughed easily, talked a *lot*, and seemed content to let me make decisions about things like places to camp. There was an iron quality to him, though, that I sensed would be quite willing to knock me over the head and bring me to Arentia trussed and thrown across my saddle if I gave him too much grief.

We guided the horses onto the raft and poled it across the Hornfisher. The looming shore had thick forest down to the waterline, and I wondered if there was room to land even this tiny vessel. The dock, when we touched it, was actually disguised as a pile of driftwood, and only when I stepped onto it did I realize it was solidly anchored to the river bottom.

I don't know what I expected to happen when I set foot on Arentian soil again—maybe for it to burst into flames beneath my feet or something—but of course it was just dirt, like any other dirt.

We pulled the raft out of the water, tucked it into a depression dug for it and covered it with leaves. Then, leading our horses, we weaved through the trees until at last we hit a trail. I'd have had a hard time following the path in broad daylight, let alone at night, but Anders worked from memory and landmarks I didn't bother to try to map out.

As we led our horses down the narrow trail through the woods, Anders asked, "Feel strange to be home?"

"This ain't my home," I muttered.

"Oh. Right. Sorry." He seemed genuinely contrite. "I didn't mean to bring up—"

"Do you hear that?" I snapped, and when he stopped to listen I pushed past him. He didn't say anything else for a long time.

By sunrise we'd emerged from the woods onto a wide highway that led eventually to Arentia City. These roads were Arentia's pride, layered with flat, smooth stone dredged from the Hornfisher and other rivers. Creating them had been a tedious process that almost led to a revolution against then-King Hugh II; his insistence on good infrastructure earned him the nickname "Highway Hugh," and of course the roads themselves became "Hughways." But once completed, everyone suddenly realized the advantage they gave: they didn't become impassable muddy tracks after each heavy rain, and trade between towns became so easy that within a generation Arentia went from a cesspool not unlike Muscodia to the thriving center of commerce it was now.

At least, that's what they taught us in school. What they left out, naturally, was that the roads were built by press gangs of Fechinians who, after they'd done their jobs, mysteriously died of a disease that left marks almost identical to sword wounds. This massacre was quietly swept under the tapestry, and when Hugh III ascended to the throne two centuries ago, all mention of it was expunged from the official history books. Only the diligence of the Society of Scribes, who made copies of *everything*, kept the memory alive in their hidden archives.

It was a glorious spring day, and everything seemed to be in bloom beneath the wide blue sky. Everyone we passed, whether farmer, trader or soldier, waved or said something friendly. Children laughed, dogs barked. Birds sang. My mood grew more and more foul.

Suddenly I noticed that the road beneath us was not one of the original Hughways, but a new construction; the rocks were a completely different color. "Hey, wait a minute. Didn't the road used to turn right here and go all the way around old Hogenson's place?" I asked.

"They've built a whole new series of roads," Anders explained. "The king bought rights-of-way across some of the big landholdings to cut travel time down, and trade picked up a lot as a result."

"Huh." That explained all the traffic, although not how the king had managed to sweet-talk the various big shots into something that gave the appearance of patriotism. Arentian nobles weren't known for being altruistic, and old Baron Hogenson was especially self-absorbed.

As we traveled, I learned that young Sir Michael was the eldest son and namesake of an army general who'd earned his rank the hard way, protecting the border Arentia shared with San Travis to the west. Mike junior attended military school and then took a commission in the regular army. Since Arentia wasn't at war with anyone he found the distinct lack of action mind-numbing, until a superior suggested he apply for the special operations branch. The screening process alone took three months. His tests included being tossed naked from a ship off the coast of Romeria with orders to retrieve a certain piece of jewelry from a nobleman's house and return with it by a given date. He'd done so by convincing the scullery maid's young daughter that he was a merman, and she hid him long enough for him to learn the layout of the house and acquire the jewelry. He even sculpted a copy from melted sugar to give himself more time, and arrived back in Arentia three days early. He seemed very proud of this, and if it was all true, he had a right to be. I'd been to Romeria a few times, and it was a cold, ragged, lawless place where strangers weren't welcome and thieves were routinely blinded.

Anders had two younger brothers, also in military school, and a sister who still lived at home. Because of the nature of his work, his brothers believed he'd actually been drummed out of the service and now worked as a kind of liaison with merchants who sold things to the military. Once they reached a high enough rank they could learn the truth, and he anticipated that day with intense glee. "Cornel, especially, loves giving me hell when we're home together at the holidays," he practically giggled. "I can't wait to tell him that while he was learning to turn left on command, I was out sabotaging Ashatana's naval construction yards."

"Should you be telling *me* that?" I asked.

He laughed. "I think, given your status in Arentia, it's safe to tell you anything."

"My status isn't quite what you think it is," I said.

"Not to dispute you, but your status is whatever the *king* tells me it is. And after what he told me, I don't have any worries about you keeping state secrets."

There seemed no point in contradicting him further, so I let it go. The conversation (monologue, really) next turned to his romantic life. He was unmarried, although there was a certain young lady in Arentia City on whom he had his eye. Her name was Rachel, she had long dark hair and a bosom of surpassing perkiness. I gathered she was also quite intelligent, and had goals for her life beyond simply marrying some man who'd keep her fed and pregnant. Anders approved of this, and encouraged her education and training as an architect.

"She's really good; I wish I could tell her more about my own job, because there are times I know she could help. That little shack where we got the raft? I sort of tricked her into designing it for me. I told her I needed a place to store trade goods where no one could find them, and after I gave her a map of the area, she designed the thing so that it worked with the forest to provide camouflage. Pretty smart, huh? There's nobody in special ops who could've figured that out, that's for sure."

He continued telling me about Rachel, how they'd met at an art exhibition in Arentia City, and carefully implied that their first date ended the way boys always hope they will. This didn't give him a bad opinion of her, though; just the opposite. Her willingness to act on impulse was apparently one of her best qualities.

But solemnizing the relationship was on indefinite hold. "It wouldn't really be fair to marry her while I was in such a dangerous job, would it?"

"I ain't the guy to ask."

"Never been married?"

"Nope." He was just trying to be friendly, I reminded myself. "Never was lucky enough to find a girl like your Rachel."

"She's a jewel, all right. Whenever I have doubts about my job, I remember that I'm doing all I can to keep her and her family safe. That's all the encouragement I need."

We stopped in Mahaleela for the night. The town was pretty much the same as I remembered it—one long central road with an inexplicable right angle in the middle of it. The Serpent's Toe Tavern and Inn was the best accommodation in town, and the desk clerk certainly fawned enough over Anders when the boy flashed his money bag. We sent our horses to the stable, dropped our saddle bags in the room and went downstairs to eat.

Perched on the main road like it was, the Serpent's Toe catered to a more varied clientele than the regular taverns. Single adult travelers and wealthy families both stopped there, and it dealt with this dichotomy by dichotomizing itself. The main room, where you could get dinner and warm yourself by the fire, was designed to be acceptable to prudish parents: the barmaids wore necklines to their chins, the ale served with dinner was frighteningly watered down, and there were even wet nurses available if the parents didn't bring their own. Off to one side was the true tavern where you could ogle the girls' cleavage and arrange for an evening's companionship while you drank yourself idiotic on the real stuff. It was an interesting approach to attracting customers, but judging from the crowd in the dining room, it worked.

One family, a Mishicot livestock trader with two wives and a half-dozen kids, occupied a corner table. The kids, as Mishicotian children tended to be, were regimented little mechanicals who lifted their spoons in unison under the watchful eye of their mothers. This kind of iron-fisted parenting was necessary when you might have twenty kids in a household. The younger of the wives, a shapely blonde with dark circles under her eyes, nursed a fussy infant and stared blankly into space. Each time the baby made a particularly loud noise, the other wife, dark-haired and portly, would shoot the blonde a disapproving look. Through all this the head of the household ate ravenously, ignoring everything around him. He was tall and handsome, and scanned the other women in the room with the same rapacious gaze so many Mishicotian merchants possessed. In Mishicot a man measured success by wives and children, and he was clearly on his way up the ladder.

Our waitress, far too young for me but just about right for Anders, brought us drinks and bread. The menu was scrawled in chalk on a board on one wall. As we studied the fare, I caught the voices of two tradesmen at the table behind me.

". . . worst domestic scandal we've ever had."

"It's not a scandal, it's just the inevitable result of dealing with women."

"You're too cynical. *My* wife isn't so bad. Certainly not a child-killer."

"Well, you know the government's not telling us everything. *I* hear that she's a moon priestess; I bet it was all part of some spell."

"To do *what?* She married the king of Arentia, she's the most powerful woman in the country now. What more did she need?" His voice dropped. "I bet there's another man involved, and the king found out it wasn't his child. This is just his way of saving face."

"I just know that I don't believe they're being straight with us."

"This king isn't like that. He doesn't hide in his castle behind guards and soldiers, he's never had a scandal, and he's never been caught in a public lie."

"Maybe he's just better at hiding it than his father was."

That tied in with the message Anders had given me, and I began to understand its urgency. After we ate, I excused myself and went into the tavern for a nightcap. I couldn't imagine sleeping in Arentia while sober.

The tavern was half the size of the dining hall, lit with a few oil lamps and the smoldering fireplace. But the nearest waitress wore a blouse so low-cut the brown circles around her nipples poked above the hem, and the slit up her thigh went nearly to her waist. She tossed her hair as she turned and gave me the kind of professional smile that promised many pleasant surprises, if my money pouch was heavy enough. Then she looked me up and down the way a butcher might appraise a steer.

"Hi, handsome," she said. She held her tray with one hand and put the other on her hip, which emphasized her narrow waist. "Like a table?"

"No, thanks, I'll just sit at the bar."

"Your loss," she said with a mischievous wink. For a

moment I considered that it really might be. I felt too old, though, to need her kind of distraction.

One thing I hadn't expected was how weird it was to hear so many Arentian accents. My own had faded into a kind of neutral regional one, but I was slipping back into it with each word I spoke. Usually if I heard someone say "loss," or "coin," or any of those words that really emphasized the way Arentians talk, it would be a novelty. In Arentia, of course, everyone spoke that way, and it inexplicably made me nervous.

I sat at the bar. It took my eyes a while to adjust to the dimness. I saw a half-dozen fellow patrons, four clustered around a single table, one at a table by himself and one at the far end of the bar. They were from all over: Suamico, Trego, Winneconne. The other guy at the bar had a tattoo on his arm marking him as a wizard from Colfax, even though he wore neither the robe of his calling nor the insignia ring. Either he was incognito and just not very good at it, or he'd broken their vow of chastity and been formally derobed. I suspected the latter, given the speed with which he put away the ale. Poor bastard, that's what he gets for signing up with a group of men who decried sex as the world's greatest evil. The moon priestesses, now, *they* had the right idea.

The woman behind the counter, a tall, cool blonde with a scar along her jaw that somehow made her more attractive, served me without a smile. I downed it in one swallow, asked for a refill and prompted, "Pretty bad about the queen, ain't it?"

"Shit happens," she said as she poured. She wasn't going to make this easy.

"I've been out of the country for a few years. What's this Queen Rhiannon like?"

"Blonde, blue-eyed, gorgeous," she said, as if reciting the ingredients of a recipe. "Sings like a bird, dances like the wind. Can heal the sick, raise the dead, make the young men talk right out of their heads. Or so they say."

"She's a healer?"

She looked at me with disdain and blew a strand of hair from her face. "That's exaggeration for effect. Sarcasm, I think they call it."

I raised my drink. "Here's to 'they.' " After I took a sip, I asked, "You believe she did it?"

She leaned her hands on the bar and fixed me with her best no-nonsense stare. "I don't care, mister. I thought King Philip was doing a bang-up job before she came along, and if she made him happy, I was happy. Now I just wish we still had a death penalty, because the bitch deserves to hang."

That pretty much ended the conversation. I finished my drink and went upstairs, where Anders was already asleep, fully dressed. His sword lay on the floor atop its scabbard, and a dagger handle peeked out from beneath his pillow. I took off my shirt and boots, washed my face in the basin, then dropped off asleep from trail exhaustion more than peace of mind. I dreamed of screams and fire.

FIVE

W e reached the outskirts of Arentia City at noon the next day. Again, I don't know what I expected—a storybook castle, the brightly colored child's-eye view I remembered—but what I got was a city like any other, filled with people trying to get by and buzzing with the latest scandal.

The city walls loomed at the end of the road, a great rectangle across the horizon. Legendary for their thickness and impregnability, they rose from the Eagle's Plain (once known as the Vulture's Plain, due to the inconclusive battles fought there in ancient times) like artificial cliffs. The city's population believed it could never be sacked because of them, and that sense of safety led many to forget how much bloodshed still existed in the world beyond those walls.

Outside the walls a second city had grown up, peopled by the merchants and farmers selling their wares. This population was seasonal, but at its peak, as it would be in a couple of months, it rivaled the permanent citizenry of the city proper. With the first spring harvest out of the way and the second planting well into its season, this extended shantytown encircled the walls to a thickness of over a mile, and the straight roads split into little side paths, like a river's delta, that wound through the wagons, buggies and semipermanent stalls of this alternate Arentia City.

This was one advantage of peacetime that the more belligerent kingdoms envied: a strong economy based on agriculture and manufacturing, not preparation for, and recovery from, war. It took Arentia a while to achieve this, but it became a sort of economic beacon to show other kingdoms that conquest was not the only way to grow riches. Arentia could certainly defend itself—ask the queen of Shawano, especially any of the few survivors of the Battle of Frog's Lip—but had learned over time that economic security trumped the military one. A lot of this came about because of the courage of Queen Gabrielle, mother of the great King Dominic and grandmother of the man I was being brought to see.

My thoughts returned to the present as we entered the great mass of merchants. Vendors yelled and waved as we passed, holding up goods and hawking services. Anders, at least, looked like he had money to spend, and that made him a prime target. He politely refused each and every offer without once losing his temper over the constant supplication, something I know I couldn't have done. The people who did approach me got only an angry glare in response; few of them were Arentian, and their goods were either substandard or sublegal.

Traffic was heavy, and my stolen horse reacted to the crowds by growing more and more anxious. By the time we got to the big gate that allowed passage through the wall, she was almost too skittish to control. "Country horse," Anders observed disdainfully.

"I didn't exactly have time to comparison shop," I said. Truthfully, my horsemanship had always been pretty bad, a source of embarrassment to my father and amusement to everyone else. That's why I didn't own one of the vile creatures.

Inside the walls the socio-economic levels went up dramatically. People who could afford to live in the city could also afford the best of everything, and this was where they found it. The shops and dealers inside the walls sold overpriced jewelry, furs, tanned hides and elaborately dyed cloth. Merchants dressed like courtesans, and courtesans dressed in whatever ridiculous fashion was current. Noblemen and their entourages wandered among the goodies, and fancy buggies carried them to and from whatever they did between shopping trips. Anders blended in with this crowd; I did not. They probably thought I was his newly indentured servant, being brought in for a flea bath and etiquette training.

I sensed an uncomfortable undercurrent to a lot of the conversations, and noticed more soldiers than usual posted on the corners and striding the parapet at the top of the walls. Given what Anders's message said, this made sense. A captain of the bowmen walked past and yanked down a broadsheet tacked to the stone wall around a public well; I couldn't read the message, but the illustration showed a woman with an excess of red lipstick around her mouth, like blood. The glimpse I got of the words implied a mocking, hateful tone.

We continued down the main thoroughfare toward the palace itself. The grand stairs that led up to the main hall were now gated off and guarded by lancers in dress uniforms. The gates were new; in my time, those steps were public areas where people with grudges against the government, religious axes to grind or the simple need to be the center of attention could draw crowds of sympathetic or mocking listeners. To block them off this way spoke of a serious crisis that had rattled the palace's sense of safety. It also, if I recalled my civics tutoring, violated one of the articles of the King's Charter signed by Arentia's original monarch, Hyde the Grand.

We passed the gates, turned the corner by the Grand Stone set by King Hyde when the original palace was built, and proceeded down the Avenue of Wolves. I couldn't quite recall the folklore that provided the street's name, but it had something to do with King Hyde clearing the forest that once grew here of those nuisances. Now it was a row of houses and mansions crammed together on the street opposite the palace, occupied by noblemen and those appointed by the king to special tasks. Each house had an underground entrance to the palace, and the king could easily summon his advisors any time of day or night. Guards stood by the doors of each house as well.

"Was there a coup attempt?" I asked softly as we rode beneath the carefully groomed trees.

"Rumors," Anders said with equal discretion. "No action taken, just handbills posted, a few protests and so on. This is just a visible precaution to make any impulsive types think twice."

"So you only get the well-organized revolution?"

He chuckled.

We turned down an alley at the back of the palace. I knew it led to the kitchens, where garbage and other refuse was removed by the wagonload daily and new supplies were delivered. There was a new iron gate here as well, guarded by two big men in uniform. There was no visible evidence of *why* this gate had been installed, and the soldiers themselves didn't appear too concerned with their job. That, at least, I knew to be a trick: only the toughest guys watched the palace's back door. You'd stand a better chance of storming the throne room itself.

Anders stopped and dismounted. One guard stepped forward, and the other discreetly put his hand on his scabbard. "State your business," the first one said.

"King's orders," Anders said, and held out his right fist. He wore a signet ring, and popped it open to reveal the second insignia, the one that showed his true rank.

"Huh," the first man said, then looked up at me. "And you, fuzzy?"

I nodded at Anders. "I'm with him."

The man started to say something, then stopped and stared at me as if I'd grown another nose. Then he turned to Anders. "Is that—?"

"Yeah," Anders said quickly, and snapped his ring closed. "And we don't want to keep the king waiting."

"No, of course not," the guard said. He gestured to the other man, who produced a key and unlocked the gate. I dismounted and followed Anders.

The first guard preceded us through, and unlocked a nondescript wooden door set into the palace's foundation. It looked like a servant's entrance, and the ground outside it was stained after years of chamber pots, leftovers and worn-out linens being stacked for collection. He pushed it open, and we stepped inside.

"What about our horses?" I asked.

"They'll be attended to, sir," the guard said. He sounded nervous now. "Well fed, brushed down and put away dry. And, hey—sorry about that 'fuzzy' crack. No harm done, right?" He closed the door behind us before I could answer, and I heard the key turn the lock again.

Anders was clearly on familiar ground, because even though we were in total darkness, he began humming. I said, "What the hell was *that* all about?"

"They knew who I'd been sent to fetch. People still talk about you here."

"They do," I repeated. My stomach fell into a pit and I was suddenly queasy. "What do they say?"

A spark flared in the darkness, and then a torch burst to life. Anders held it at arm's length while the harsh residue burned away. "They talk about that day at the lake, when you fought all those guys," Anders said as he waited for the flame to settle. "Whenever someone's facing odds like that, they call it 'getting LaCrossed.' "

"I can think of a few better words for it." *Failure* came to mind. "We're not allowed to use the front door?"

"People watch the front. The king wants your visit to be, ah . . . discreet."

We were at one end of a long passage. We walked down the tunnel to another door and Anders, still humming, tapped the stones in the wall, looking for the false one. I reached past him and pushed the correct one, which slid in to reveal a key in a small depression. The castle had dozens of these secret passages—every castle did—and it made me smile to think that I probably knew them better than Anders. After all, I'd grown up around them.

The passage beyond was lit with widely spaced torches, so that we had to pass through deep pools of darkness between them. I knew that in some of these shadows, soldiers could hide in invisible notches in the wall, a security precaution to defend against enemy infiltrators. Heavy iron gates could also drop at a moment's notice, trapping intruders between them. Ordinarily, though, these spots would be unmanned, because Arentia had been at peace with its neighbors for over forty years, since the reign of the previous king. Now, given all the precautions outside, would these niches be occupied by soldiers ready to defend the palace from attack? I thought about reaching into one just to see, but figured that was needlessly provocative. If I got run through before I even talked to the king, I'd never find out the truth.

The tunnel dead-ended at yet another door. Anders knocked, and a slot opened. Hard eyes peered at us. Anders held up his identification ring again, and after a moment the slot closed, and the bolt inside slid back. Anders snuffed his torch in a bucket beside the door and gestured for me to precede him.

We entered a small antechamber with a desk and two chairs. When the door shut behind us, it became almost invisible in the wall's stonework. Another much more modern door was directly opposite the one we'd just used. A soldier, a major according to his uniform, sat behind the desk and looked up at us. When he saw Anders, he jumped to his feet and saluted. The man who'd opened the door stood at stiff attention beside it.

"As you were," Anders said calmly. "Has the king been informed that we've arrived?"

"Yes, sir," the major said. "He's expecting you in his office."

"Very good." The soldier who'd admitted us leaped to open the other door.

I realized I was sweating, and my hands shook as we walked down the hallway whose every brick and tapestry was familiar to me. This was the passageway to the king's private family quarters, and you could only enter through the secure door we'd used, or the two other hidden ones known only to the family and its closest friends.

We reached the big double doors at the end of the hall. Anders knocked. The door opened partially, and a white-haired man peered out beneath thick, still-dark eyebrows.

"Brought him," Anders said simply, and stepped aside.

The old man squinted at me. I knew him, of course— Emerson Wentrobe, advisor to the king of Arentia for the last sixty years, the one great constant in Arentian government. Some uninformed wags always insisted that Wentrobe was the apocryphal power behind the throne; the rest of us knew that, while his advice was often heeded, he never made the final decision. At least that had been the case with the previous king; I couldn't imagine Phil being any different.

Wentrobe had only been an advisor for forty years the last time I saw him, and his hair had been stone gray, not white. But his eyes were still as sharp as ever. "Young master Edward," he said to me.

"Not so young," I replied, and offered my hand. "How are you, Mr. Wentrobe?"

"Not so old," he said with a grin. His grip was still firm, although not as bonecrushing as it had seemed in my youth.

He stepped aside, and this time I gestured for Anders

to precede me. But the young man shook his head. "I'm just supposed to deliver you. This is where I get off. It's been a pleasure traveling with you, Baron LaCrosse."

I winced a little; it was the first time anyone had ever used that title in reference to me. "Yeah, well, you can still call me Eddie. Thanks, Mike."

SIX

Wentrobe closed the door behind us. The office was decked out with all the gilt and glitter expected of a king, but for the moment we were alone in it. I dropped my saddlebags next to the door and hung my jacket on the coat rack. I felt seriously underdressed.

"Would you like a drink?" Wentrobe asked, moving to the bar.

"Sure. Rum if you have it."

"We do indeed." As he poured, he glanced at me. "You appear to have grown accustomed to hard work."

"Yeah. Who'd've thought, huh?" I took the drink gratefully. "So. How are . . . things?"

Wentrobe sipped his own drink. "What do you know?"

"What was in Phil's note, what Anders told me, and what I picked up from gossip on the way. Phil met some mysterious beautiful woman, married her, and now everyone thinks she killed their child."

He nodded. "That's what everyone thinks, all right. Almost everyone."

"Is that what happened?"

He made a grand shrug. "Their son is dead. The queen was found with the body, covered in blood that wasn't her own, inside a locked room. Those are the only facts everyone agrees on."

"So the queen murdered the prince."

He nodded and poured himself another drink. "There seems to be no other logical explanation."

"But *Phil* doesn't believe it."

He looked down into the goblet. "No," he said with the weight only a disillusioned elder can manage. "He doesn't."

I picked up a framed portrait from the big desk. About the size of my hand, it was a colored line drawing of a woman with wavy blond hair, blue eyes and a mouth that seemed about to smile. She had the look of fresh air and forests after a spring rain, probably because she wore a crown of flowers. "Is this her?"

"Yes," answered a new voice. It had grown deeper, but I'd know it anywhere.

He stood across the room from me, in a casual jacket and shirt. He wasn't wearing his crown, which for some reason surprised me, although I knew it was too heavy and uncomfortable to wear except on formal occasions. I guess I just expected him to look more *royal*, like King Philip, instead of so much like my old best friend Phil.

Phil. Fucking *King Phil*.

He grew taller than me when we were fourteen, and still was. His hair was cropped short, and touched with gray at the temples, but otherwise still had that annoying disheveled quality that made all the girls sigh. He wore a mustache, also shot through with gray, and there were deep lines at the corners of his eyes. He wasn't fat, though, and he still moved gracefully.

Still looking at me, he said, "Pour me one of those, will you, Emerson?"

"Of course, Your Majesty," Wentrobe said.

I put the picture back on his desk. "Not bad. Not as cute as that Danner girl you chased after when we were fourteen, but not bad."

"The picture doesn't do her justice," Phil said. He took the drink from Wentrobe, downed half of it and then managed a small grin. "Remember when we stole that bottle of rotgut from your dad's wine cellar and drank it in the woods, then tried to sneak back in without anyone noticing?"

"Yeah. I'm a better drinker now."

"Me, too." A real smile finally cracked his cool demeanor, and suddenly there was my old pal Phil, who'd once puked in my lap and set me up with his sister and taught me to play cards and was the worst dancer I'd ever seen. Something fell away inside me, too, and we grabbed each other in a long, intense bear hug that once would've embarrassed us both. A whole bunch of emotions I'd stuck in that dark spot under my stomach threatened to burst out, but with great difficulty I kept them in their place. Finally we broke apart and just grinned at each other.

"You smell like a pond," he said.

"Where I live, everything's been flooded for two weeks. *You* smell like a damn bouquet."

"It's called bathing. All the kids are doing it. So did you have any trouble getting here?"

"Not with that super-patriot you sent to find me."

Phil nodded. "He's a good one, for sure. I've had my eye on him for a while." He swallowed the rest of his drink and handed the goblet to Wentrobe for a refill.

"Well, I'll leave it up to you. We can drink and reminisce first, or I can tell you why I needed to see you."

"Why don't you tell me what you want *while* we drink?"

"That works." He gestured at an overstuffed high-backed chair. I sank into it while he sat on the corner of the desk and picked up the picture of his wife. "You didn't come to the wedding."

"Had a previous engagement." In truth, I avoided information about Arentia so successfully that he'd been married for eighteen months before I even knew about it.

"Well, that was six years ago, anyway. We tried to start a family right away, but it took a while. Eventually, though, we did have a son. Last year." He met my eyes. "We named him Edward."

I must've had a great expression, because Phil only kept a straight face for about ten seconds. "No, I'm just kidding, we named him Pridiri."

"Good, *that* won't get him picked on in school."

"Ree wanted it. She said it means, 'relief from anxiety,' and it was very important to her. I call him 'P.D.' for short." I assumed "Ree" was what he called his queen, Rhiannon. Girls could get away with strange nicknames like that, especially girls who looked like the one in that picture.

"So what happened to him?"

"The official version," he said with a glance at Wentrobe, "is that she killed him."

"Why?"

"I don't know. There are all sorts of rumors, including that she was a moon priestess doing a spell to bring down the government. My favorite is that she hated changing diapers so much that she lost her temper when she couldn't find a nursemaid." His smile was not amused. "But there's no denying she was found covered in his blood, and the only remains were bones." He said this with the practiced calm of royalty, betraying no emotion. "She was violently ill afterwards. The consensus is that she ate part of the corpse."

"What does *she* say?"

"She says she can't remember. We'd been at a state dinner, and she left early to go put him to bed. Her maids said they left her alone with P.D., and when they came back they found her passed out, covered in blood, surrounded by moon priestess paraphernalia. Candles, knives, incense, the works."

"Could it be a setup?"

"I wish it could be, but how? She was in the nursery, in the middle of the most well-protected building in the whole country. And *why?* If someone breached our security and got into the castle, why kill a baby? Why not her, or me?"

I nodded. "Yeah. 'Why' is a good question, all right."

He was silent for a moment as he met my eyes. "I was hoping you could find the answer to it."

"Figured as much."

"I need someone from outside, who I can trust, and who's up to the challenge. Believe it or not, you've got quite the reputation for cleverness. In some circles, at least."

I held my goblet out to Wentrobe for a refill, then tossed it down. "I don't normally work in circles this high off the ground."

"But I can *trust* you, Eddie," he repeated, so simply that I was both touched and infuriated.

So this was it. My best friend, who I hadn't seen in

twenty years, wanted me to help prove his wife wasn't a child killer when everyone else seemed sure that she was. To do that, I'd no doubt have to move around through these places loaded with memories for me, memories I'd gladly cut out of my brain with a rusty butter knife if I knew it would get rid of them. And I knew he wouldn't offer me money, just like he knew I wouldn't accept any. My only reward would be helping a friend.

I stood. "Well . . . ah, hell, you know I'll do it, so we can skip all the hemming and hawing. I'll need to see the official reports on it, the witness inquisition notes and everything."

"All waiting for you," Wentrobe said, "in your room."

I managed half a grin at Phil. "Pretty damn sure of yourself, aren't you?"

"That's why they let me wear the fancy hat."

I put the goblet down on his desk despite the temptation to ask for another refill. "Okay, then. Guess I'll go get cleaned up a little. Think I could get some food?"

"Yes. Emerson, I know it's a little beneath your standard duties, but would you show Eddie to his room?"

"Certainly, Your Majesty. And I'll send up something—ham and cheese were your favorite, as I recall."

I nodded, and picked up my jacket and saddlebags. "Once I've read through this stuff, I'll probably want to talk to the same people. Hopefully I'll have some new questions for them."

"Sure," Phil said.

"And then . . . I guess I need to meet your wife."

SEVEN

I hadn't enjoyed such swanky accommodations in a long time. When we were kids, Phil and I watched his father's guests go in and out of these elaborately appointed rooms, often accompanied by a train of assistants and servants. Once we planned to sneak our dates into one of them, but his mother busted us and we both got grounded. And once I *had* sneaked into one, with Janet. So even though I was a grown man, I still felt like I was about to get in trouble as I sat on the edge of the ridiculously soft bed.

After a bath I changed into clean clothes and ate two of the huge rolls, packed with ham and cheese and brought by a serious-looking, matronly servant. Two thick parchment folders were stacked next to the reading lantern on the desk. I finished the second roll, opened the top folder and began to read.

Two hours later I'd finished the files, and the rolls weren't sitting too well alongside what I'd learned. I closed the second folder, walked to the window and opened the wooden blinds. It was dark, and although the night was filled with city sounds, the breeze seemed cool and clean. I certainly didn't feel the same way.

All the guests at the state dinner the night of the murder agreed that Queen Rhiannon had seemed in her usual good spirits, charming the visiting bigwigs and even, once the after-dinner wine started flowing, favoring them with a song. She'd left at around 9:30 and gone upstairs, ostensibly to feed her son before retiring.

The head nursemaid, Beth Maxwell, reported that the queen arrived just before ten. I knew something about the layout of this castle, and nearly thirty minutes seemed a long time to get from the dining room to the nursery. Still, why would she hurry? Dawdling certainly wasn't a crime.

Nurse Maxwell left the baby with his mother and went to fold some linen in the laundry. Next, one of the maids, Sally Sween, entered the nursery to refill the night lamps with oil; the queen appeared to have dozed off in her rocking chair, with young Pridiri asleep in her arms. This, evidently, was not unusual, and the maid left them alone. And they stayed alone for the next hour. So from about 10:30 to 11:30, the queen could've done anything.

At 11:30, Nurse Maxwell returned to the nursery to put away the fresh bedclothes and diapers. She found the door locked, which according to her had never before happened. Miss Sween joined her in pounding on the door, but they got no answer. When they smelled smoke, they summoned a captain of the guard, Thomas Vogel, who forced the door open.

Here I found the guard's report most illuminating, because he was a trained soldier who could observe accurately in a crisis. The queen lay on the floor, naked, covered in "a red substance that appeared to be blood."

Marked on the floor was a circle, with "various ideograms inscribed along its border with chalk." He also described a knife, a stick with three feathers attached, and a bundle of what he correctly judged to be sage. In the center of the circle, a cauldron had been set up over a small brazier. This, plus the incense, supplied the smoke the two women smelled.

As the women attended to the fallen queen, Vogel examined the cauldron. Inside it he saw "boiling water and several pieces of bone, one of which appeared to be an infant human skull." The window was open, but he stressed that no one could have gained access through it, as the window was barred and opened onto a sheer four-story wall well inside the castle's guarded perimeter.

The queen awoke then, and was immediately violently ill. Vogel, in some sort of triumph of observational skill, mentioned that "she expelled large chunks of what appeared to be boiled meat."

Vogel dispatched Nurse Maxwell, the calmer of the two women, to immediately fetch King Philip. He then shut the door to the room and insisted nothing be touched. He spent the few minutes before the king and Wentrobe's arrival sketching the designs and placement of items within the circle. He also provided a list of banquet guests, along with capsule summaries to help jog people's memories: *Lady who bark-talked to her poodle, Blond man with the ugly chimpanzee, Countess with flatulence problem, Baron and young footman with family resemblance.*

I smiled; with a dozen men as cool-headed as Vogel, I could rule the world.

And so the king and Wentrobe arrived, and pieced

together—no pun intended—what must have happened. The queen, who had never before shown any interest in mooncraft, had, for reasons unknown, ceremonially sacrificed her son and cannibalized his corpse.

The queen claimed to remember nothing other than falling asleep while she nursed. This obviously wasn't much of an alibi, and the scrutiny Phil knew he'd face if he tried to delay action left him with only one option: he arrested her for murder and had her held in the prison tower reserved for the most dangerous, or most important, criminals. And then secretly, he sent for me.

Queen Rhiannon had been in that tower a week now, with no visitors except for the staff and no contact with the outside. Not even Phil had been to see her, since that would give the wrong appearance. No date had been set for her trial, but Phil would have to announce it soon.

I let the night's wind blow through my hair. I could just make out the top windows of the prison tower, visible over the peaked roof of the king's main audience chamber. I thought I saw a figure move across one of the windows, but it was too far and too dark to be sure. My first glimpse of this mysterious Queen Rhiannon?

THE NEXT MORNING I got down to work.

I pushed open the nursery door. The hinges, well-oiled as everything else in the castle, made barely a peep. The door swung slowly back and bumped softly against the wall. I stood on the threshold, absorbing the scene for a long moment before I finally entered the room.

I wasn't sure if this was the "official royal nursery from time immemorial," but Phil had been nursed in this room, and Janet. One of my earliest memories was of Phil and me repeatedly slamming our thick little skulls against the slats of his crib. Now the room was empty, the lamps unlit, and the smells of smoke and dried blood still hung in the air. The light through the window fell on the scene of the crime like the blazing finger of some god.

The cauldron had been removed, and the brazier, but the designs chalked on the floor remained, and the big red stains. I carefully walked around them, remembering that moon priestesses cast their spells clockwise. They wrote in a symbolic language I couldn't quite translate, but that usually had some sort of common theme. For instance, almost every symbol might feature a bird, if the spell had something to do with the primary magical element of air. But these designs meant nothing to me; one featured a bird, the next two a dragon, and the one after that a mermaid. To me, and I suspected to any real moon priestess, it was gibberish.

I walked to the window and looked out. Vogel's report had been accurate; the bars were close enough to keep any small inquisitive bodies from accidentally tumbling through, and the wall beneath the window was sheer straight down to the courtyard. I shook the bars and examined the corrosion around the bolts that held them in place; they were anchored into the stone as securely as the day they'd been installed. No one, or at least no human being, had entered through them.

A soft knock and cleared throat got my attention. I turned to see a tall, portly man with a long mustache standing at attention in the door. "Thomas Vogel, Sergeant of the Palace Guard," he announced stiffly, "reporting as ordered, sir."

"At ease, sergeant," I said. "I'm a civilian."

"Yes, sir," he said, and clasped his hands behind him in military at-ease. He was about as relaxed as the bars over the window.

"Come in and close the door," I said, and he did so, standing in front of it. I sat on the window ledge. "Your report was very thorough. I didn't ask you here because I found any fault in it, I just wanted to walk through the scene with you. Does anything look like it's different now?"

He took a slow look around, moving his head from left to right. "The cauldron and brazier are gone. The linen on the crib's been changed. The cushion on the rocker is different. And one of the pictograms is smeared."

I smiled. I'd deliberately smudged the corner of one drawing with my boot to see if he'd notice. "Damn," I said softly, "why are you just a sergeant?"

"I notice things," he said flatly.

I nodded. "Okay, help me out now. Where was the queen, exactly, when you came in?"

He stepped forward and pointed. "Kneeling here, in the middle of the circle. She was facing the door. The cauldron was in front of her."

"And she was naked?"

He actually blushed a little. "Yes, sir, she was."

"Where were her clothes?"

"In a pile right there. As if she just undid them and let them fall."

"Including her shoes?"

He squinted with thought. "Yes, sir, her shoes were under the pile."

I nodded. That was odd; a formal gown around your knees would make it hard to then step out of the kind of shoes a queen would wear. I hadn't yet met her, but the Rhiannon I'd heard described seemed far more graceful than that. "What did she do the moment you opened the door?"

"She looked up and gasped."

"In surprise?"

"No, sir. More in satisfaction." He took a deep breath and went "*Ahhhhh,*" imitating her response.

"Did she protest the interruption?"

"No, sir, she seemed intoxicated."

"How long did that last?"

"Until the king arrived. Then she seemed to sober up."

"He does have that effect on people."

"Yes, sir."

I walked around the circle. "Did you find the chalk she used to draw this?"

"No, sir, we did not."

"How do you explain that?"

"Two possible explanations, sir. One, she used all the chalk she had for the designs. Two, she threw the chalk out the window, and it shattered below. I found no fragments, but the courtyard has a lot of traffic. They could have been thoroughly crushed before I was able to search."

I nodded again and returned to the window. "Sergeant, is there anything, any detail, that was left out of your report? I know it might seem inconsequential, but you never know what might be crucial."

He stared straight ahead, resolutely formal. "I'm aware of that, sir. My report is as thorough as I can make it. I wrote down everything I observed. The questions you've asked me here are more matters of interpretation."

"True. And you've been invaluable, thank you."

"Will that be all, sir?"

"Mostly. Except . . . do *you* think the queen did it?"

" 'Think,' sir? I'm a soldier. I don't think."

"You must have an opinion."

"As do we all, along with a certain orifice."

Vogel clearly was not going to commit himself; perhaps he had done just that at some point in the past, which explained why he was still a mere sergeant. "Yes. Well. Thank you again. And please keep this conversation just between us for the time being."

"Of course, sir." He bowed and left with the same precision he'd arrived.

I looked down at the bloodstain on the stone. I knelt and ran my finger across it, then smelled my fingertips. It was blood, all right. Something had died in this room. But that was the only thing that might truly be what it seemed.

NURSEMAID BETH MAXWELL was a cheery, round young woman who would no doubt make a good mother herself, should she ever run across a man whose tastes ran to acres of rolling white flesh. She wore a neat, spotless uniform and a little cap over her tight brown curls, and looked up at me with guileless eyes. Phil let me use his office for these interviews, which conveyed a lot more authority than I'd command on my own.

"I appreciate you seein' me on such short notice," I said, exaggerating my country accent so she'd feel less threatened. "Just want to ask you a coupla things 'bout that night in the nursery."

She shuddered at the memory. "I'll never forget a thing from that night."

"That's what I'm hopin'. When the queen came in from the dinner party, did she seem upset or anything?"

"No, just the opposite. She seemed almost *silly*. I assumed she'd overindulged a bit on wine during dinner, although that wasn't like her, especially since Diri was born—that was our nickname for the prince, you know. The king called him P.D., but he was our little Diri." She sniffled and dabbed at her eyes with a handkerchief. "But she certainly didn't seem depressed."

"Did you say anything to her?"

"Just reported that Diri had spent a quiet evening, and had only just begun to fuss because he was hungry."

"Fuss?"

"Yes, you know how babies are."

"Not really."

"Oh. Well, their little tummies know when things are supposed to happen, and if they don't get fed right on time, they let you know they're not happy about it."

"So she was late, then?"

She thought for a moment. "A bit, I guess. No more than a few minutes."

I thanked her and showed her out. I was starting to get an idea, but I tried not to dwell on it until I had more information. I wanted the theory to fit the facts, not the other way around. I made some quick notes and stared at the battle scene painted on the ceiling until the next timid knock on the door.

THE MAID SALLY Sween was way too pretty to work in a bachelor household. Had she been in service back when Phil and I were teenagers, I shudder to think of the lengths to which we'd have gone to win her favors. As it was, her exquisite face was puffy with fear-spawned tears, since being summoned to the king's office was almost never a good thing.

"Would you like a drink?" I asked. Her uniform worked hard to control her décolletage, which distracted me more than I wanted to admit. She shook her head. I poured myself one. She crossed enviable legs as she waited.

Finally I said, "You stated that when you first checked on the queen and the baby, she was asleep in the rocking chair, right?"

"Yes, sir."

"Was the baby asleep?"

She blinked. "Well . . . I assume so. He wasn't crying or anything."

I nodded. "Now I need you to think real hard on this one. Did you actually *see* the baby in the queen's arms?"

She thought so hard I was afraid her eyes would pop from her face. "She had a bundle in her arms that I thought was her son, but . . . I can't swear to actually seeing him. Is that important?"

"I don't know," I said honestly. But inside I felt another click as more things aligned.

I KEPT MY gaze as even as I could. What I'd asked was horrendous even to me, but I couldn't let Phil know that, or I knew he'd talk me out of it. He stared at me over his desk, speechless.

Wentrobe finally spoke. "Baron LaCrosse, are you sure that's needed?"

The use of the title made me grit my teeth. "Pretty sure," I said, although I kept my eyes on Phil.

"Well, I don't know if I can condone this," Wentrobe said. "It's . . . it's *sacrilegious*."

"It's necessary," I said. "I just need one workman to help me. No one else has to know."

Phil looked down for a minute. "Okay," he said at last. "I did ask for your help, so I have to let you do your job." Then he looked up and added, "But no workman. You and I'll do it."

Wentrobe looked stricken. "Your Majesty, I don't think—"

"No one is going to desecrate my son's tomb," he snapped. "If I do it, then I know it'll be done with respect." He stood up and took a deep breath. "Exactly what do you think you'll find?"

"The last piece of the frame," I said. I didn't want to give him my entire theory just yet. "Then maybe I can see the whole picture."

EIGHT

⌐∼∽⌐

The tombs for Arentia's royal family were in a crypt deep beneath the castle. We waited until night to make our descent, when theoretically no one would notice that the king was up to anything so screwy. The air grew cooler and damper as we wound our way down the spiral stone steps, and my nascent discomfort at closed spaces began to flare. Despite the chill air, I was sweating like a pig.

Phil noticed and grinned at me. "Not scared of the dark, are you?" he teased, using any excuse to avoid expressing the feelings I knew churned within him.

"No, scared this half-assed castle might fall on my head," I said. "Some kings build brand new ones, you know."

"Hey, remember when you snuck down here thinking Tasha Ghent was waiting for you?"

"Oh, yeah, I remember. I still owe you for that one." Phil had told me Tasha, a buxom young brunette who worked in the kingdom's taxation office, had developed a crush on me even though I was six years younger. I received a note telling me she'd wait for me in the catacombs, along with a map showing me exactly where. At the time, my little head exerted more influence than my big one, so I followed the map and ended up in a disused, dead-end corridor; when I tried to backtrack my way out, I discovered that Phil had blocked me in with a fake wall. I didn't know it was fake, of course, and to this day I swear I got my first gray hair screaming like a girl until he let me out.

We reached the final door. It was a huge iron-barred affair, ten feet high and locked at the center. Beyond it, our torches illuminated the first of many rows of sealed royal crypts.

Phil slipped the key into the lock, but paused a minute before he turned it. "You have any kids, Eddie?" he asked softly.

"No."

"It changes the way you look at things. You completely stop living for yourself; you live for them." He took a deep breath. "I can't tell this to anybody else. I don't know *how* to be a father who's outlived his son. Not like this."

"I wish I could help," I mumbled. I didn't want to let on what I suspected; even though it might have eased his mind a bit for the moment, it would be even worse if I turned out to be wrong.

"I completely trusted my wife," he continued. "With everything—state secrets, personal secrets, even things I've never told anyone else. She was the mother of my child. If I could be *that* wrong about her . . . how can I ever trust my judgment again? How can I expect anyone else to trust it?"

"Things aren't always what they seem," I said as reassuringly as I dared. "C'mon, let's go do this and then we can go get drunk."

The gate creaked the way a mausoleum door should. I followed him past the bones of his ancestors, until we reached the most recent additions. He stopped before one whose capstone was still white with its newness. It bore his son's name, and the beginning and end dates of a criminally short life. We placed our torches in holders on the wall behind us.

I opened the canvas bag and pulled out a hammer and chisel. Phil ran his finger down the line of fresh cement that sealed the tomb.

"Really have to do this?" he asked one last time.

"Really do."

"I'm sorry, P.D.," he said softly, and stepped back.

Removing the seal was a one-person job, so I didn't begrudge Phil not helping. It took awhile to chip the cement away; it was still fresh and solid, unlike the crumbly stuff around older tombs. By the time I finished, my shoulders were in knots and I was drenched with sweat.

I dropped the tools back in the bag and pulled out two crowbars. We wedged them on either side of the stone and, accompanied by a great grinding sound, pulled it out and carefully lowered it to the floor.

Phil drew out the heartbreakingly tiny coffin. He placed it on the floor, took a deep breath and then lifted the lid. I leaned down to examine the contents.

I knew within moments that I'd been right. "I've got good news and bad news," I said as I scrutinized the scattered, fleshless bones retrieved from the cauldron. "The good news is, this ain't your boy."

Instantly Phil was on his knees next to me. "What are you talking about?" he demanded.

I picked up one of the skeletal arms, intact from the

elbow down. "Look at the hand bones. Baby bones are short and round, because they're not fully formed yet. These are the finger bones of an adult. But here's the clincher." I picked up the skull, which was conveniently missing its lower jaw. "Look. Somebody was in a hurry, and they got a little sloppy. That look like a baby tooth to you?" I pointed at the single molar at the back of the jaw that had been missed when the gum was altered to look more infant-like.

"What *is* this?" Phil whispered, astounded.

"It might be a dwarf, but I'm betting it's a monkey. Changed around a little so it would pass the kind of inspection it would get in a crisis. It wouldn't occur to anyone that these bones *wouldn't* be your son, especially since he was gone." I dropped the skull into the coffin, where it landed with a dry clatter.

Phil sat heavily against the wall. "My God. I don't understand all this. . . ."

I scooted the coffin aside and sat beside him. "It's a setup. I suspected it when I realized how long it took your wife to get from the banquet to the nursery; no way it should take thirty minutes. Something happened to her."

"But . . . what? And why?"

"Only she can answer that."

He turned to me. "If this counts as good news, what's the bad?"

"The bad news is that someone wanted it to look like your wife killed your son so badly that they'd go to all this trouble. They were able to get into and out of this castle with no one noticing it. Even if he's not dead, your boy's still gone. Somewhere out there, you've got one hell of an enemy."

"*Who?* Arentia hasn't been at war for nearly fifty years. The crime rate's lower than it ever has been. We don't even have a death penalty anymore. And I don't mean to sound egomaniacal, but everybody seems pretty happy with the job I've been doing."

"Maybe it's not you, then. Maybe it's *her*."

He nodded; I'd expected him to resist the idea. "That's the only possible explanation. Like you said, that's the picture inside the frame."

We replaced the coffin and the cover, then resealed it with some cement from my bag. I stood and stretched my back, then put my hand on the wall for balance while I pulled on my hamstring. My eyes fell on the name chiseled into the capstone next to Pridiri's, and suddenly a razor sliced out my heart. "Shit," I whispered.

Phil turned. "What? Oh . . . damn, Eddie, I'm sorry. I didn't think about it. I was so far into my own problems, I didn't—"

"It's all right." I turned away, shaking like I'd been drunk for weeks, and seriously considered smashing my head into the other wall just to banish the unbidden images of her laugh, her touch and, worst of all, her screams.

Phil didn't say anything for a long moment. Finally he said, "It's weird to think she'd be thirty-five now."

"Yeah." He was her brother, after all, he had the right to talk about her.

He put a strong hand on my shoulder. It reminded me of the way my dad's hand had felt there. "If you need to—"

I cut him off. "Can we go now? I need to talk to your wife."

He tilted his head back against the wall and let out a long breath. "Okay, but . . . I don't know how much help she'll be."

"Why not?"

"There's something about her that isn't widely known."

"What's that?"

"She doesn't—*claims* she doesn't—remember anything from before the day we met."

NINE

⟅⟆

Getting discreetly into the prison tower took some finesse. I had to dress as a guard and go through the motions with the shift change; hopefully no one watching noticed the second shift had six men instead of the usual five. Once inside and divested of my helmet and armor, I was led up the stairs and frisked very thoroughly by the matron entrusted with the imprisoned queen's care. Since she outweighed me by a good thirty pounds, I didn't complain.

Then she snapped out the rules. "Sit in the chair by the door and keep its back against the wall. Don't pass anything to the prisoner or accept anything from her. If she reaches through the bars for any reason, pull the cord by the chair. It drops an iron barrier between you and her. If you violate any of these rules, you'll be arrested." Despite my friendship with Phil, I had no doubt she meant it.

Finally, weapon-bare and winded from the climb, I was let into the cell that took up the entire top of the tower. The visitor's area was a narrow section blocked off by bars. On the other side of them, staring out the window, stood Queen Rhiannon of Arentia.

She wore a prison tunic that was too big for her and didn't do a damn thing to make her unattractive. Her golden hair was tied back in a ponytail, and of course she wore no make-up. Three small, shimmery birds sat on the sill as if they expected her to feed them.

She had her back to me when I entered, then turned and gazed at me with calm eyes so blue it was like looking directly into the sea. And it was a look I *knew*.

I just stared. If she'd had two heads and bat wings, I don't think I could've been more surprised. The door slammed shut behind me, and the noise snapped me out of my moment of shock. The shiny birds, startled, flew away. "*Eppie*," I said, my voice flat with shock.

She frowned. "Eppie," she repeated, as if it were some strange greeting. "Do I know you, sir?"

"Epona Gray," I said in the same blank, astounded tone.

Her eyes looked around the room, as if to make sure I was speaking to her. "Is that a color? Are you here to paint?"

I dropped heavily into the chair. All my careful theories and concepts vanished. "No," I said.

After a long moment she pushed self-consciously at the tunic's hem and said, "You're staring at me, sir."

"Yes, I am," I agreed.

"It's rather rude, don't you think?"

I continued to stare for a long minute before I finally asked the only question I could. "Don't you recognize me? I'm Eddie LaCrosse."

She nodded. "Philip's friend from childhood. The one who was there when his sister was killed."

"No!" I exclaimed. "Cathy Dumont's friend! Thirteen years ago, remember?" I spoke more quietly, although

I still felt like I was shouting. "You and I got to know each other *very well,* remember?"

She looked me over, then said, "I'm sorry, sir, I have no memory of you. Perhaps without the beard—"

"*I had the beard then!*" I shouted for real, and she backed away from the bars.

"Please, sir, you're scaring me," she said, and wrapped her arms around herself. "I swear I don't know you. Could you possibly be mistaken?"

Even the voice was the same, with that slight trill of amusement under everything. "Maybe so, if you don't have a horseshoe-shaped scar on the inside of your left thigh, and don't enjoy having the back of your neck licked."

She blinked, startled. Now she was politely outraged at my insolence. "Sir, I assure you, I have no memory of you."

"But I'm right, aren't I?"

She turned away from the bars, and a red shine crept up her face. Only the best actresses, or con artists, could manage a blush on cue. "About the scar, yes. About the other . . . I don't feel it would be polite to say."

My heart began to return to its normal rhythm, although I was sure it had burned a good six months off me in those brief moments. "So the name Stan Carnahan doesn't ring a bell? Or Andrew Reese?"

She shook her head and looked down. "Didn't my husband tell you? I'm an amnesiac, Mr. LaCrosse. My life began six years ago. I recall nothing before that."

The woman I'd known as Epona Gray sported straight, dark hair, and as they say, I was mighty damn sure it was her natural color. This Queen Rhiannon had cascading, wavy hair the color of sunbeams. Moreover, if this was Epona Gray, she didn't look a day older than when I last saw her. Could this be a relative? A daughter, perhaps?

But no, the resemblance was *too* close, too identical. Every instinct told me this was the same woman. "So you never went by the name Epona Gray?"

"I can't say for certain." She met my gaze with those big, innocent eyes that could probably convince the devil he needed an extra blanket. "I suppose it's possible. The name Rhiannon just came to me shortly after I awoke. I assumed it was my own, but I could be wrong. No one's suggested another one until now."

I took a moment to regain my composure, and began again. "All right. We'll assume for the moment that I'm mistaken, although the resemblance is astounding. I'm here to help Phil, who wants to know the truth about what happened the night your son died."

The confusion and queenly reserve were instantly—almost as if on a well-rehearsed cue—replaced by a touching vulnerability. "You have to believe me, Mr. LaCrosse, I'm innocent. I didn't kill my son."

I was on firmer ground now, questioning a suspect. "Then who did?"

"That's just it, he's *not dead*," she said urgently, and stepped toward the bars. She caught herself just before touching them, apparently remembering the rules. "I'd know if he was. I'm his mother, I'd be able to feel it. But no one believes me. They're too busy convicting me to make any effort to find him."

"*I* believe you," I said.

"Do you?" she almost cried.

I nodded, my practiced cool bouncing off her histrionics. "The body in that coffin was not your son. It wasn't even human, probably a monkey or something. But that doesn't get me much closer to knowing who's behind this, or what to do about it."

Relief, fear, desperation and finally cagey intelligence played over her exquisite face. I'd seen that same sly look on Eppie Gray, too, and it took all my concentration to stay on topic. The breeze through the window blew a strand of golden hair in her eyes, and she absently tucked it behind her ear. "Then what may I do to help you, sir?" she asked.

"Here's what I think happened. Somebody hates either you or Phil an awful lot to go to this much trouble. And since this couldn't have been a spur-of-the-moment thing, it was probably someone who's had a grudge simmering for a long time. Maybe even further back than six years."

Her eyes met mine, and there was no denying their candor. "Let me tell you *my* version of how I met Philip, Mr. LaCrosse. I awoke in the woods, lying in the sun in a patch of clover, naked and with no memory of anything except my name. Philip was hunting, and he'd broken away from his guard, and found me." She held my gaze. "And that is truthfully my earliest memory, as ludicrous as it may sound."

"Phil always knew how to meet the girls. So were you injured?"

"No. I seemed to be fine. I *always* seem to be fine. I've never even been sick a day since. I was only in labor for an hour with Pridiri. I can't explain it."

Epona's voice rang in my memory. *Ripping myself open reminds me there is life.* "Maybe you're just living right. So have you pissed anyone off in the last six years?"

"No one of whom I'm aware. We lead a very sedate life, for royalty. And I don't really participate in the government, I'm more of a public relations person." She smiled, but her eyes remained sad. "There are schools named after me, did you know that? They'll probably change that now, though."

If this was genuine, her real personality showing through, then I was baffled. It was like she had none of the skills everyone else in the world had developed to mask her emotions; whatever she felt came through as pure and clear as sunlight after a summer rain. I felt bad questioning her, like you might feel kicking a puppy. And that annoyed me. If she *was* Epona Gray, she was reeling me in like a suicidal bass.

"Then let's try something different. On the night of the, ah, incident in question, why did it take you thirty minutes to get from the dining room to the nursery?"

She blinked in surprise. "It did?"

"People know when you left, other people know when you arrived. I could *crawl* that distance in half an hour, so why did it take you that long to walk it?"

"I don't know." She seemed genuinely surprised by this information.

"Nothing unusual happened? No one accosted you or spoke to you or anything?"

"No. In my memory, I went straight to the nursery. You're right, though, it couldn't possibly take that long."

She overdid the sincerity just a hair, but it was enough for me to catch it. She knew something she wasn't telling me. I decided to change tactics.

"Look," I said, resting my arms on my knees, "I don't know *what* the hell to do here. I want to help Phil, but I've got jack to go on. Nobody hates him, nobody hates you, so why the hell would someone go to this much trouble? And if they did get into the nursery undetected, why *fake* a murder? Why not just go ahead and kill the little bozo? No offense."

I watched her closely, but the only thing she let show was confusion. With all apparent honesty, she answered, "Mr. LaCrosse, I don't know."

I sat back. So much for polite tactics. "You're lying to me."

"You think I'm this Epona person," she said.

"I don't know. I *do* think something scares you so bad that you'd actually *prefer* people to think you'd killed and eaten your son."

"That would be insane," she said to the floor.

"If you'll be honest with me, I promise I won't tell anyone else. Not even Phil. And if he's told you anything about me at all, you'll know that's true. I keep my word."

She looked down at her bare feet for a long moment, one elegant toe tracing idle circles on the stone floor. Finally she asked, "Are you helping Philip because of what happened to his sister?"

Epona knew about it, and it also made sense Phil would tell his wife. However she found out, though, it was still a low blow. "I want to help because he's my friend," I said through my teeth.

I stood. I really wanted out of that room, and a big drink, in that order. When I reached for the door, she cried, "That's all? You're leaving?"

I almost laughed. "You either can't or won't tell me what I need to know, Your Majesty, so this is pointless. I'll have to do this without you."

"You're going to find my son?" Now she sounded hopeful.

"I'm going to find out the truth. Because like I said, Phil's my friend. If I find your son in the process, great. If I find out why you're lying to me, I'll be sure to let Phil know so that he can decide if it's for a good reason."

Of all things, *that* finally broke her facade. "No!" she almost screamed. "You can't tell him—" Then she caught herself.

But I was already across the room, clutching the bars and inches from her face. "Tell him *what?*" I hissed. "I know you're Epona Gray, or at least you used to be. You know *me*. Who did all this? And *why?*"

Tears rolled down her face, and she wrapped her arms around her upper body. "What I *know*, just as I know the sun will rise tomorrow and that a dropped apple will hit the ground, is that I'll die if Philip doesn't love me."

"Do you love *him?*"

"Oh, God, yes," she sobbed. "With all my heart. Like I could love no other man."

Enough time had passed that this statement inspired no jealousy. Well, okay, only a bit. "Then who hates *you?*"

She didn't answer, just repeatedly shook her head. She began to cry in earnest, and sank to the edge of the hard bunk, still hugging herself. I smacked the bars in frustration.

"When I find out the truth," I almost snarled at her, "it better be damn well worth all this shit. *Eppie.*" Then I turned and knocked to be let out of the room.

TEN

Wentrobe gave me directions to the spot where Phil originally met—or found, rather—Rhiannon. It was deep in the woods on the royal hunting preserve. I could've gone with Wentrobe, or Sergeant Vogel, or even Phil, but I wanted to see it alone. I needed some time away from Arentia City and the palace to sort through what I'd learned, and not learned, from the queen.

The preserve was usually a bastard to sneak onto and off of. But I'd learned a lot of the old trails when I was a kid, and it seemed the current crop of guards knew even fewer of them than they had back then. I only had to duck off into the trees once to avoid an oblivious game warden on patrol. Poaching only became an issue when there was some famine, and Arentia was anything but starving.

It seemed unlikely I'd find any clues after six years, but I still wanted to see the place. I was reasonably certain that the plot surrounding the mysterious queen originated in her life before Phil met her; and since she claimed to remember nothing prior to that meeting, I had to work backwards from day one.

I found the area easily enough; a soft, low clover-covered hill in a clearing next to a stream. A good hunter like Phil would've checked this area for deer tracks, because the slope down to the water showed several in sharp, clear relief. I dismounted and tied my horse to a low branch; the beast looked at me with her typical equine arrogance. She seemed to have no trouble changing her loyalty from whichever border bandit owned her before, to me. Fickle tramp. I walked up the hill, scanning the ground for . . . I had no clue what.

The blue and gray clover flowers shone in the bright sun, and a light breeze made them wave a little. I sat down and surveyed the stream, the forest, even the sky. They all seemed normal, as any crime scene would after half a decade. Especially when you're not sure of the nature of the crime.

I picked one of the gray clover flowers. I stared at it, and something went *ping* way back in my head. I couldn't quite drag it forward, though, and sat there for a long moment until it hit me.

Clover doesn't have gray flowers.

I bent and looked at the plant very closely. A gray one grew next to a purple one, and other than the color of the blooms they were identical. Then I stood and looked at the whole hill.

Atop the rounded peak was a circle of gray clover about nine feet across. From one point, a narrow trail of the gray flowers led down the hill into the woods. The trail ended at the leaf litter, where the overhead branches blocked the sun.

A large crow *cawed* from a limb overhead and flew away into the forest. My eyes inadvertently followed the movement, which seemed to sparkle like the birds

I'd seen on Rhiannon's window sill. On the tree he'd vacated, a trail of silver-tipped moss grew in a narrow, thick line down the trunk, in the dead center of a burn scar from an old lightning strike. It, too, disappeared under the leaves. When I kicked the litter away, I saw that the moss continued in an unbroken line along the ground, green and alive despite being covered. I followed it, knowing it would eventually turn into the trail of gray clover. It did.

Okay, I'd found a clue. But it told me nothing. Actually, it took away some certainties, so it was more of an anti-clue. Eddie LaCrosse, reverse investigator.

So, divorced from its context, what did this tell me? Something apparently came down the tree, across the ground and landed on the very spot where my pal Phil had found his bare-assed bride, and left a trail conducive to the growth of slightly off-kilter flora. Had the lightning scar been there before the moss? Could whatever left the trail have also split the bark of the tree? I'd seen burning rocks fall from the sky; I'd seen lightning. I'd encountered all manner of animals that flew. What combination could result in what I now saw? Nothing came to mind. Except the obvious idea that Queen Rhiannon herself had left the trail after she'd fallen from the heavens and crawled out into the sun. But I wasn't ready to put my weight behind that.

"Hey!" a harsh male voice said behind me. "Hands where I can see 'em!"

I slowly complied. "I'm not a poacher. I've got authorization to be here."

"Not without me knowing about it, you don't," the voice said much nearer. I hadn't heard any steps; the guy knew his way around the forest. Suddenly I also recognized the voice.

"Terry?" I said. "Terry Vint?"

"Who's asking?" he said, now right behind me.

I grinned. "Someone you still owe three bucks to."

"I don't owe anybody any money."

"Not money bucks. *Deer* bucks."

He was silent for a moment. "Eddie LaCrosse?"

I turned. Terry's dad had been the head warden when I was a kid, and Terry had run around with Phil and me whenever he could. Now he was older, and had inherited his father's lean leathery look along with his job. But the smile was all Terry.

"Well, goddamn," he said, and lowered the crossbow he'd held pointed at my back. He wore the warden's camouflage clothes and carried a short sword at his waist. His hair was mostly white, a combination of gray and sun-bleached blond. A deep scar marked the left side of his neck. "You are the absolute last person I expected to see here. When did you get back?"

"I'm not back, and you haven't seen me. I'm working on something private for the king."

"Private?" he repeated, puzzled. Then he nodded. "Ah. The mysterious Queen Rhiannon."

I waved at the hill. "This is where they met, isn't it?"

"Yep. I was with him that day, although he'd gone ahead to scout for tracks. He'd already found her by the time I caught up."

"Do you remember anything unusual about that day?"

"Other than finding a drop-dead gorgeous blonde laid out naked like a picnic?"

"Yeah, other than that."

"No. But I noticed some weird stuff afterwards."

"Like what?"

He nodded toward the hill. "See anything strange about the spot?"

"Besides the trail of gray clover that turns into silver moss and runs up that tree?"

"Not bad. Clover doesn't grow gray flowers, and moss doesn't grow silver tips, yet here they are. Like they're marking a trail, wouldn't you say?" Without waiting for a response, he walked over to the moss-lined tree. "And I've got something else to show you, that I never showed anybody. Tried to show the king once, but he couldn't be bothered. Haven't looked for it in a few years, so it may not be there, but let's see. . . ."

He walked to the base of the tree and began kicking away the leaves. In a few moments he'd uncovered an area of bare, dark dirt about ten feet square, bisected by the silver moss. "Whadda ya think of that?" he asked, gesturing at the ground.

He'd uncovered a line of carefully placed rocks marking the impression where something big and heavy had hit the ground. Weather and time had blurred some of the edges, but the rocks, placed soon after the initial impact, clearly showed the object's unmistakable outline. The trail of silver moss ran right through it.

"It looks," I said obviously, "like a horse fell out of the sky."

"Yep," Terry agreed.

"Horses don't do that, as a rule."

"Not usually."

"I don't suppose anyone saw a horse fall from the

sky, turn into a beautiful woman and then lay down in the grass to wait for passing royalty to pick her up?"

"Horses generally don't do that, either."

"No," I agreed. "So Phil never saw this?"

"*Nobody* else has seen it. I marked it out after the hubbub died down, figuring some day someone might want to know, and pretty much forgot about it myself."

I looked at him. "It might be important that you forget again."

"Hm. I got a pretty good memory. Except when I drink."

I grinned. "Well, let's get to work on your memory, then."

TERRY VINT HAD inherited his family home from his father, and moved his already-considerable brood into it. I counted five children playing in the yard, and when Mrs. Vint came out the door, she held the newest future woodsman in her arms. For such a prolific breeder, Shana Vint was still very attractive in an earthy, sensual way that went well beyond physical appearance. I imagined that, had I married her, she'd have spent a lot of time knocked up, too.

Terry introduced us, then he and I adjourned to chairs in the back yard beneath the shady trees. Shana brought us two tankards and a big bottle of wine, poured the first two drinks and then left. We could hear the children playing in the front yard, and the smell of dinner drifted from the kitchen.

"So you came all the way back from wherever you

were to help the king get his wife off the hook?" Terry asked.

"He wants me to find out the truth," I responded. I didn't feel comfortable giving out more details than I had to.

"I thought she was caught red-handed. Literally."

"That's true," I said. "But sometimes things aren't exactly what they seem to be."

He looked at me. "You're being cagey with me, Eddie. And I guess that's okay, we haven't hung around each other in twenty years, we probably don't have much in common anymore. Me, I got my home, my five sprouts and my wife, and no ambition to be anything else. I mean, I like Phil, and the queen was never anything but nice to me. But it's hard for a parent to find a lot of sympathy for her. You got any kids, Eddie? Wife, family?"

I shook my head.

"She killed her own child. Pretty brutally, from what I hear. The king's got to do the right thing by his people, or he'll lose 'em. He's only the king because everybody acts like he is."

Terry's political insight, while accurate, didn't help me much. I turned over the known facts in my head, looking for ways they might connect. So far, though, the threads eluded me.

I threw out a wild card. "You ever heard of anyone named Epona Gray?"

He thought it over, and his response seemed genuine. "Nope."

Something else nagged at me, another of those small off-kilter details, but this time I couldn't catch hold of it. The wine unsurprisingly didn't help, although I made sure I thoroughly explored that option before I left.

I was a little wobbly by the time I excused myself from Terry's hospitality. I had to hug each of his five mobile offspring in turn, while the baby settled for a simple kiss atop his fuzzy head. Terry's wife was even more attractive once I got some alcohol in me, so I knew I'd picked the right moment to leave. As I rode away, Terry stood behind her nuzzling her neck, which made her smile. I wondered how soon she'd be pregnant again.

THE BEST VIEW of the sunset anywhere in Arentia was from a certain part of the castle roof, where you could see for twenty miles in any direction. The roof was higher in other places, but in none of those could you also drink yourself stupid in peace. Phil and I had used the spot often as teenagers, and now we sat with our backs against a chimney, two empty bottles beside us, and a third destined to join them.

Phil took a long drink then passed the bottle to me. "I can't do it, Eddie," he said. His eyes were heavy, but otherwise he betrayed no sign of the fact that he was almost, as they say in the provinces, too drunk to fish.

"You gotta," I repeated. We'd gone around this issue for nearly the entire three bottles, and I was at the end of my patience. "You're only king because everybody acts like you are, you know."

He ignored my stolen wit. "Could *you* do it?"

"I could if there was a good reason. Think about it, man. If you don't let whoever did this think they've succeeded, then they'll just try something else. This way, they'll be off guard."

He looked at me seriously. "Ed, that's my *wife* you're talking about."

That made me mad, and yet again I almost told him about Epona Gray. Each time, though, Rhiannon's words about love rang in my head, and somehow this made me keep it to myself. "Hey, y'know, you're the goddamn king. You don't want to take my advice, then I'll just pack my stuff and go home."

"C'mon, Ed, I'm serious."

"So am I!" I was drunk enough to take his resistance as an affront to my professionalism. "You *asked* for my help, you know. I didn't come bustin' in here sayin', 'Oh, Phil, you must listen to me!' I can go back to my old job and be quite happy." I started to get to my feet.

"Whoa, man, sit down," Phil said. He grabbed my arm and pulled me back hard against the chimney. "I didn't mean anything by it, it's just . . . how do I sentence my wife to prison when I know she didn't *do* anything?"

I met his eyes as well as I could. "I wouldn't say she hasn't done anything. I don't think she's been honest with us, for one thing. But I'll bet my left nut she didn't kill your son."

He took another drink. In a small voice I'd never heard from him before, he said, "I miss him."

I couldn't think of anything to say to that.

"Losing Janet was tough," he continued. "And you'd think it would somehow, I don't know, prepare me for losing P.D. But it didn't."

I took a long drink from the bottle.

"You ever think about her?" he asked me. "What she'd be like now?"

"Nope," I lied.

"Think you would've married her?"

"Nope," I lied again.

"Mom and Dad never blamed you, you know. Never. Neither did *your* dad."

I stared at him. "You talked to my *dad* about it?"

"After you ran off, I felt bad for him. I used to visit him while he was sick before he died. He wanted me to tell you, if I ever saw you again, that he regretted all that stuff he said."

"That a fact." *You failed to protect the goddamn princess of the goddamn country*, he'd roared. *If you'd died too, then maybe we'd have some dignity left, but you couldn't even do that right.* "Well, he always tended to speak before he thought."

"Something I noticed *you* don't ever do." He took another drink. "What do you really think happened, Eddie? To my wife, to my son? Please, man." The pleading was so honest it damn near broke my heart. I never expected to hear Phil beg anyone, let alone me, for anything.

"I think," I said carefully, "that your wife knows more than she's telling, and that someone from her past, from before you met her, is out to get her. I don't know why they picked *now*, and I don't know why they chose *this* particular way." I took another drink. "And that's why she has to go to jail. I have to do some poking around outside Arentia, and that may take a while. I need all the cover I can get. The *best* cover is to let whoever did this think they got away with it."

"But I can't even tell Ree."

"*Especially* not Ree."

"She'll think I hate her."

"And so will everybody else, which is the important part. She has to believe it, or no one else will."

"How long will you be gone?"

"As long as it takes me to find the answers, or at least find better questions to ask." My sympathy got the better of me. "I'll go as fast as I can, Phil. I promise."

We stopped talking then, but kept drinking. Eventually we staggered downstairs, gave each other drunken hugs and stumbled off to our respective rooms. Mine kept spinning whenever I lay down, so I paced for a long time, trying to burn off enough buzz to get to sleep.

I snuck back out and made my wobbly way to the royal portrait gallery, where paintings of the Arentian rulers and their families had hung for generations. I wanted one look, just for a moment, to see if my memory had embellished itself or if she'd really been as beautiful as I recalled.

The gallery was dark, of course, since it was the middle of the night, but the moonlight shone through the huge windows and illuminated the paintings on the opposite wall. I'd entered on the far end, where the legendary founder of Arentia, King Hyde, began the progression. I quickly moved down to the most recent paintings.

And there she was. Dark hair cut shorter than was fashionable at the time, framing a face that was still a little too round to be striking. And yet she was still the most beautiful thing I'd ever seen. Never mind that she was a child when this was painted, barely two months before her death; I'd been a child, too. Both of us six-teen, full of the certainty of our own immortality. And the moonlight in the painted eyes seemed an especially cruel reflection of the trust I'd once seen in them, a trust I failed in the most horrendous possible way.

Hell, Janet, I wanted to say. *I did the best I could. I'd do it all so much better now*.

The painting was too high on the wall for me to touch. I stared at it for a long time, marveling at how accurately the artist had captured her smile, the cocky tilt to her head, the way she'd lean her weight onto her right hip as if readying for a scrap. We should've had a lifetime of scraps; but we never even had time for one.

I fell asleep fully dressed, and dreamed the worst dream ever, of Janet screaming for me to save her while the men who'd killed her laughed at me. I hadn't had that dream in years, and hoped the wine would dull my head enough to avoid it now. I awoke in tears, but luck-ily no one was there to see it.

ELEVEN

I left Arentia before dawn, two days after my interview with Queen Rhiannon. I slipped out of the castle with the morning garbage detail, and waited at the dump outside town for an hour to make sure no one had followed me. My adversary, whoever he was, clearly had his fingers on a lot of spider webs. I wanted to make sure mine didn't quiver.

A day's ride on my stolen horse brought me almost to the Arentian border, where I made camp. That night I stared up at the stars and imagined a wide-eyed horse tumbling out of the sky, its hooves pumping madly as it plummeted toward the ground. I looked over at my stolid, arrogant horse, tied to a low tree branch. The absurdity of the idea made me smile.

If you wanted to say anything was possible, it *was* conceivable that Rhiannon had fallen from the sky in the shape of a horse and then transformed into a beautiful woman. And I guess it was also conceivable that the fall could've knocked her memories from her head. But none of that explained how a horse got up in the sky in the first place. Or why Queen Rhiannon was the spitting image of Epona Gray, the Queen of Horses.

Hell, I chastised myself, *don't be catty about it.*
Queen *Rhiannon* is *Epona Gray*.

Epona Gray, and Cathy Dumont, and Stan Carnahan
and the mysterious Andrew Reese. I hadn't thought of
those names in over ten years. It was from a time in my
life when I made foolish alliances far too quickly, and
often found myself stuck with obligations I couldn't
fulfill. I'd learned a lot since then.

They say too much introspection is as bad for you as
too much drink. The folks who say this spend a lot of
time introspecting, so I guess they'd know. *Forced* introspection can be even worse, because no one is ever
compelled to contemplate the good things in their past.
You look to history to avoid the same mistakes, not repeat the same joys. That's why defeats are clearer than
victories, funerals more vivid than weddings.

I hated my past. Yet in it was my only clue to the disappearance of Phil's son. The resemblance between
Rhiannon and Epona Gray was too striking to be mere
coincidence. But how had a woman who'd been dying
when last I saw her traveled all this way, in both time
and distance, to emerge as the sun-infused beauty I
met in that tower?

The trail to Epona Gray stretched back thirteen years,
almost as far as the one to Phil and Janet. I seldom
thought about that time in my life, but now I had to re-
trace not just my footsteps but my memories and feelings. Something, some miscellaneous detail, *had* to
provide the connection. And if I knew why Epona had
become Rhiannon—never mind *how*—I might know
why someone hated her.

So by day I headed toward Cazenovia, eventually
crossed the bridge at Poy Sippi, and traveled through

the dense forests to the hidden place that, long ago, had sheltered Epona Gray. And each night, I gave my thoughts renewed access to those days as well, hoping that some vital clue might shake loose from the memories. The past washed over me like the flood that hit Neceda, leaving behind the debris of pain, failure and death.

THAT FIRST NIGHT on the trail, my thoughts returned to the other time I'd skulked out of Arentia, after Janet's death. I'd been sixteen, and sure of absolutely nothing except that I never wanted to see anyone I knew ever again—not my parents, not my friends, especially not Phil. As soon as my injuries had healed enough for me to travel, I caught a ride with a flannel merchant heading for the border, and spent the next three months drunk off my ass, fighting and whoring my way as far as my money took me. I wasn't trying to burn Janet's memory from my mind, or seeking death so I could be with her. I was creating a new Eddie LaCrosse, one who'd never been rich or brave or happy. Eddie version two was mean, selfish and took no shit from anyone.

Finally, several months into my transformation, I awoke in some strange girl's bed, broke and bruised and monumentally hung over. When the girl started screaming for her money, I smacked her, and knew I'd achieved what I wanted. I'd reached a point where no one else existed for me, where my own brutality was simply the way I operated. I was a bully and a jackass, and people better stay out of my way.

Even a jackass needs a job, though, and what better

one than signing up for someone else's army? My dad had insisted I learn to handle a knife and sword, and it turned out I had a real knack for it. Since I didn't care which side won, I had no problem hacking down anyone designated as my "enemy," and so I spent five years bouncing around various small countries, once rising to the rank of major. I drank too much, killed people for all the wrong reasons and generally behaved like most of the career soldiers I knew. I saw things so brutal they would give a lesser man, or any man with a conscience, nightmares for life. It was a liberating experience.

Once again, though, the change came when I awoke one morning with a girl. Only this time she was dead, and so was everyone else in the whorehouse, including my entire unit.

It remains the spookiest dawn of my life. A noise awoke me, but I never found out what it was. I winced at the sun through the window. The girl's body had stiffened during the night, and I had to struggle to get free of her cold, clutching arms. A single sword thrust went through her back and emerged between her breasts, bisecting her heart. Blood soaked the mattress beneath us. Her expression was one of slack-jawed surprise, although her eyes were closed. When I threw her aside in momentary panic, I dislodged two dozen flies already claiming the body.

My head thundered from drink, and I quickly checked myself for injury. Not a fresh mark showed among the old pink scars. Had the murderer been after only the girl? And had I been so drunk that someone could come into the room and stab her without waking me?

I got dressed, and found my money was still in my pockets; robbery hadn't been the motive. I searched each room on the second floor and found the same thing—a soldier and a whore, both dead from a single sword thrust. Nothing seemed to be taken from them, either.

The bar downstairs was empty. I helped myself to enough drink to dull my headache, then went into the street. Our horses, tied to the post the night before, were gone. The manure piles told me they'd been away for over six hours. The rest of the tiny crossroads town was deserted, although I found no other bodies, or any indication when the native population left. It was as if they'd just vanished.

I didn't make a really thorough search because the whole thing was too damn eerie. I got out of there as fast as my wobbly legs would carry me. At first my wine-addled brain convinced me I was marked for death, that who or whatever had slaughtered everyone else would realize it had missed me and follow me to the ends of the earth. Later, after I'd thrown up a lot and choked down some half-cooked rabbit, I realized I'd just been incredibly, almost mythologically, lucky.

To this day I don't know for certain who killed them all, or why. We were fighting in a disputed territory with lots of guerrilla units as well as regular troops on the prowl, none of whom were above ambushing us while we were drunk or asleep. Later I heard a faction loyal to the local king may have killed everyone and burned the town; I must have accidentally slipped out while they were off readying their torches. Either way, that day loaded with real death marked the symbolic demise of Eddie the Mercenary. Although I wasn't a religious guy, I couldn't shake the notion I'd been spared for a reason, and once I'd sobered up enough to think straight, I decided I'd be an idiot not to honor my luck.

I spent two aimless years doing odd jobs for meals and learning various quirky trades. I was still young, and didn't really look like a soldier, although I still had my sword and sundry other hidden weapons. I also still despised horses, so I traveled everywhere on foot. It kept me lean and alert.

And so it was that one day thirteen years ago I strolled along the empty road between Antigo and Cazenovia, minding my own business, when I heard the distinctive clatter of swords in combat.

I instantly slipped off the road and into the thick forest. A woman's voice snarled, "Goddammit!" accompanied by three quick clangs. I followed the sound to its source.

Three men, rough-clad ambush robbers by the look of them, surrounded a fourth figure. The bad guys had huge battered swords and wielded them with casual, vicious skill. They stood around their quarry in a practiced pattern that kept one of them always out of their victim's field of vision.

In the center of this triangle stood a slender, red-haired girl, as tall as me but with that willowy quality so many country girls possess. She had short hair and was dressed like a man, which actually made her look more feminine. But this was certainly no helpless maiden.

As I watched, one of the men grabbed for her jacket. She spun, and something smaller than their weapons flashed in each of her hands. They were too big to be knives and not wide enough to be swords, but they clearly did the job. The man howled and jumped back as the girl blocked not only his awkward sword thrust but the straight-to-the-mark jab of another man now directly behind her.

She aimed a kick at the backstabber's knee, but he dodged it. She used her momentum and spun, catching the third man's sword in the crossed blades of her own long, thin weapons. She rolled her weight onto her back foot and slammed her other one into his crotch. As he fell, she kneed him hard in the face. He dropped, out cold. Then she whirled on the other two, trying to keep them both in sight.

"Who's next, huh?" she demanded. There was no fear in her voice.

She was, however, outnumbered, and these guys were pros. They'd already slipped up by underestimating her, and they wouldn't make that mistake again. They slowly circled, moving into opposite positions so she couldn't watch them both at once. Neither of them had noticed me, however, and I used the trees and shadows to cover my approach.

"Look, fellas," the girl continued, "this doesn't have to get any uglier. I don't have any money on me, so this is just a waste of your time."

"You got something on you, all right," one of them said. "It may not be money, but it don't mean we can't sell it somewhere."

"Yeah, I bet you're awful cute under all that," the other agreed. "And I know one way to find out."

She snorted. "What you see is nothing, I got a Falinese dancing girl tattooed across my back." Then, surprising me as much as them, she *attacked*.

She feinted toward the weaker-looking of the two,

and when the bigger man tried to take advantage of this, she was ready for him. She kicked him hard in the nuts, then spun and slashed him across the throat. It wasn't just a casual blow, either; she windmilled at him, so that if the first blade missed, the second would not. In this case, neither did.

But even the best plans can be foiled by sheer dumb luck. The bigger man was *so* big, his momentum carried him forward faster than she could react, and he plowed into her, blood gushing from his neck. His weight drove her to the ground, and the remaining thug lost no time stepping forward to take advantage of this.

That is, he would have if my throwing knife hadn't struck him in the heart. He never knew what hit him or where it came from, and he stumbled a few feet before collapsing. I waited to make sure he wasn't faking before strolling over to the scene.

The girl, still pinned beneath the big man, looked up at me. "So are you gonna do anything other than gawk?" she gasped in annoyance. "I could use a little help here."

"I already gave you a little help," I said, and retrieved my knife from the dead man's chest. I wiped the blood on his clothes and slipped it back into the side of my boot. "I figure you can get out of there on your own."

She glared at me, but didn't ask again, and after a couple of moments of concerted wriggling, she emerged rumpled but unhurt. Blood streaked her clothes, but none of it was hers. The first man moaned, and she kicked him in the head hard enough to knock him out again. Then she faced me, and I got my first close look at her.

She had wide shoulders and the kind of trim, narrow

body that spoke of hard muscle beneath her baggy clothes. A deep scar cut through her right eyebrow and touched her hairline, where a streak of white sprang from it. She was cute rather than pretty, and I just bet she knew that and it bugged the hell out of her. "So what happens now?" she snapped, challenge in her voice. For all she knew, I was another bandit.

"Can I see that tattoo?" I asked with a grin.

"Is that why you jumped in?"

"Nah. You looked like you needed a hand. Hand given. We'll leave it at that. See ya."

"That's it?" she exclaimed as I walked back toward the road.

"That's it," I tossed over my shoulder.

She made an exasperated noise. "Will you wait a minute?"

I stopped.

"Where are you headed?" she asked as she caught up with me.

"Nowhere," I said honestly.

She paused for a deep, calming breath before she spoke again. "Here's the thing. You're pretty good with a knife. I assume you're good with that sword. And you seem to be a decent guy. At least, you didn't try to get into my money bag *or* my pants." Then she stopped, scowling as if her openness embarrassed her.

"Either say it or don't," I prompted.

"Well, it's just . . . I'm not a fighter, I'm a delivery man . . . girl. *Woman.* I'm new at it. And I've had six fights like that one in five days, most of them not even over the package I'm supposed to deliver. They were over this package." She gestured at her body. "Know what I mean?"

"Ah."

"And damn it, I don't want to have to either pretend to be a teenage boy for the whole trip or just 'lay back and enjoy it,' as they say."

"Understandable."

"So. . . ." Again she paused, working up the nerve to say what she wanted. "I would like to hire you to go with me the rest of the way."

"The rest of the way to where?"

"I'll tell you when I know I can trust you. Until then, all you'd have to do is just tag along and look unpleasant." She put her hands on her hips and waited for my reply. Her skin was flushed from exertion, and it made her freckles stand out.

"You don't even know me," I pointed out.

She rolled her eyes. "No, I don't, and I don't have time to check your damn references, either. I'm a pretty good judge of people, and my fast decisions tend to be my best ones. If you're in, let's go; if not, say so."

"Okay, so what's in it for me besides your charming company?"

"I have half my fee in advance. I'll give you half of that, which means I'm out a quarter of it."

"I can do math, you know. But how much actually goes into my pocket?"

She told me, and it was certainly a respectable amount. I didn't have to think about it for long. "Okay, you got a deal. Where are we going?"

"Uh-uh. I'm the boss, so we're in the world of need-to-know. Until, like I said, I know I can trust you."

"It ain't very smart to hire a bodyguard you don't trust," I pointed out.

"You're not a bodyguard," she almost snarled. "I can

guard my own damn body, thank you very much. You're just along to expedite things."

"So I'm your arm candy," I said with a grin.

She scowled, but I saw amusement in her eyes. "I'd say you were arm spinach. It's good for you, but nobody enjoys it."

"In case you stop eating healthy, then, maybe I better get half *my* fee in advance."

She shrugged. "If it makes you feel more secure." She took out a handful of money and counted out half of the agreed amount.

"You can trust me now," I said as I put the money away.

"Only halfway," she fired back, but she grinned when she said it.

And so I met Cathy Dumont, proprietor and sole employee of Dumont Confidential Courier Service. Since we were far enough from Arentia that she'd probably never heard of my family or my own connection to scandal, I gave her my real name, and we shook hands on our bargain. She told me nothing about our destination, or about the "package" she carried in her backpack. As for where we were headed, she said only that we had to cross the Wyomie River sometime within the next three weeks. We could've made better time on horses, but neither of us had the money to buy them or was sleazy enough to steal them. So we walked.

We fell into an easy traveling rhythm those first few days. Cathy proved to be quite loquacious, but unlike a lot of people, she actually had something substantial to say. She explained that she'd come from Bonduel, the daughter of a blacksmith who encouraged her to both master some form of weaponry and never allow herself to be dependent on anyone. She married young, and was widowed shortly afterwards, a memory that seemed to call up no regret on her part; I didn't ask the obvious questions about just *how* her late spouse had met his end.

Yes, she was attractive. And yes, I noticed, and yes, it had been a while for me. But besides the fact that she was not very encouraging (she insisted we always sleep with the fire between us), I just wasn't motivated that way. Although I'd visited whorehouses with my fellow soldiers, Janet had been my only "lover." Even after seven years that memory was still too fresh.

TWELVE

Ten days later Cathy and I reached the public bridge over the Wyomie River. The spring thaw upstream had swollen it high above flood stage, and great foamy waves churned mere inches beneath the span. The banks, thankfully, were so steep and rocky the water had not flooded the town. But if it rose another eight inches, folks in Poy Sippi would be rolling up their pants legs.

Too deep and swift for boat traffic on a normal day, the Wyomie was an impassable border slicing between the last of the foothills and the irregular Ogachic Mountains beyond. Over time it had carved a famously deep canyon, and the bridge at Poy Sippi was the only way across for miles in either direction.

About a hundred years before, a land speculator had paid for the bridge, assuming the real estate on either end would quickly increase in value. But because the location had *only* the bridge to recommend it—the surrounding soil was too rocky for farming, and despite years of effort, nothing useful could be mined from it—Poy Sippi was slow to become a real family-friendly town. At the time Cathy and I passed through, it was just a ragged settlement of the kinds of people who could make a living off bridge patrons.

On the day we arrived, it was crowded with travelers funneling into, or fanning out from, the ends of the bridge. There was no charge to use it, so for lots of folks it was the only way across the Wyomie. The local constabulary was supposed to police it, but like all isolated officials, they spent most of their time enjoying the illicit spoils of looking the other way. You crossed at your own risk, and if you got beaten, mugged or worse, you were on your own. Lots of bodies washed up downstream.

Before crossing, we stopped for lunch at one of the roadhouses clustered around the ends of the bridge. The sign proclaimed it *The Sway Easy*, and beneath that was what appeared to be a motto: *Pain Don't Hurt*. After the waitress delivered our drinks and food, Cathy leaned over to me and said softly, "My instructions are really clear. We have to be sure no one follows us across the bridge. Specifically, no women on white horses."

"Okay," I agreed. That seemed easy enough. "But why?"

"I think my client is a little paranoid."

"So who *is* your client?" I asked. "Seriously. We've spent every minute of the last ten days together, surely you can trust me now."

She bit her lip thoughtfully, then nodded. "Okay. I had taken a set of property deeds to Cape Querna down on the coast of Boscobel. While I was there, I was approached by a messenger with this job. He wouldn't tell me who it was for, but he paid up front. When I'm done, I'm supposed to go back to Boscobel and check into the same boarding house. They'll contact me then about the balance due."

I scowled. "And you wouldn't trust me," I said sarcastically.

"Got nothing to do with trust. It's how couriers operate. We never get paid everything in advance, and a lot of times we don't know who's hired us." She shrugged. "It's the business."

The back of my neck suddenly tingled. I looked around at the other travelers in the roadhouse. None of them seemed interested in us, yet I knew someone was studying us with more than idle curiosity. It's a skill, or a sense, that develops quickly in battle, when two eyes just aren't enough. "Maybe your mysterious client isn't paranoid," I said quietly. "I got that prickly feeling."

She nodded and muttered, "Me, too. Do we run or try to draw them out?"

"You're letting me decide?" I teased.

"I'm asking your opinion." She kicked me sharply under the table. "This is my *job*. Be serious."

I grinned. "Okay. Since even I don't know jack about your job, how likely is it that someone else knows what you're carrying?"

"Not very."

"So unless it's some woman on a white horse, they're probably no more interested in us than they are in anyone else who might wander through. Probably think we're newlyweds with pockets full of wedding cash. If we let 'em pick the fight, we'll draw an awful lot of attention."

"So we should just valiantly tiptoe away?"

"You're the boss."

She smiled. She did that seldom, but when it happened, it was dazzling. It made her eyes crinkle at the corners and completely eliminated the hard, no-

nonsense warrior-bitch look she cultivated. It also made her, momentarily at least, quite beautiful. I'd never tell her that, of course.

"Prudence over passion, then," she said, and dug out money to pay the check. "Just like my daddy always said. Let's at least let 'em know we're not complete morons, though."

Outside she casually joined the pedestrian traffic moving toward the bridge, pushed aside by the bigger wagons and horses. I headed in the opposite direction, looped quickly around a smithy shop and watched two thuggish men emerge from the roadhouse. They saw Cathy walking away alone and instantly looked around for me, knowing they'd been smoked. I stepped out so they could see me, tapped the side of my nose to indicate I knew exactly what they were up to, and watched them shuffle back inside. Evidently they weren't up for such hard work.

I caught up with Cathy. "Just a couple of bums thinking they'd surprise us. Gave up when they saw we were on to 'em. Good call."

She just nodded, but I saw her blush slightly at the compliment. It was so adorable that, combined with the smile she'd given me over lunch, I found my thoughts turning in a surprising direction. But I kept them to myself, out of respect for Janet, and Cathy.

THAT HAD BEEN a long time ago, before traveling all day made my lower back throb like it did now. Now Poy Sippi was huge, and new gates controlled the bridge traffic. There was still no charge, but pedestrians could only cross at certain times, wagons at another, and so forth.

The old roadhouse we'd stopped at for lunch was long gone, replaced by a brand-new tavern advertising gourmet dinners and great-looking waitresses. I tried lunch, which was adequate, and admired the waitresses, who were attractive. But then again, so were the girls in the place next door. And across the street. The individual quality was gone, replaced by cookie-cutter roadhouses owned by far-off noblemen. I missed the individual touch.

"Everything good?" the waitress asked brightly. Her name tag said *Trudy*. "Shall I freshen up that ale for you?"

"No, thanks," I said. "You know, I haven't been here in a while; the place is really built up."

"Oh, yes. There's talk of putting in a whole other bridge to handle the traffic. If they do that, this place'll explode." She was young, so the thought excited her. I bet she'd be bored to tears by the town I remembered.

"You live here long?" I asked.

"All my life." A guarded tone slid into her voice, probably because she thought I was about to proposition her.

"Did you ever know a woman named Epona Gray?" To aid her memory, I put money atop my check and a sizable pile next to it for her tip.

Trudy thought about it, her serving tray balanced on her hip. "No, I don't think so. A lot of the old-timers left when it started getting crowded, maybe she was one of them."

"How about Andrew Reese?"

"No, haven't—" She stopped and looked puzzled. "Do you mean the children's rhyme? 'Andrew Reese is broken to pieces'?"

Those words, said so casually, sent a chill through me. The only time I'd ever heard them before was from Epona Gray's own lips. "You know that one?"

She smiled. "Everyone here knows it. We all learned it when we were little kids in school." She closed her eyes and softly sang:

"Because he had no manners,
She pounded him with hammers.
Because he was so rude,
She fixed his attitude.
Because he was so mean,
She made him scream and scream.
And now Andrew Reese is
Broken to pieces."

She laughed a little. "Wow. It must really stick in your head if I can remember it after all this time."

The last couplet, in Epona's drunken voice, echoed maddeningly in my mind. "Yeah, I bet it does. So there's no real person with that name?"

"Oh, I'm sure there is somewhere. But not in Poy Sippi. Nobody would be cruel enough to name their kid that. That'd be just asking for him to get beaten up."

After she left to attend other customers, I sipped my ale and mentally kicked my own ass. I'd assumed, for no good reason, that Andrew Reese was a real person. I don't know why, given the lunacy of everything else Epona said, that I'd seized on this one thing as an indisputable fact. Had she just been drunk, singing some nursery rhyme?

No. I was certain she'd said Andrew Reese sent the package Cathy delivered. And whether or not she meant it symbolically—*an* Andrew Reese instead of *the* Andrew Reese—it still counted as a clue. If my trip into the mountains crapped out, I'd pursue the origins of this children's song. It was only a slightly longer shot than my current course of action.

I came out of the roadhouse and started down the street when a voice said, "Hey, mister."

I turned. A tiny young girl stood in the alley between the livery stable where I'd left my horse and a ramshackle swordsmith's shop. I guessed she was around four, with matted hair, a dirty face and clothes that were little more than rags. You saw kids like this in every town, especially those on trade routes like Poy Sippi: orphans or junior criminals, sometimes both. When I'd first passed through town with Cathy, the gangs had been adults; now, with security to keep the grown-ups in check, the streets fell by default to the kids.

This girl certainly looked more like a victim than a crook, but the voice that called me had belonged to an older child. As soon as I'd had time to make solid eye contact with the girl, a hand appeared behind her and yanked her out of sight down the alley.

"Help!" the other child's voice called.

I looked around. None of the other passersby seemed to have heard, or else had sense enough to ignore it. I sighed, unsnapped the catch on my scabbard and strode toward the alley. I'm sure they counted on finding someone unable to just walk away from a child in danger, preferably a stupid do-gooder with a wallet full of gold and a naive belief in his own invulnerability. They'd soon find out how wrong they were—I had very little gold on me. My only advantage was that I knew exactly what I was getting into.

I peeked around the edge of the swordsmith building. The girl now waited at the alley's far end, and again a hand yanked her out of sight once she knew I'd seen her. I was being drawn into the wider alley at the rear of the buildings, where the garbage and other refuse, some of it human, always collected.

I wanted to smack myself. *Of course* I was being suckered, and I was on an important job, but the infinitesimal chance that a child might actually be in danger made me proceed anyway. I hugged the wall down to the far end of the building, then stopped and listened. I heard nothing. I drew my sword, held it down beside my leg and stepped around the corner.

Luckily I'd also crouched, so the wooden board slammed against the building above me instead of into my head. I used my left arm to grab the kid who swung it. He was about ten, and struggled with well-practiced panic. "Hey, help! This guy wants to bend me over a garbage barrel! Let me go, you pervert!"

I got a good grip on his hair, yanked him back against me and raised the sword blade to his throat. He froze when the metal touched his skin.

I faced his gang. Three grubby boys, the oldest about fifteen, watched me with wide eyes. The little girl they'd used as bait ran over and hid behind them.

The boy in my grasp burst into renewed struggles, trying to catch me off-guard. I pressed the blade harder against his throat. I wasn't going to kill him, but I didn't care if he got cut a little. "Shouldn't you kids be in school?" I said over my hostage's head.

"Uh . . . give us your money," the tallest boy said, falling back on routine.

I almost laughed. "I don't think so. Why don't you give me *your* money?"

He blinked. "What?"

"You heard me. On the ground, right here in front of me. Come on."

The kids looked at each other.

I leaned close to my prisoner. "Better get 'em moving," I snarled in his ear.

"Give him the damn money!" the kid squeaked.

The tallest boy, evidently the leader, stepped forward and said, "No. I don't think you'll hurt him."

I slid the sword just enough to slice my hostage's neck. It was no more than a glorified shaving nick, but the nice thing about those harmless, shallow cuts is that they sting like a bitch and bleed quite freely. This one did both, and the kids gasped. The little girl began to cry.

"Hell, Scotty!" my captive screeched. "Give him the money!"

"All right!" the boy Scotty said. He tossed a small bag to the ground at my feet. It jingled when it hit. "There. That's all we have."

"Is that the truth?" I asked the kid in my grip.

"Yeah!" he shrieked.

I slowly withdrew my sword. The boy was sure I was about to cut his throat all the way, but I wasn't. When I released him his knees collapsed, and he crawled over to Scotty's feet. He put his hand to his throat, and when he saw blood he passed out.

I picked up the money. It was maybe enough to buy a couple of meals. I looked at the raggedy idiots, sighed and tossed the money back to Scotty. "Here. This was embarrassing for all of us."

Scotty caught it and stared at me. "Are you going to kill us?" he asked, his voice low but steady.

"No, you moron. But I should, just to save some other sword jockey from having to put up with you. Do you have any idea how close you came?" I sheathed my sword. "You guys are *really bad* at this."

"You're mean!" the bait girl said, then ducked back out of sight.

"Yeah," I agreed, and turned to go. And that should've been that. But I never saw the blow coming, since whoever struck me did so from behind. I felt only the rush into that big black pool where nothing hurts and nobody bothers you.

THIRTEEN

M y first thought as I awoke was that my head
hurt so much, if anyone spoke to me, I'd cry.
The second was that the room was way too small for
my head.

This was the third time in my life I'd been knocked
out. Those who make their living relaying tales of
heroic deeds at fancy banquets would have you think
this was no more than an inconvenience, to be shaken
off as easily as raindrops. Their heroes always snap
wide awake and rush off to make up for lost time. I can
guarantee that the folks who come up with those stories have never been seriously whacked in the head.

"Is he alive?" a woman's voice asked. I couldn't
place it, but I'd heard it before, and recently.

"I didn't hit him *that* hard," a boy replied with a
child's superior impatience. "He's breathing, isn't he?"

"Quiet," a new voice snapped. It was older, rougher
and female. "He's awake. Now get out."

Door hinges protested, wood scraped against wood
and I felt that slight change in air pressure that said a
heavy door had closed. I decided to open my eyes.

The back of my skull felt like mashed potatoes. I blinked, groaned and tried to make sense of the confusing lights and shadows. Luckily the room was dark, but a table lamp provided some dim illumination. I blinked, tried to rise and found I was on my stomach, my hands tied to my ankles behind me.

"Don't try to move," the older female voice said. She sat just out of the lamp's illumination.

"Okay," I rasped out. The room was very small, and I lay on what felt like a blanket spread across uneven wooden crates.

"You were asking about Epona Gray."

"Yeah," I said. I didn't know this one, but I realized where I'd heard the other woman's voice before. "I guess I didn't give Trudy a big enough tip, huh?"

"She knows I'm always interested in certain things."

"Like Epona Gray?"

"Always." She leaned forward. I saw frizzy hair backlit so that her head resembled a dandelion gone to seed. "You're a smart guy, I'd guess. So I don't think I have to explain too much. Whether or not you leave this room depends on what you tell me about Epona Gray."

"What do you want to know?"

"Where is she?"

"Dead, as far as I know."

The frizzy head leaned back. "Then why are you asking about her?"

I wriggled as much as I could. "This is really uncomfortable," I groaned. "I'd feel a lot chattier if you'd untie me."

"And I'd feel a lot less safe," she said. "You can answer my question just fine from where you are."

I squirmed some more, but couldn't reach the knife in my boot, or even tell if it was still there. "I knew her once," I said. "I just wondered if anyone else around here might remember her."

"Everyone that knew her is dead," the woman said with deep certainty. "Except me."

"Not everyone," I replied.

"So you knew her?" she asked derisively. "When?"

"Right before she died."

Again she leaned forward, and her frizzy hair caught the light. "And how is that possible?"

"Hey, lady, I'm not trying to convince you of anything. I met her the night she died, I only spoke to her for a few minutes, but since I was back in the area I asked a waitress a harmless question. This seems a lot like an over-reaction."

"Nothing to do with Epona is 'harmless.'" She leaned back again. "Tell me how she died."

I saw no reason to keep it a secret. "She was poisoned."

She paused for a long moment.

I took advantage of the silence and asked, "And what the hell do *you* know about it? I was the only person who walked away from it."

The smile in her voice had no warmth. "Not the only one," she said, imitating my tone. She reached over and turned up the lamp.

I could not begin to guess her age. Her face was a mass of scar tissue, and her hair grew in ragged white patches. "I crawled out of a burning house. I was on fire as well, but I made it to a creek and put out the flames. Did you know that, if you're burned badly enough, you don't feel it?"

"Yeah," I said. I recalled those same flames myself, and the blood-soaked beast roaming through them.

"My parents died. My friends died. Everyone died because of Epona. On the very day I was initiated into her mysteries."

I went cold. It took a moment to find my voice again. "You're only about eighteen years old, aren't you?"

She crossed her legs, deliberately letting her wrap-around skirt fall open. Her legs were a little hairy, but had the smooth lines of youth. "How could you tell?" she asked sarcastically.

"Because I saw you that day," I said. "I saw you pass your initiation."

"Bullshit," she snapped.

I rose as much as my contorted position allowed. "The horses should have killed you, but they didn't. Your dress was too big. And you wore ribbons."

The silence grew heavy over the next few moments. Finally, in a voice so quiet I barely heard it, she said, "Who are you?"

"Name's Eddie LaCrosse. I'm from Neceda, in Muscodia."

"Where is that?"

I told her.

"And you. . . ." She took a deep, shuddering breath in the darkness. "You remember what happened?"

I nodded. "And I tell you the truth: I killed the monster who did it that same night, too."

The position they had me in was really killing me by now, so when she stood and cut the ropes that tied my wrists to my ankles I let out a loud groan. She undid the rest of the bonds, and I sat up stiffly.

"I'm sorry," she said.

I worked my numb fingers and toes. "No problem," I said out of habit. I gently felt the back of my head. The lump, tender and hot to the touch, swelled behind my right ear, but I felt no dried blood. The little bozo that smacked me had a light touch, at least. "Who hit me?" I asked.

"His name's Leo," the scarred girl said. "He always stays back to see how the robbery goes. He's only seven, but he's tall for his age and totally fearless."

"He's got a future," I agreed. I'd never even heard him coming. A spasm of queasiness went through me, but I blinked it away. I wiped the sweat from my face with my sleeve. "So what kind of scam do you have going here?"

"Not many jobs for someone who looks like me, so I've learned to work the edges. I take in the orphans and the runaways, teach them how to survive. And when the boys get old enough, like Scotty, I teach them about women. If it's dark enough, they can pretend I'm anyone."

"And you've been here ever since . . . ?"

"I traveled around. Some people helped me, some didn't. I settled here because these old mines under the town make it easy to stay in the shadows. For obvious reasons, I prefer that."

"Yeah."

She leaned forward into the light. What expression her injuries allowed was pitiful. "*Why* are you here? Please, tell me the truth. I deserve it."

"I'm trying to find a line on Andrew Reese."

"You mean he's real?" she whispered.

"Maybe. If he is, he's the one ultimately responsible for what happened to you."

Her eyes were clear and bright blue, the beautiful eyes of a sad and tormented child. "Will you kill him if you find him?"

"Yeah," I said. Truthfully I didn't know what I'd do, but the lie seemed a small enough reparation for the life she'd been given.

Someone knocked on the door. "Come in," she said.

Trudy the waitress stepped into the light, followed by the boy Scotty. "I have to get back to work, and—" She froze when she saw I was no longer tied.

"Relax," I said. "We're old friends."

"He's free to go," the scarred girl said. "Trudy, show him out, will you?"

"He knows about me," she said dubiously. "About all of us."

"And I know about *him*," the scarred girl said. "He's been honest with me. There's no reason to hurt him."

Trudy scowled at me.

I looked at the scarred girl. "Can I do anything for you?"

"We don't need your help," Scotty snapped.

"We don't," the scarred girl agreed more evenly. "We've found our niche here."

I started to protest further, but I sensed the futility. "Maybe I'll check in on you again, if I'm ever in town," I told her. "And if I find Andrew Reese, he'll pay for what he did to you. To everyone."

"But not Epona," she said emphatically. "Epona gets no vengeance."

"Why?"

"Because Epona lied to us. She claimed to be . . . well, you were there, you know. I believed her. I believed *in* her. That lie was the hardest thing to accept."

I nodded.

"Come on," Trudy said impatiently and grabbed my arm. She was clearly anxious for things to get back to normal. "I'll take you to your stuff." Scotty stayed behind with the scarred girl, standing protectively beside her and glaring until the door closed. As I followed Trudy down the dim passageway of what had been a played-out mine, I faintly heard the scarred girl singing that damned maddening tune. "Andrew Reese is broken to pieces. . . ."

My sword and other belongings lay in a pile near a curve in the old mine tunnel. I buckled my scabbard and counted the money in my pouch. It was all there, and it turned out they hadn't even thought to check for the knife in my boot. Well, they were just trainees. Then I trailed the waitress some more, having to stoop in many places. At last light shone down an overhead shaft and illuminated a ladder that led to the surface. My head still throbbed like a drum at a harvest festival, and finally I had to say, "Whoa, wait a second." I leaned against a wooden support beam and made myself breathe slowly and evenly. I was in no shape to climb a ladder until the tunnel stopped wobbling beneath me.

Trudy impatiently put her hands on her hips. "Come *on*," she snapped. "You've been lucky enough today."

I wanted to lie down right there, but I knew I needed to get out of the tunnel and back to my job. I shook my head to clear it, a move I immediately regretted. Then I realized the soft voice I heard was not, in fact, my conscience chewing me out for being an idiot. It was a child's voice softly repeating something.

It came from behind a tapestry hung over a crossing

tunnel we'd just passed. If we hadn't stopped, I never would've noticed it. I lifted the heavy fabric and peeked around. The area was just a tiny side room, originally carved to allow miners to step aside when ore carts needed to pass. Small candles illuminated it, their light hidden by the thick curtain. The little bait girl knelt before an altar, her pudgy hands clasped together in prayer. "By Epona's white mane, I ask that my wish come true," she said in her singsong voice. On the altar was a single horseshoe, and on the stone wall it faced someone had crudely drawn a white horse.

Trudy pulled me back. "That's none of your business," she snapped.

"You're right. Let's go." Some lies took longer to accept than others, evidently.

I stepped ahead of her, and realized she lagged behind for just a moment too long. I dodged sideways, and her knife stabbed right through the spot my kidneys occupied a moment earlier. I punched her with the heel of my palm right between her eyes. The blow stunned her, and the knife clattered to the stone floor. The noise carried, and would soon bring her preteen reinforcements.

I slammed her against the nearest wall. I was pissed off now, and took her knife hand by the wrist. "Your boss and I had a deal, you backstabbing little bitch," I snarled. "Did she tell you to do this?"

"No," she said, too dazed to lie.

I bent her last two fingers back until the bones snapped. She cried out in pain, and her eyes opened wide. I slapped her to keep her attention. "I'm not going to kill you because your boss was straight with me. Next time be a good soldier." Then I shoved her to the ground and went quickly up the ladder. No small, lethal hands reached to pull me back.

I RETRIEVED MY horse and crossed the bridge at the next open time for folks mounted on horseback, and eventually found the spot where, long ago, Cathy and I had departed from the road. Most of the forest had been cleared to build the newer buildings in Poy Sippi, but I still wandered for two days, trying to hit upon some familiar landmark that would orient me to the old half-remembered trail. Finally, just as I was about to admit defeat, I found the sign that had originally guided us.

I'd learned about that sign, and the others, after that first Poy Sippi lunch thirteen years earlier. Back then Cathy and I had crossed the bridge without incident and, after most of the traffic had dispersed onto other roads, we ducked into the woods that grew thick and heavy along the main highway.

We hunkered down out of sight behind a huge fallen tree. Cathy took a drink from her canteen and leaned back against the bark. Sunlight through the leaves dappled her face, and a breeze rustled her bangs. "I need a bath."

"You're not so bad yet," I said as I took off my boots and stretched my toes.

She made a face. "Compared to that, I'm not. Did something die in your socks?"

"Keeps the bugs away." I reclined and looked up at the patches of blue sky. I hadn't noticed the color of the sky in a long time.

She closed her eyes. "I hate feeling skanky. Always have. It's been the hardest part of this job."

"Harder than fighting off grabby yahoos?"

She laughed. "Yeah, definitely." Then she sat up and looked at me with careful, measuring eyes. I pretended I didn't notice, but I did. She studied me for a long time before she said with certainty, "Eddie, you were right back at the Sway Easy. I should be able to trust you now. If I'm wrong about it, I deserve what I get."

She dug inside her pack and pulled out the small map she'd previously consulted only in private. She unfolded it on the mossy ground between us.

"Here's where we are," she said, indicating a spot next to the river's wiggly outline. "And here's where we're going. There's no road or path; we have to look for landmarks."

The destination seemed to be high in the Ogachic Mountains ahead. "What's there?" I asked.

She shrugged. "Have no idea. Except that it's where I'll find the person I'm supposed to deliver this package to."

"Do you know this person's name?"

She nodded. "Epona Gray."

"A woman?"

"Sounds like it."

I looked at the map. Our destination really was in the middle of nowhere. "Does it seem odd to you that a woman would get a package way out here?"

"Depends on the woman, I guess," she said. "Or the package."

"I don't know anything about either," I pointed out.

She looked at me again for a long, quiet moment. Something had changed in her expression. "Yeah," she said at last.

She peered over the log to make sure we were alone,

then unbuttoned her shirt. Strapped around her stomach was a soft fur-lined belt, and in it she'd stuck a thin sealed parcel no bigger than my hand. She pulled it free and handed it to me.

I examined the box. It was a faceless wooden case, tied with string, and the knot had been sealed with unembossed wax. It could hold nothing bigger than my hand. When I shook it, a single large heavy object slid around inside. "Sounds like a rock."

"Might be," she said as she put it back and buttoned up her shirt. I realized I hadn't even glanced at her to see what skin she might reveal.

We waited until dark, then crept back onto the road. There wasn't much traffic at night, and the nearly full moon provided plenty of illumination. A breeze blew from the east, keeping the air cool and clear. Something about the combination of wind, moon and silence made us speak softly; it was the kind of night that, in retrospect, earns the name "magical." At the time, though, it was just another night on the job.

Cathy told me about her first delivery, escorting a valuable show dog through fairly harmless territories to the home of its new owner. It had been just her and the dog, a medium-sized wolfhound, walking together for two weeks. The customer tried to stiff her for her fee because the dog had replaced so much flab with muscle. He was not successful.

"That poor dog used to howl at the moon for hours every night," she said wistfully. "It was the saddest, loneliest sound you can imagine. She never had a proper home, just kennels and dog shows and such. The lady who sold her had never even petted her. I would try to calm her down, comfort her, and it would work for a while. But then she'd move away from the fire and just howl some more."

I had my hands in my pockets and looked out at the trees tinted blue by the moonlight. Our footsteps were the only unnatural sounds. "Sounds like she had a tough life," I agreed.

She kicked at the road's surface. Without looking at me she asked, "Want to know a secret?"

"Sure."

Her voice grew softer. "One night, when she seemed so alone and pitiful . . . I howled with her. I took off all my clothes, danced around in the moonlight and *howled.* . . ." She smiled at the memory.

For some reason this made me uncomfortable. "How much had you been drinking?"

She laughed quietly, musically. "Oh, I was cold sober, Eddie, just like I am now." She twirled slowly, like a child, and looked up at the sky. "You think she's a goddess?"

"The dog?"

"No, the moon. Priestesses say it's the light of the goddess. They say her tug makes women bleed once a month so we can have kids. What do you think?"

"I dunno."

"I hope she is. I hope there's a goddess somewhere who hears all those howls in the moonlight."

"It's not my area of expertise."

She laughed again and danced ahead of me. Her long shadow reached down the road. I'd never seen her like this, so . . . uninhibited. Janet had the same paradoxical quality, as if more life experience somehow made her more innocent. A big knot of conflicting feelings fought unsuccessfully to untie itself in my gut.

After that little outburst, we walked in silence until, past midnight, we made camp. I watched her sleep for a long time, enjoying the play of firelight on her features. She had great lips, I belatedly decided—full enough to be delectably pouty in the right circumstances.

A wolf howled in the distance, too far away to be a threat. And I had to admit, the urge to howl along was pretty damn strong.

FOURTEEN

Following the map, Cathy and I hiked into the Ogachic Mountains. There was no existing trail, so we had to work with the terrain. It grew harder as we climbed higher, rocks replacing dirt and trees giving way to bushes and scrub. It seemed unlikely that this was really the most efficient way to get to our destination, but the map gave us no alternatives, and I knew nothing of this area.

At last, just above the tree line on one rocky face, we found the first landmark: a horse's head, in silhouette, painted in white on black granite.

The image was about four feet across, and right at eye level. While Cathy checked the map, I scratched at the paint; it did not flake off. "This is some heavy-duty artwork. Whatever they used, it sealed pretty good."

"Have to be to survive the weather up here," Cathy said. "The winters get vicious."

I knew a bit about art from my childhood tutoring. This wasn't in the usual regional style, which favored a flatter, more abstract approach. The horse's silhouette was entirely realistic, down to the slightly parted

lips and flying mane. Then I noticed something unex-
pected.

I got very close to the fine detail work along the
mane's fringe and squinted. "Wow," I whispered.
"Cathy, this isn't paint."

She looked up from the map. "What do you mean?"

"This is . . . quartz or something. Some other kind
of rock. Inside the granite." I ran my hand over it, and
only the slightest bump marked the border of the image. "This is a natural formation."

She joined me and peered at the seam between the
two rocks. I was suddenly, uncomfortably aware of her
proximity. "Rocks can do weird things sometimes,"
she agreed. "Back in Bonduel, there's a mountain in the
shape of an old man's profile. It looks just like somebody
carved it, but it's all natural." She turned, and our faces
were inches apart. She looked into my eyes, glanced
away, and looked back. "Nature can be pretty powerful,"
she said.

Her eyes were hazel flecked with gold. I asked softly,
"Weren't we supposed to avoid a white horse?"

"Only if a woman was riding it." She licked her lips,
and I realized my own were suddenly dry.

I broke the moment and stepped away. My face felt
unaccountably hot. "So which direction now?"

"Northwest," she said quickly, looking down at the
map. "The next landmark is about a day's walk away,
if the terrain's not too much more difficult."

The landscape cooperated and we made it halfway
before darkness forced us to camp. It was one thing to
use an open road at night, but neither of us wanted to
climb over unfamiliar ridges and chasms we couldn't
see. We picked a hidden area next to a small stream,

sheltered on three sides. If we kept our fire small, we'd be invisible.

OVER A DECADE later, I stood before that same flat rock again. The weather was a little cooler, but the sunlight shone on its surface just as brightly now as it had done on that long-ago day. The white quartz deposit still stood out starkly against the gray-black granite. But the equine shape I remembered as so definite was now . . . vague. It could still be seen as a horse's head. It could just as easily be a wolf, or the bow of a ship, or a random geological formation that resembled any one of a dozen things if you looked at it cockeyed.

I put my hand flat against it just as I'd done thirteen years earlier. It felt weathered and smooth. No marks of workmanship showed; no one had altered it. Either I remembered it wrong, or . . .

There was less point in speculating now than there had been then. Then, our ultimate goal had been a mystery tugging us on. Now I knew where I was headed, and what awaited me.

I climbed back onto my horse. I don't know when I began to think of her as "mine," but somewhere between Arentia and here, I'd actually grown a little fond of her. I still didn't trust her, but I felt I could turn my back to pee without risking a kick to the head. That was a big change. As we picked our way along, I considered names for her. None of the possibilities clicked.

By nightfall, I reached the stream where Cathy and I had camped before. Given what happened, there was no way I'd use the same spot, so we crossed the stream and continued on until it was so dark my nameless horse refused to proceed. But ultimately, it didn't matter where I slept. The memories were just as vivid.

IT HAD BEEN a warm night back then. As always, Cathy and I put our bedrolls on opposite sides of the fire. I lay awake staring up at the stars. Tendrils of smoke from the dying fire made gray shifting shapes in the moonlight. I felt tense, and couldn't place the reason for it. I was absolutely sure no one followed us, especially no mysterious woman on a white horse, and this whole delivery trip should be over in a couple of days. I'd get the rest of my money and be free to continue wandering. And if I wanted to return to Bonduel with Cathy, to help her with her business or for any other reason, there was nothing stopping me. But did I want that?

No. I *wanted* Janet. But Cathy was everything I *should* want.

Shit, I thought as I rolled onto my side. I couldn't believe I was actually losing sleep over this. This was just a job, after all. Cathy was my boss, not my damn soul mate. I was making way too much out of it.

I looked through the smoke at Cathy's bedroll for a long moment before I belatedly realized it was empty. I sat up and heard splashing in the creek. I pulled on my pants and went to check on her.

Cathy lay crossways in the shallow water with her back against a rock. She was naked, of course, and as I watched she ducked her head under and came up with a gasp of happiness. I'd never heard that sound from her before. If a sound like that could still exist in the world, I thought, maybe fate was telling me I'd suffered enough.

I called out, softly so I wouldn't startle her. "Sorry, but I saw you were gone and came down to see if you were okay."

"I just couldn't pass up the chance for a bath, even a primitive one," she said. She made no effort to cover herself, although the moonlight twinkling on the water preserved her modesty. She kicked her feet like a child. "You have *no* idea how good this feels."

"Probably not," I agreed.

She turned onto her stomach and crossed her ankles above the water. For a moment only the creek made any sound. Finally I said, "Guess I'll go back to camp."

"I couldn't sleep, either," she said. "I can't help thinking this is all some big, elaborate game, and we're pieces the players would gladly sacrifice. Not a good feeling."

"No."

She looked back over her shoulder at me. "So since we both can't sleep, why don't you come out for a swim?"

"Not much of a swimmer."

"Oh, come on. Those feet of yours could use it, if nothing else. Do it for me."

"I'll pass."

She stood up in the knee-deep water, hands at her side, unashamed. Her short red hair swept back from her face. The moon cast highlights on her straight shoulders, the tops of her breasts and the sides of her hips. The rest of her body glowed pale gray against the sparkling river.

I'd seen plenty of naked women, but never one who seemed *so* naked, exposing not just her skin but some aspect of herself hidden far beneath her tough-girl personality. That was it, I realized: she was a *girl* now, untested and untouched in the ways of adult women. It had nothing to do with physical virginity and everything to do with a heart filled with things that had long ago been driven from my own.

"I have a surprise for you," she said.

"I'm already pretty surprised."

"It's the only thing you've ever asked me for."

She turned her back to me. There was, indeed, a tattoo of a dancing girl across her shoulder blades, the legs extending down her spine. "Worth the wait?"

"I dunno. Can you make it dance?"

"Not sober, I can't." She faced me again. "So," she said after a moment. "What do you think?"

"Nice ink."

"And the canvas?"

I bit my lip. The rest of the evening played out before me now; I'd undress and join her in the river, we'd make love until the cold water drove us out, then we'd return to the fire and continue until we fell asleep. And tomorrow everything would be different.

"The canvas is nice," I said. "But I really only know about ancient art."

She walked toward me, making little bow waves with her shins. "Some of the modern stuff can be pretty exciting."

"My taste is for the classics."

She stepped out of the water in front of me, shining and soft and very, very desirable. Even though she was tall for a girl, she had to tilt her head up to see me with those big guileless eyes, unashamed of anything in her life. Then she smiled. "Even the classics were new once."

I took the deepest breath I'd managed in years. She put her hand on my chest, stepped closer and gazed into my eyes. "Care for a little art appreciation?" she said softly, then tiptoed so she could kiss me.

I let her, but I didn't respond. She settled back on her heels and scowled. "What?" she asked, in her old voice.

I couldn't look at her. I mumbled, "I'm not really up for this right now."

She grabbed me around the waist and pulled her body tight against mine. Her smile returned. "That's not true," she said in a soft growl.

"Hey, it's nothing personal, he always gets up a half-hour before I do." Instantly I regretted it. Even in the moonlight—maybe because of the moonlight—I saw tears fill her eyes. She strode quickly back to the water's edge and stopped, her back to me, arms wrapped around her sides. Her voice did not weaken. "You're a jackass, LaCrosse. And you just missed your chance."

With that she splashed back into the water and swam away downstream. I sighed. I had no idea at the time whether I'd been noble or idiotic.

Now, though, I know.

FIFTEEN

The second marker was another horse head silhouette on a rock face. To reach it Cathy and I traveled a fairly tortuous route along a narrow canyon ledge shadowed by mocking crows and silent, watchful buzzards. Once, as we negotiated a sharp turn, we surprised a wildcat, or rather it surprised us. I almost lost my balance and tumbled to the forest below, but Cathy caught me, the cat scrambled up out of sight, and we continued on without incident. The map did not indicate the path's increasing danger, and I wondered what other important information it omitted.

This second horse image was formed of shiny black obsidian inside a wall of whitish slate, a reverse image of the first. Cathy also discovered that, if you stood in the right spot, a tiny chink reflected the sun so that the beast appeared to have one glowing, vaguely malevolent eye. This one also looked like a natural formation, but it seemed unlikely that two such identical mineral deposits would be found within a day's walk of each other. We consulted the map again and set out for the third and final marker.

Cathy never spoke of that night by the stream. She came back to camp fully dressed, went to sleep without a word and awoke at dawn just like always. She acted as if nothing unusual had happened, and I did the same. I couldn't believe she was letting me off the hook so easily, and kept waiting for the blow I knew must be coming. But it never did.

BACK IN THE present I murmured, "Easy, sweetheart," to the horse as we reached the remains of the third marker. I'd taken an alternate route around the mountain's base to avoid the treacherous ledge. "Nothing's gonna gitcha." Her hooves clacked nervously against the rocky ground, and she repeatedly tossed her big head. I didn't understand why this one bothered her more than the other two, but I finally gave in and led her down the slope a ways before I returned to look more closely.

When we first found it thirteen years earlier, the third marker had been a relief carving of a woman on horseback, done in the style of Delavan, far to the east. That puzzled me then, although I later learned the explanation. Hidden in a crevice like a shrine, it would've been invisible had Cathy's map not been accurate and precise about its location. Once we found it, we knew our destination was near.

But now that marker had been utterly obliterated. Someone had thoroughly chiseled the image out of its rock home and left a shallow, ragged crater. I could imagine how difficult carving it must have been in that narrow, tight space; getting both the tools and the elbow room to destroy it so completely must have been equally hard. Obviously none of Epona's people could have done it, but who else would hate it so much?

The area outside the crevice shrine provided a spectacular view of the mountains ahead. In the distance the tallest peaks, including Mount Ogachic itself, sported snowcaps testifying to their height. Nearer, the low ones cut jaggedly into the sky, so close together it seemed impossible anyone would travel, let alone live, here.

Our old trail showed no sign of recent use. For all I knew, I was the first person to travel it since I used it to leave after the encounter with Epona. Here in the thin, dry air change came slowly; what changes waited in the hidden valley below?

I was putting off the inevitable, but it seemed the right moment for reflection. I needed to make sure my head was on straight before I made the final part of the journey. I knew what I'd left in the valley ahead; I was less sure what I'd find now, or how I'd feel about it.

My horse took me away from the shrine with all the alacrity the terrain allowed. We headed down into the complex series of passes and gullies that had once deposited Cathy and me at the doorstep of the Queen of Horses.

OUR TRIP BACK then took quite a bit longer because we were on foot. Following the map, we descended from the mountains, emerged at last onto a tall, narrow ridge and stopped, breathless from both the exertion and the sight that greeted us.

Below us stretched a small valley completely encircled by ridges and peaks. Unlike the rest of the Ogachic range or the land around Poy Sippi, this valley was alive with verdant foliage. Meadows and forests alternated on the rolling hills, and a network of small ponds and streams twinkled in the sunlight. It was so awash in trees and grass that it reminded me of the old stories of the Summerlands where folks waited between lives. "Wow," I said.

"How does nobody know this is here?" Cathy asked softly. I knew what she meant; the journey was arduous, but not unreasonably so, and with a paradise like this at the other end the path should've been well-worn by now. Hell, Poy Sippi was only three days' hike away. But the trail we followed showed no sign of recent traffic.

"I guess there's no chance we're in the wrong place," I suggested.

"I can read a damn map," she fired back.

"But there's no roads, no trails, no smoke from fires." The implication was plain: however beautiful, the valley appeared to be uninhabited.

"We're in the right place, according to the map," Cathy insisted. Her fists clenched in frustration. "But so help me Goddess, if there's no one here—"

I pointed. "Look. *Someone's* here."

A human figure appeared at the top of the nearest hill and descended the grassy slope. Something about its vaguely awkward movement held my gaze until suddenly I realized what I saw. "It's a *kid*. A little girl."

The distance made it hard to guess her age, but the way she flounced down the hill implied she was about five. She had long dark hair decorated with multicolored ribbons, and her dress seemed too big for her.

Cathy and I both scanned the surrounding hills and forests, but saw no other people.

"She's all dressed up," Cathy said. "You think she's lost?"

I shrugged. "Maybe."

"We can't just let her run around loose, she'll get hurt."

"Let's just watch a while," I said guardedly.

Without warning, a herd of horses topped the same hill and bore rapidly down on the little girl. They were huge, wild animals, with no sign of the sleekness brought on by domestication. At the front of the herd, clearly its leader, ran a snow-white beast I assumed was a stallion. I estimated about two dozen of them, and the sound of their passage over the soft ground reached us like thunder heard beneath a thick blanket.

Cathy and I both started forward, and simultaneously caught ourselves. We were several minutes away, at least; rescue was out of the question. The herd was on the child in seconds, swarming over her in a rumbling wave of hooves and snorts. "Son of a bitch," Cathy muttered, expressing our mutual frustration.

The horses turned at the bottom of the hill, ran along the flat, narrow gully and vanished. The soft grass bore the marks where they'd torn divots from the earth. My eye backtracked their passage, looking for the trampled corpse of—

The little girl stood intact, upright and happily twirling right where she'd been before the horses appeared.

"You see that?" Cathy asked, her voice soft with disbelief. "They missed her. They all missed her. What are the chances?"

I shook my head. "I'd give a year's pay for that kind of luck, though."

People appeared at the top of the hill. Even at this distance we heard the cheers and applause. Everyone crowded around the child as if she'd accomplished some miracle, which from our vantage point was certainly true. The adults were from a variety of races, and wore colorful clothes like you'd see at a festival. It was the wrong time of year for the harvest, and late for a spring fertility dance, but there was no doubt they were ready to celebrate. One woman scooped the girl in her arms and kissed her like only a mother would. The people disappeared back down the opposite side of the hill, the little girl perched on the woman's shoulders, everyone still cheering. No one even glanced in our direction.

As the noise faded, I said, "*That* was weird. Were you expecting this?"

Cathy shook her head. "No way. I assumed I'd find Epona Gray alone."

"Well . . . I suppose it's possible they have nothing to do with her."

She glanced skeptically at me. "You wanna bet?"

I didn't. We picked our way down the rocks to the tree line, and eventually emerged onto the crest over which the crowd had disappeared. And we saw where they went.

A small village, hidden by the hills until you were right on top of it, awaited us. A dozen homes and some obvious common buildings circled a large central well. Each structure was in a similar style, bordered by either a small livestock pen or household garden. Neat stone paths connected them. In fact, the whole vista was so damn neat it raised hackles on my neck, because it was completely empty.

"Where is everybody?" Cathy asked.

The valley forest bordered the far side of the village, and a dark opening indicated a wide trail into it. The grass appeared trampled in that direction, as if many people had entered the woods. "Must've gone in there."

"*All* of them?"

"Maybe."

"Then we can at least go down and look around," she said, and started forward.

I grabbed her arm. "Hold on. This whole thing is creepy. We're outnumbered, on unfamiliar turf and not even sure who we're looking for. That's not the best time to be caught snooping. I think we should just sit down here and wait for them to come to us."

She glared at me, then down at my hand, until I released her. "I know it's weird," she agreed. "That's why I want to get this over with and get out of here. But you have a point." I could tell admitting it was difficult for her.

So we sat on the top of the hill, clearly silhouetted against the sky. We both kept one eye out for the rampaging wild horses, but they did not reappear. I also belatedly noticed that none of the livestock pens held anything larger than a goat; nor, I realized, *could* they. Even taking into account the odd ceremony we'd witnessed with the child, it seemed strange that an isolated settlement would allow a herd of such monumentally useful animals to run wild.

Hey, I thought. That's it. It wasn't a near-accident, it was a *ceremony*. But what did it signify?

The sun passed midday and descended, blinding us since the village lay to our west. Cathy yawned and stretched out flat with her arm over her eyes. "Wake me if anything happens," she muttered, then began to snore. A big butterfly landed on her knee, basked there for a while, then flew off.

At last, near sundown, the people we'd seen earlier emerged from the forest trail. It was a bastard to see through the glare, but they appeared to have returned from a community picnic or party. Many of them seemed a little drunk, young couples walked arm in arm, and fathers carried weary children. Most reached their homes without even glancing in our direction, but at last, one very tall man pointed at us. Several others joined him, and finally a dark-haired woman strode out of one of the houses. She looked in our direction, listened to something the tall man said, then started up the slope toward us. The tall man followed.

I lightly kicked Cathy. "We're on."

She awoke instantly. We stood, drew our visible weapons and placed them on the ground at our feet. Cathy stepped slightly in front and crossed her arms. "I'll do the talking," she said. "You just look mean and keep your eyes open." That was fine with me; I could watch more closely if I didn't have to be charming.

The woman was in her late thirties, dressed in a low-cut purple gown. Festive flowers dotted her straight, thick hair. She had a strong face, and when she got close enough, called out neutrally, "Hello."

"Hi," Cathy said as they stopped before us. "We have a package to deliver. We're looking for an Epona Gray."

"Then lucky for you we have one." She smiled, and

the seriousness melted. I got no bad vibes from her at all; although she bore an unmistakable air of authority, she seemed earthy, self-assured and, at heart, kind.

The tall man, however, was a whole different story. He stood over six and a half feet, wore his hair military-short and had the knack of watching without appearing to be. His arms were bare and, like mine, bore a network of fine pink scars from sword cuts. We both knew fellow soldiers when we saw them.

He nudged my sword with his foot. "Zuberbuhler Warmonger with a weight-balanced hilt. Big knife for a delivery boy."

Nothing clever came to mind, so I let it go. Cathy said, "He's just hired muscle, tough guy. There's no need for a pissing contest."

"There never is," the woman agreed. "Mr. Carnahan's old habits die hard."

"That's how they get to be old habits," Carnahan said. He slipped his boot under my sword's blade, then kicked it up into the air. I reflexively caught it without breaking eye contact, a feat I was never able to manage again in my life. But at least the one time that I got it right, it counted. Carnahan's eyes widened in surprise, but so slightly only I noticed.

I slipped the weapon back in its scabbard. "Thanks."

"Come on, you two," the woman said patiently.

"Yeah, don't forget who's paying you," Cathy added, but I saw from her glance that she agreed this Carnahan bore watching.

"Sorry," the big man said. "Guess that's not very friendly." He offered me his hand. His grip, even restrained for politeness, could twist off a crocodile's head.

Cathy cleared her throat and he turned to her. "Cathy Dumont," she said as she shook his hand. "Dumont Confidential Courier Service."

"You've picked a fine day to visit," the woman said. "We're finishing up a celebration, and it's almost time to open this year's sacred wine. Why don't we go down and relax a little."

"Is Epona Gray celebrating?" Cathy asked.

The woman looked at her carefully for a long moment. "She surely is," she answered enigmatically.

We followed them down the hill into the village. Giddy people milled about, watching us but not making a big deal of it. One little boy fell into step beside me; I noticed that he mimicked the way I walked.

"Get outta here, Randy," Carnahan told the kid. His voice was gruff but not mean. The boy instantly ran off.

The woman led us to one of the larger common buildings. On the closed door was a white horse head symbol identical to the first marker we'd encountered. The woman stepped onto the small porch and opened the door, then stepped aside in a formal, practiced way for us to enter.

We both stopped. Cathy said, "Just so you know, we're not planning to stay for church," and glanced back at me. I saw the tense, suspicious look in her eyes, and wished Carnahan wasn't directly behind me, blocking any quick retreat. But we had no real choice. I followed Cathy into the temple with every sense straining for danger.

SIXTEEN

Inside was a quaint little temple big enough for perhaps twenty people at a time. A huge white horse head silhouette in mosaic tile dominated the far wall, with a low altar before it. A cauldron, charred from much use, sat over a fire pit in the center of the room. Half-moon benches circled the cauldron. The woman closed the door from the outside, leaving us alone in the room with Carnahan.

Then another woman emerged from a side entrance carrying a fresh bundle of grain, oats by the look of it. She placed it on the altar then turned to us. She had long wavy hair streaked with gray, and wore several symbolic necklaces. "Hello," she said. Her slight accent identified her as Ginstrian, from the far west.

"Epona Gray?" Cathy asked, all business.

The woman looked carefully at her, just as the other one had done on the hill. "If I am . . . what happens?"

"If you are, I give you a package, you make your mark on a receipt and we all go our merry way."

"What sort of package?"

Cathy sighed impatiently. "Ma'am, I am tired, and frustrated, and really just want to be rid of this thing, okay?" She pulled the small box from her pocket. "This is it. I have no idea what it is, or even who sent it. I just got paid to put it in your hands."

The woman reached for the box, but just as her fingertips touched it, Cathy yanked it back. "*If* you're Epona Gray," she added.

The woman smiled contritely. "All right. I'm not Epona. I'm her assistant. My name is Nicole Ritter."

"Assistant?" Cathy repeated disdainfully. She gestured at the temple. "Then is she the priestess here or something?"

"Something. She's also very ill." She said this as if the words didn't quite convey the meaning.

"Then maybe we should get this to her quickly," Cathy snapped as she returned the box to her pocket.

"I could sign for it," Nicole said. "Epona wouldn't mind."

Cathy shook her head. "Sorry. From my hand to hers. That's what I was paid for."

"We could take it from you," Carnahan said. There was no malice or threat in his voice, just a simple statement, and that made him scarier.

I turned to him and kept my voice just as neutral. "Might be harder than you think."

"Mr. Carnahan, we're not that way here," Nicole said firmly. To Cathy she said, "I would really prefer not to take you to Epona right now, miss. Both for her sake and yours. But . . . " She bit her lip as she thought.

Then she stepped close and looked intently into Cathy's eyes. Cathy tensed but didn't move away, almost like the woman had instantly transfixed her to the spot.

"Do you know the goddess inside you?" Nicole asked, so softly I barely heard it. "Are you a spiritual woman?"

Like a contrite little girl Cathy said, "I don't . . . " The she blinked to break the moment. "I'm a *busy* woman," she said in her normal voice. "If it'll simplify things, we can leave my muscle-boy here. He gets in the way more than he helps, anyway."

Nicole pondered this a moment, still looking Cathy over. "Very well," she said at last. "I'll take you. Give me a few minutes to change clothes. Mr. Carnahan, since you and this gentleman seem to have so much in common, why don't you entertain him until we return?"

Carnahan looked at me like you would an ingrown toenail. But he said, "Sure."

Nicole excused herself into a back room. Cathy put her hand on my arm and leaned close. "If it seems like I've been gone too long, don't wait for an invitation. Come find me."

"My plan exactly," I replied quietly.

Cathy nodded, then said for Carnahan's benefit, "Then go play with your new friend. But don't get so drunk we can't leave when I get back."

I grinned at Carnahan. "Reckon I'm all yours."

"Hmph," the big man replied. With a last look at Cathy, I followed him out the door.

The sun had dropped out of sight behind the tree-tops, and torches now illuminated the paths and door-ways. I smelled meat cooking and incense. A crowd gathered near the central well, and I heard music and dancing. Between two other buildings children too small to celebrate played and laughed, watched over by two hugely pregnant teenage girls.

"What's the occasion?" I asked Carnahan.

"Ah, when their daughters turn five, they send them out to get trampled by the wild horses. But I've never seen it happen. The horses always miss, and the kid is therefore 'blessed by the goddess Epona.'" His sarcasm was thick.

"Epona is a *goddess?*" I asked.

"You betcha." We reached a long, narrow building with a sign over the door proclaiming it *Betty's Place.* "The great goddess Epona, who lives in the forest with her spirit birds and magical horses." He snorted. "It's a bunch of horse *shit* if you ask me. Somebody trains those animals not to run over people. And if Epona's a goddess, then I'm the damn King of the Monkeys."

The door opened just in time to catch his last words, and the same woman who'd led us to the temple smiled at us. "Your majesty," she said with a mock curtsey.

"Oh, stop it. Betty, this is—?"

"Eddie," I said, and bowed slightly. "Pleased to officially meet you."

"Likewise." To Carnahan she said, "You have a friend with manners, Stan. How'd that happen?"

"Nicole told me to entertain him," the big man mumbled. "C'mon, let's sit down."

"Just pick a seat, I'll be right with you," Betty said, and I followed Carnahan to a corner table. The place wasn't exactly a tavern or entirely a restaurant; parchment books lined the walls, and board games were available. Small candles on the tables kept the room dim and somehow mysterious. Three teenage girls talking in low, intense voices sat at the only other occupied table. Music filtered in from outside.

"So what kind of place is this?" I asked softly. It may have been a bar, but it felt more like a library or church.

"It's some damn place for thinkin' instead of drinkin'," Carnahan confirmed. "They serve watered-down beer and tea so strong it'll slap you." He shook his head. "You put women in charge, this is what you get."

Betty appeared next to us. If she took offense at Carnahan's comment, it didn't show. She put some bread on the table. "I'll be right back to take your orders, gentlemen."

When she was out of earshot I observed, "You seem a bit out of place here, Stan."

He ran his fingers through his short hair and nodded. "Yeah, you could say that. No matter how much I try, I still stick out, and not just 'cause I'm tall."

Then he looked at me with surprising sincerity. "You ever kill anybody? Hell, course you have, I could tell the minute I looked at you. Well, I killed one too many people. He wasn't any different than anyone else, except that when I looked in his eyes, I didn't see an enemy. I just saw a guy just like me, man. With everything inside him—" He slapped his chest for emphasis. "—that I have inside me." He looked down. "After that, I went looking for something different."

"And you found it?"

He shrugged. "If you like rule by committee, kids underfoot all the time, and some woman who claims she's a goddess living in the woods calling the shots, then yeah, I found it. I thought these folks were all here for the same reason as me, to get away from all the meanness in the world. And they're mostly decent people. But they're so cut off here, I don't think they realize how fragile all this is. They think anyone who shows up has been divinely drawn here by Epona. But eventually someone's gonna top that hill who ain't lookin' for peace and love."

"So why do you stay?"

"Gave my word," he muttered. "All I got left, so I have to make it worth something."

Betty returned and put down two tankards of wine. "Compliments of the house. We have to finish this old stuff before we open the new cask Epona gave us. Enjoy."

Again I waited until Betty was across the room. "Epona gave them wine?"

He nodded. "She keeps the good stuff to herself, and when her worshippers hold their mouths just right, she gives it to them. *Us*," he corrected.

"She sounds more like a bartender than a goddess."

He took a long drink. "I'm bein' too cynical. Epona's something, I gotta admit. She started this place. A spot away from everything, away from all the troubles of the world. People hear about it, but supposedly you can't find it unless you're meant to."

"So I'm meant to be here?"

"Hell, I'm just repeating what she told me. She lives in a little house in the heart of the woods out there, and every full moon, people go up there to ask her advice, her blessing, and so forth. Nicole is sort of her day-to-day manager here in town, making sure everything runs smooth. Most of the jobs are done by women, unless something needs lifting or killing."

"Lots of things need lifting?"

"No. And nothing *ever* needs killing."

"You sound disappointed," Betty said from behind me.

Carnahan looked up. "Got nothing to fight against here, Betty. Nothing to measure yourself against."

"We fight against what's inside of us. That's the scariest stuff of all, don't you think?"

"That's Epona talking," he snorted.

"*No*," Betty said with surprising, sudden intensity. "It's *me* talking. Every person here believes in what Epona represents, but we think for ourselves. We believe we can exist without conflict, in harmony with nature and—"

"—in connection with spirit," Carnahan finished with her. "Yeah, I know the words."

"But not the meaning. Stan, we all took a conscious leap of faith when we came here. I won't have it denigrated by someone like you."

"Someone like me?" he repeated. He glanced at me and winked.

"Yes. Someone who says he believes, but doesn't. Someone who says he wants to change, but not really. You're a liar, Stan, and you and I aren't the only ones who know it."

Stan smiled at me. "Sense of humor is the first casualty of enlightenment."

Betty rolled her eyes, grinned and mussed his hair like a boy.

"You believe this Epona is a goddess?" I asked Betty.

She thought for a moment. "Do you know what I was before I came here? Nothing. Well, that's not strictly true, I bore my late husband's children, then raised them to be men like him and women like me. We left no mark on anything. Every special jagged edge had been smoothed away by time and our sense of propriety. I knew that when I died, I'd leave no trace behind. Even my children would forget what I looked like. But I was resigned to being a woman, a *person*, of absolutely no consequence."

Her whole demeanor changed. The amusement was replaced by a look of wonder, all the more powerful for its completeness. "Then I met Epona. She didn't try to convince me my life was wrong, or my choices bad. She just . . . she showed me I could be *more*. I could *matter*."

"By moving to the woods and opening a tavern?" I asked, with as little sarcasm as I could manage.

She smiled one of those infuriating, patient grins the enlightened always have for the rest of us. "I understand why you say that. After fire ants, cynicism is the most difficult thing to kill. But look around. Every tile, every crossbeam, every book and decoration and piece of furniture is there because I put it there. This place is *mine*, in a way my life never was before. And a cynic could never see that, or even comprehend it. But once the cynic inside us dies, the idealist can dance in the moonlight. Epona showed me that. That's why I love her, and worship her. So yes, I believe she's a goddess." With that, she left to attend to something in her kitchen.

"She feels pretty strongly about it," I observed to Carnahan.

"Ah, they all do. I tell you, if I hadn't promised to stick it out for a year, I would've already blown this place like a port city whore."

"How much longer do you have?"

He shrugged. "This is boring," he said abruptly, and stood. I followed him to the end of the counter. He removed the darts from the dart board, then nodded at a big bowl of apples. "Grab those."

We went outside. It was completely dark now, and the enormous full moon rose in the east. Orange torchlight illuminated the whole town.

Carnahan stuck all the darts but one into the wall by the door. He readied the remaining one in his hand. "We can at least try to keep our skills sharp, right? Those apples won't feel anything. Toss one up."

"Which way?"

"Surprise me."

I threw one high into the darkness above the torches. Carnahan's eyes flashed upward, his arm jerked, and the dart stuck neatly into the fruit as it came down.

Betty, watching from her tavern's back door, said, "Not bad."

Grinning, Stan reached for the bowl. "You try."

I plucked a dart, and he hurled an apple higher and harder than I'd done. I made myself relax; no conscious skill could help me with this, only the instincts I'd honed over the last few years. My elbow flexed before I even knew it, and my apple landed with the dart fully embedded.

A few other townsfolk stopped to watch and politely applauded. The three girls we'd seen inside joined Betty in the doorway. I took the bowl back and threw another apple. Carnahan hit it dead center. I did the same on my next turn.

By now we'd attracted quite a crowd, including several charming young ladies. Miraculously we both hit our next two apples, to much appreciative clapping. At last one girl, a shapely lass with long red hair, took an apple from the bowl. She wobbled a little, tipsy from the celebration, but the gleam in her eye was unmistakable.

She took a big, voluptuous bite from the apple. Torchlight glinted on the juice as it ran down her chin. "I have an apple-flavored kiss," she said, "for whichever of you puts their dart closest to the center of this bite."

Carnahan and I exchanged a look. This was more like it. We each plucked a dart, his red and mine green, and waited.

The girl looked up into the clear, starry sky and took a deep breath. "By Epona's white mane, I ask that my wish come true," she called to the night. Then she threw the fruit as hard as she could.

The moment grew silent and immobile. No one breathed. Again my arm snapped, and the fruit hit the ground on the open space between the girl and us.

With a sly smile, she bent and picked it up. The crowd gasped.

Our two darts could not have been closer together. The flights were interlaced and the shafts side by side in the exact center of the bite.

The crowd cheered. Carnahan and I both grinned. The girl pulled the darts from the apple and, holding them side by side, licked the juice from their tips. "Looks like," she said with an unmistakable smile, "I owe two kisses."

My grin grew wider. Heck, I could grow to like this place.

A familiar voice suddenly cried, "Will you people get the *hell* outta my way!" Cathy pushed roughly through the crowd, oblivious to who she shoved. Behind her,

Nicole almost ran to keep up. Cathy seemed uninjured, although her hair was tousled, but something bad had clearly happened. She marched right up to me and faced me with cold, suddenly haunted eyes. The crowd fell into a murmuring semi-silence.

"I've done my job and made my delivery," she snapped. "I am now going to take the longest, hottest bath of my life, and then I am leaving. What you do is entirely your business, but I advise you not to go anywhere near this Epona."

I stepped close to her, aware that all eyes watched us. "Are you all right?" I asked softly. "Did something—"

"I don't want to talk about it," she muttered, and pushed past me. I started to go after her when I felt a hand on my shoulder.

"Mr. LaCrosse," Nicole said. Her eyes were even sadder than they had been before. "Epona would like to see you."

"I've just been told that wasn't a good idea," I said. I didn't know if I should pursue Cathy or not.

"Miss Dumont will be fine," Nicole insisted with gentle authority. "She wasn't hurt in any way. And neither will you be. Epona merely wants to meet you."

A murmur went through the crowd.

"Why?" I asked.

Nicole stepped closer. "She said to tell you," she whispered, "that she knows how hard you tried to save Janet."

I went cold inside. Cathy knew nothing of my past; certainly I hadn't seen anyone from Arentia in the village. There was no way, no *fucking way*, this Epona could know about Janet.

Nicole smiled sympathetically at my reaction. "She is a goddess, you know." She pointed at my sword. "You won't need that."

"I usually need it the most right after someone tells me that."

"You're going to meet a lone woman half your size. Who's also deathly ill."

"I thought she was a goddess."

"Then going armed won't matter, will it?"

"Don't worry," Stan interjected. "Seriously. Being with Epona is the safest place in the world."

I unbuckled my sword. I would've preferred to leave it with Cathy, but I handed it to Carnahan. He took it easily, the weight barely registering. "Keep it clean for me, okay?"

He nodded. "Like it was mine."

Nicole took my arm. For the benefit of the crowd she said, "Now come into the forest, Mr. LaCrosse, and meet the Queen of Horses."

SEVENTEEN

I'd spent a lot of time in forests all over the world, but I'd never seen one that looked, or felt, like the one into which Nicole led me that night. This was a virgin forest, almost a jungle. No ax ever struck home in this place, nor any natural fires swept it clean. Vines and undergrowth shrouded the roots and formed intricate lattices in the spaces between the trunks. They kept travelers on the trail far more efficiently than any man-made fence. In no time the glow of the village vanished behind us, and only the bright moon overhead showed the way. The music and noise quickly faded as well. Insects, frogs and birds filled the air with their cries.

It took a moment, but the presence of birds finally hit me. I was no expert, but I could recognize most normal bird cries, and the ones I now heard were new to me. They almost sounded like fragments of composed songs, rather than the calls of living animals. "What kind of birds are those?" I asked Nicole.

"Just birds," she said with a dismissive wave. "What else would they be?"

"That's why I'm asking," I said. I didn't press the

issue, but I knew she was evading my question. Owls, loons and mockingbirds sang at night, and this was none of them.

The trail was broad and clear, as it would have to be to regularly accommodate the town's entire population. But it wasn't expedient. It curved around some truly gigantic trees, no doubt allowing pilgrims sufficient time to contemplate their upcoming meeting with the goddess.

Nicole's crack about Janet had put me on edge, and the further we traveled, the more annoyed I got. How could Epona know about that? How could anyone? I never told a soul, not even Phil, how truly hard I'd fought that day. I took a fucking sword hit to a lung and continued trying to save her. When my own sword broke, I fought on barehanded. I killed seven of them, and injured a dozen, but they outnumbered me and eventually beat me down. And then they made me watch what they did to Janet. But damn it, I did fucking *try*.

Something large moved in the woods to my right. I turned in time to see a shadowy form, far too big for either a wolf or deer, leap nimbly through the undergrowth. It was so stealthy I barely heard its passage. Another one, whatever it was, ran laterally through scrub that should've tripped anything larger than a raccoon. Then I realized these huge silent shapes were everywhere, moving parallel with us. I was just about to ask Nicole what they were when one of them emitted an unmistakable equine *whinny*.

"Looks like you've got horses in your trees," I said.

Nicole laughed. "You make it sound like an infestation. Like roaches or rats."

I shrugged. "If the horseshoe fits."

"You don't care for horses?"

Moonlight gleamed off the eyes of a great equine shadow as it paused to watch us. "Not as a rule."

She nodded. "All that speed. The grace. The strength. That can be intimidating, I suppose."

I scowled. "Saw a guy get his jaw kicked clean off once. That was intimidating."

"Did he deserve it?"

"Maybe. I'd just prefer that my work animals not make that kind of moral judgment."

"See, that's your problem. A horse by its nature is not a 'work animal.' "

"Then what is it?"

"An equal. A friend. A symbol of the goddess."

I smiled. "Yeah, you gals always get into horses, don't you? I never knew a girl who didn't obsess about horses until she discovered sex."

I'd intended it as a joke, but Nicole didn't laugh. Instead she walked in thoughtful silence before replying, "I guess that's true. Something about horses appeals to the adolescent feminine nature. That's very astute."

"I was mostly kidding."

"I know, but I think you may be right. There's an undeniable sexual thrill for a woman to wrap her legs around a horse, and that gets replaced by the thrill of actual sex. So we do lose that first rush of chaste awareness once we begin making love." She thought some more. "The act of love mirrors the act of creation. Perhaps, for women, the feeling we get before we know physical love is the closest we get to knowing the goddess. Because a goddess is everything at once, eternally sexual and eternally virgin. So even as the virgin, she's still aware of her power because she's also the wanton. And perhaps *that* is what girls feel."

"You got all of that from one bad joke?"

She laughed. "As Epona's hands-on agent in daily mundane life, I spend a lot of time trying to think like she does. I know she considers horses her sacred symbols and avatars in this world, so I guess I do, too."

I watched more horses flit through the trees. They were quick and graceful in a way totally at odds with the terrain; were they even real? "So all your children get the chance to be trampled by these sacred horses on their fifth birthday?"

"No, not children. Just daughters. A taste of the nearness of death, before they grow old enough to give life."

"Do any ever get more than a taste?"

"Yes," she said sadly. "That's what gives it value. Some are lost. But most survive. Epona is not a cruel goddess."

"You did say she was a *dying* goddess."

Nicole stopped and faced me. The moonlight hid her eyes in shadow, so I couldn't read her expression. "Mr. LaCrosse, do you have any sort of spiritual life?"

"I'm usually too busy."

"There are many gods and goddesses worshipped in the world. Most are no more substantial than the icons used to represent them. But the greatest gift a true goddess can give those who believe in her is the reality of her presence. Epona chose to become one of us. A human woman. And like all of us, she is prey to the frailty of the flesh she inhabits."

"That sounds a little like a dodge," I pointed out. "Not much of a goddess if you have to make excuses for her."

Nicole did another one of those patient grins. "Her compassion and wisdom are the true signs of her divinity, not her mortal form. Death won't part her from us. And the time she's spent among us will become our legend, our mystery, the story that binds our hearts together, and to her."

"You realize how that sounds."

She shrugged. "I'd rather believe in something than nothing. I get the impression you feel the opposite."

She had me there. We resumed our trek in silence, engulfed by the night. The fact that Epona knew about Janet did not convince me of her divinity; after all, news of the death of a princess tended to get around. I'd seen far too many unlikely things to simply accept divine insight without question. I had no doubt that, at the end of this trail, I would meet only some half-crazed mumbling wisewoman with a lot of stage presence, but I almost wished Nicole were right. To behold a goddess in the flesh might almost cure me of my bitterness.

We rounded a corner and found our path blocked by the same immense white horse I'd seen leading the herd that nearly trampled the little beribboned girl. This close I saw I'd gotten the gender wrong; this was a mare, and she regarded me with black, fathomless eyes. I recalled the apple-flavored redhead's prayer: *"By Epona's white mane."*

The horse allowed Nicole to gently stroke her cheek, and the woman whispered something so softly I couldn't catch it. Then the huge white head turned and again fixed its dark eyes on me.

Sweat popped out all over me as the mare scrutinized me. I knew what those slashing hooves could do.

I forced myself to breathe as the mare took two casual steps closer and stopped inches from my face. She snorted at me, as if asking a question.

Time froze for the moment we gazed into each other's eyes. Beyond the obligatory equine haughtiness, I saw real intelligence and certainty of purpose that could, it seemed at the time, easily turn violent. The mare shifted her weight, and the massive flanks rippled. She had a regal quality, and I wondered how this Epona person could call herself the Queen of Horses while this magnificent beast was anywhere near.

The horse actually seemed to nod, as if she'd followed that train of thought. Then she turned and walked with immense dignity ahead of us up the trail. When she disappeared around a bend, I realized I *had* held my breath. I exhaled loudly, and almost had to sit down right there on the ground.

Nicole put a hand on my shoulder. "Pretty powerful, isn't it?"

"Pretty damn nerve-wracking," I said. I took a deep breath and hoped she couldn't see my hands shake. "I'm ready to get out of the woods now, thank you."

"Just continue up the trail, then. You can't miss her."

"What about you? Where are you going?"

"I have to go back. But you'll be perfectly safe." She turned thoughtful again. "I wish I could be there when you meet her. It won't be what you think."

She touched my face much as she had the mare's. It was both unmistakably erotic and, paradoxically, maternally tender. Then she walked quickly away down the path toward the village.

I continued up the trail for another few minutes and grew increasingly apprehensive. The horses in the trees chuffed and snorted around me. Finally I turned a corner and reached the heart of the forest.

The moon bathed the clearing in bright blue light. A small cottage lay at the center, with a stone walk that led to the door. Light from a fire seeped out around the closed curtains. Smoke rose from the small chimney.

Whatever spell the journey had cast on me was broken by this prosaic scene. No goddess lived here, just a standard-issue village conjurer. I'd find her huddled over her potions, or scrawling things in a mysterious black book. Certainly no transcendental being occupied this space. I almost turned around and left, but the nagging comment about Janet came back to me. How *had* she known about that? I could discover that, at least, after coming all this way. I started up the walk.

The cottage door opened. A woman stood silhouetted against the fire blazing in the hearth. She was slender, long-haired and wore a loose gown that wasn't quite opaque. I couldn't see her face.

"Hello, Baron Edward LaCrosse of Arentia," she said.

EIGHTEEN

⟨flourish⟩

Even thirteen years later the trail leading to the cottage was still there, overgrown but easily passable. Pollen and insects danced in the afternoon sun. And the woods along the route remained the densest, most impassable I'd ever encountered. The equine creatures that once dashed impossibly through them were gone, though. Or perhaps their ghosts only came out at night.

My horse tossed her head and snorted. The irony made me smile: back then I'd traveled on foot to meet the Queen of Horses, and now I explored the ruins of her kingdom on horseback.

We'd gone about halfway when I encountered something I didn't expect. A fresh human footprint marked the muddy ground beside a puddle. I dismounted and knelt to examine it. It showed the impression of an adult-sized moccasin sole. At that same moment I heard a distant, high shout. It wasn't a scream or cry of alarm, just the kind of noise certain people make to draw attention to themselves.

My horse snorted nervously. I didn't blame her.

My own tracks weren't obvious, but I'd made no

effort to hide them, either. Discretion seemed prudent, so I led the horse into the woods as far as the ridiculously heavy undergrowth allowed. I tied her out of sight, spoke to her as soothingly as I could and gave her some berries plucked from a nearby bush. Then I crept back to the very edge of the trail, staying just inside the forest. It hadn't occurred to me that I'd find anyone else here, and I couldn't just walk up to the old cottage until I knew what might be waiting. This would take a while.

It took, in fact, until dusk for me to make my way quietly through the underbrush until I was close enough to see the ruins of Epona's home. Along the way I heard several other cries, from many different positions but all the same voice. Someone really got around. By the time I saw the house, I'd also spotted evidence of random destruction in the woods around it, and seen the glow of a big fire through the trees.

The cottage remained, although its roof had collapsed and the once-neat yard was now overgrown. Vines curled up the stone wall and in through the empty windows. This was normal, and I'd expected it. But the rest of the scene was far more appalling.

A dozen deer carcasses hung by their necks from a sagging rope stretched between two poles. They'd been field-dressed in the crudest possible way, and the decaying piles of innards still lay on the ground beneath them. Their outlines were hazy from the insects swirling around them, and I was thankful I was upwind. A huge campfire, its flames licking dangerously close to the overhanging trees, raged between the hanging carcasses and the remains of Epona's old cottage. A crude lean-to shelter had been built against the house's nearest outside wall; I wondered why they hadn't simply repaired the roof and moved into the building.

As I watched, a man emerged from the forest dragging two dead beavers. He wore ragged clothes stitched together from various hides, and his beard and hair were both long and unkempt. "John-Thomas!" he bellowed in a rough, bone-scraping voice. "Where the hell are you?" He seemed unconcerned when no one answered.

The man tossed the beavers near the hanging venison. He looked inside the shelter, then went to the fire. He stripped to the waist, revealing a tough mountain-trapper physique honed from a lifetime outdoors.

I knew the type, if not this particular guy. These dirt-crusted anachronisms roamed in all the unsettled places, living as kings among the other hairy beasts on which they fed. They were often romanticized by those disgusted with civilization, but one look at his grisly hanging larder convinced me this was no noble neo-savage. This guy enjoyed killing things whether he needed them or not.

The wind shifted, and the abysmal odor from the rotting meat hit me like a slap from an angry teacher. Combined with the dregs of nausea from my Poy Sippi head smack, it almost sent me over into a full-on fit of vomiting. It took real effort to get control, then mouth-breathe enough to continue observing.

"John-Thomas!" the big man yelled again. "It's gettin' dark! Don't make me come find you!"

I considered my options. I didn't want to spend all night hiding in the bushes, but at the same time I didn't trust this guy at all. As I watched, he cut a piece of rancid deer meat, poked a stick through it and stuck it into the fire. After a moment he pulled it out, shook it to extinguish the flames and popped the charred venison into his mouth. Something about the way he did this, strutting with his hard round belly preceding him, did not indicate a man who'd welcome a stranger. And his companion, this John-Thomas, was an entirely unknown quantity.

I could stay or go. I'd learn nothing if I left.

So I stood up, walked into the light and said, "Hi."

The big bearded man stopped and stared at me. I kept the fire between us. This close, the smell from the rotting deer was like a week-old battlefield.

"How's it going?" I added.

Again he said nothing.

"Name's Eddie. Just passing through, saw the fire. Hope you don't mind."

He said something I didn't understand. I sighed in annoyance. "I heard you yelling before, so I know you speak my language."

His expression didn't change. Neither did the utter lack of sympathy or kindness in his tight little eyes. I kept my body language casual, although I was ready for anything. "Where you headed?" he rumbled at last.

"Poy Sippi. Thought I'd try finding my own way through the mountains. I don't care much for the traffic you get on the main roads."

He scratched something under his beard, and whatever tumbled out spread its tiny wings and flew away. I couldn't tell if he was sizing me up for his confidence, or his cooking pot. "You best keep going," he said finally. "Ain't enough room for you here."

"Not even a little time just resting by the fire?"

"It ain't a cold night," he said. His voice grew darker. "And we ain't a damn hotel."

Before this banter got any wittier, I heard a familiar whinny. I looked up to see my horse coming up the trail, led none too happily by a dark figure I couldn't quite make out. This figure let out the same yell I'd heard earlier, and as the light reached him I felt a cold chill despite the fire.

He was younger than this other guy, and more slender. He had a cleft palate, and as he neared I heard the wet sound of his breath wheezing through the opening. One eye was considerably higher than the other, and his left hand sported fingers that were too small and too numerous. He wore nothing except crude moccasins.

"Hey, Paw-Paw," he said, although the words were slurred and gummy. "Lookee what I found!"

"That's good, John-Thomas," the bearded Paw-Paw said. His voice had the patient quality of an easygoing parent. "We'll butcher it up in just a bit."

"Hey, wait, that's *my* horse," I said.

John-Thomas walked up to me, put his face way too close and stared. If possible, he smelled worse than the rotting deer. I knew what inbreeding could do in animals, but this was the first time I'd seen it manifest in a human being.

"Back up a little, would you?" I said as firmly as I dared, and reached to take the reins from him.

Before I could, he let out that same screech again. This close, borne on breath that could melt rock, I nearly threw up right in his malformed face. At the last moment he turned and sort of danced away toward Paw-Paw, still holding the reins.

"He's good and plump, Paw-Paw," John-Thomas said. "Just like we always like."

"That's true," Paw-Paw said flatly.

Uh-oh. Did he mean the horse or me?

John-Thomas rushed over to me again. *"Goodanplump, goodanplump,"* he repeated. A mixture of his spit and mucus splattered on my face, and I reached up to wipe it off.

"John-Thomas!" Paw-Paw said sternly. The younger man backed away, still staring at me and continuing to hold my horse's reins.

"That's my horse," I repeated.

"Around here, things that get left belong to the people who pick 'em up," Paw-Paw said.

"Yeah, well, where I'm from, we respect other people's property."

"I get his tongue, Paw-Paw!" John-Thomas cackled. "I get his tongue all for mine!"

"Okay, that's it," I said and snatched the reins from John-Thomas.

John-Thomas let out a squeal of absolute, primal petulance and ran off into the night. The horse moved next to me, nuzzling me gratefully with her big head. I did not take my eyes off Paw-Paw. "Not tryin' to start trouble," I said. "Just didn't want him hurtin' my horse."

I was now thoroughly creeped out, and the last thing I wanted was to spend any more time with these two. The smell of danger was almost stronger than the odor of decay that clung to them. I'd return and search the cottage during the day, when hopefully they'd be out doing whatever they did. "Sorry to bother you fellas," I said, and raised my foot to the stirrup. The horse whinnied, and only that high, sharp sound gave me the warning I needed.

John-Thomas came shrieking out of the darkness, eyes wide and a crude hatchet high above his head. He swung at me with all his strength and momentum, and I felt the wind from the blow as I barely stepped aside. He tumbled past me, rolled awkwardly and almost landed in the fire. But he caught himself, got to his feet and immediately attacked again.

I had time to get set, and blocked his hatchet arm with my own. I tried to grab his wrist, but his skin was too greasy and he easily twisted free. He viciously swung the hatchet at my chest, and again I barely stepped aside. He tripped over his own feet and fell, and this gave me time to draw my sword. When he turned and attacked again I was ready, and his own forward motion lopped off his hatchet hand at the wrist.

If I thought he'd screeched before, it was nothing compared to the sound he made now. He grabbed the stump of his wrist, dropped to the ground and practically convulsed with rage and pain. His thrashing kicked up a cloud of dust that glowed orange in the firelight. I looked around for Paw-Paw, but he had vanished into the darkness.

I had no desire to prolong this. I sheathed my sword, grabbed my horse's reins again and swung into the saddle. Just as I was about to dig my heels into her ribs, a hand grabbed my jacket from behind and pulled me to the ground.

I landed right, so it didn't knock the breath from me. Paw-Paw raised a long trident-like spear over his head and hurled it straight down at my face. He roared, a full-throated adult variation on John-Thomas' horrendous shriek. I rolled aside, grabbed his legs below his knees and shoved him onto his back. He broke the shaft of his spear as he fell.

He was bigger and stronger than me, and unlike his son was not foolish enough to lose his cool. He kicked me in the chest, got to his knees and produced a long, jagged knife. I'd seen the results of that knife on those deer carcasses, and it galvanized me into action. I slipped my own knife from my boot, rolled under his first blow and plunged my blade deep into his belly. I stood, using my legs to drive a two-foot slice across his stomach, then spun behind him, grabbed him by the hair and rammed my knee into his spine, hard. The impact made his intestines burst through the incision and splatter onto the dusty ground.

I released him and jumped quickly out of knife range, ready in case he threw the weapon as a last gesture. But he only stared down at his bloody organs for a moment, then fell forward atop them with a *splat* I'll remember for a long time.

Through all this, John-Thomas continued screeching and thrashing. By now blood shot from his severed wrist, shimmering as it caught the firelight in great surging arcs. I drew my sword again and stepped over to him. "Hey!" I said sharply, and when he didn't respond I nudged him with my boot. *"Hey!"*

He froze, absolutely still. The change was so sudden it made me jump. His only movement was the steady pump of blood from his wrist.

"I don't want to kill you," I said. "I'm sorry it came to this. Let me help you."

The mismatched eyes in the malformed face showed no comprehension. He turned his head and saw his father, face down atop his own insides. He began to screech again, and flung himself at me with renewed fury.

He was weaker, though, and I was ready. I side-stepped him and brought my sword blade down in a hard, sharp blow to the back of his neck. His body hit the ground with a solid thud, followed a moment later by his head a few feet away.

I stood between the two bodies for a long time, waiting for my own heart to decide it wanted to stay in my chest. Finally I sheathed my sword and sat down on the far side of the fire. My hands shook and my head hurt. The horse came around to stand near me, a gesture that I appreciated but couldn't really acknowledge at the moment.

Sometime after midnight I tossed both corpses into the fire, followed by the deer carcasses and all the other myriad animal parts I found scattered around the area. The smell grew even more ghastly. I led the horse a short distance upwind and sat in the grass watching the fire. It faded at dawn, and by the time the sun reached the tops of the trees, it had settled down to copiously smoking embers. I figured it was now safe to search the old cottage.

I peered through one of the windows and saw the reason they'd built the lean-to instead of moving into the building. The skeletal remains of dozens, if not hundreds of dead animals had been tossed inside, and now lay in a haphazard pile that sloped down and spread from the windows and door. I saw deer, bear, beaver and a few bones I was pretty sure were human. To Paw-Paw and John-Thomas, I imagine they were all just meat for the fire. The dense, massive piles must've accumulated over several years, and perhaps that explained why no one had ever resettled the valley. I was almost sick again, but since this was my last obstacle, I choked it down and continued.

I kicked several deer rib cages aside and entered the old cottage. How had I felt all those years ago, doing the same thing? The experience had been so intense that even now I could imagine the place as I'd seen it then, the rot and debris replaced by Epona's accoutrements.

I reached the old hearth, took a deep breath and forced myself to look at the place as an impartial investigator. It was difficult, but not impossible. Beneath the carcasses, all of Epona's original belongings had decayed pretty much where I'd last seen them. Evidently Paw-Paw and John-Thomas had not bothered to loot the place before they started using it as their garbage pile. I cleared the dirt and dust from the edge of the hearth and sat in the same spot I'd occupied all those years ago, when Epona held court for me. The frame of the old rocking chair, minus its long-decayed woven seat but miraculously upright, sat like a throne awaiting the return of its queen.

That night I had continued up the trail alone after leaving Nicole, and Epona had greeted me at the door. "Hello, Baron Edward LaCrosse of Arentia," she had said then. The words still practically hung in the cottage's air.

NINETEEN

"H ello, Epona Gray of the little house in the big woods," I had replied, mimicking her tone.

"Come in," she said, and stepped aside, "before you catch your death of moonlight." Her movement was languid and yet somehow entrancing. I didn't move, but not from fear; I just couldn't take my eyes off her.

"Don't tell me the old village conjurer has bewitched the cynical young soldier," she said. Her voice was throaty, her tone gentle, so the mocking didn't grate. I saw that she was barefoot and held a wine bottle loose in one hand. "If it'll make you feel better, call me Eppie. Eddie and Eppie; has a nice lilt, don't you think?"

"That seems a little disrespectful," I said. I still didn't move. "I thought you were a goddess."

She laughed, and I got a look at her exquisite profile against the fire. "All women are goddesses, didn't you know that? Look into one's eyes sometime. Really look." Then she faced me again. "Or, since that's beyond you right now, remember what you saw in Janet's eyes. Not in that portrait in the palace; in the real eyes that looked up at you that night after the harvest festival."

I went battle-cold at that comment. The fumbling of two awkward teenagers in an unused guest room—the first time for us both—was a memory I'd never shared with anyone. I couldn't imagine Janet gossiping about it, either. I strode forward, grabbed the woman by the wrist and jerked her out of the doorway. "You goddam bitch, who do you think you are?" I snarled.

I got my first look at her gleaming, sweaty face then. It was an exquisite set of features, not so perfect as to be intimidating, yet somehow enough to make you momentarily forget all other faces. Age-wise, she seemed both a grown woman in her thirties and simultaneously a teenage girl. She had big dark eyes and brown hair that fell over her forehead. Her smile was at once rapacious and tender. "Easy, Eddie," she said softly.

From the treetops, the mysterious night birds cried out in alarm, and big shapes rustled ominously in the nearby woods. "It's all right," she murmured, and they instantly fell silent.

"Who the hell are you?" I demanded. I smelled wine on her breath, and another vague odor I couldn't identify. "Why did you want to see me?"

She rubbed her eyes with her free hand, as if struck by a sudden headache. "Wow," she whispered. "Can we continue the melodrama indoors? I need to sit down." She didn't wait for an answer, but pulled her arm from my grip and went inside.

I stopped in the doorway and surveyed the room. The place looked like a tavern after a long weekend. Bottles lay scattered on the floor, the chairs were in disarray and dirty clothes had been tossed haphazardly aside. The fire blazed so brightly it was like a sauna, which explained the almost sheer gown Epona Gray wore. She picked up an overturned rocking chair, placed it by the hearth and sat heavily. She took a long drink then offered the bottle to me.

"No, thanks," I said as I undid my jacket against the heat. "I'm not worthy to drink a goddess' backwash."

She looked at the bottle. "Your loss. About the wine, I mean. I save this for special occasions. It's great stuff."

Behind a privacy curtain I saw a large bed, the covers and pillows rumpled. The kitchen cabinets were in disarray, and dishes filled the washbasin. For a goddess, she was a slob. "Are you going to tell me what I'm here for, or *is* there a reason?"

She ran a hand through her hair. "Reason, reason, reason. That's a big thing for you, isn't it? Everything has to have a reason, everyone has to be reasonable." She turned to me. With the chair and the fire, she now looked the part of a village hedge witch. "Cathy spoke highly of you. She loves you, you know."

I blinked in surprise. If she meant something about the previous night at the river, I didn't believe for a minute that Cathy would tell this woman anything so personal. "I think that's the wine talking, Eppie."

"You people," she laughed. "Eddie, I didn't say she was *good* at it. She doesn't have a clue how to express it. She was raped as a child, again as a teenager and swore she would never feel love of any sort again. She took back power over herself, and in the process cut herself off from every tender feeling in her heart." She pointed at me with the bottle. "Until she met you, bright boy. But you turned her down at her most vulnerable."

"I suppose she told you all this?" It was hard to maintain my ironic distance with all the conflicting emotions suddenly churning inside me.

Epona nodded. "Right there in that bed. Where all secrets are revealed and all the walls come down."

Now I knew this woman was nuts. Even if Cathy was interested in women, she wouldn't just hop into bed with some drunken tart who lived in the woods. She also hadn't had time, since she'd barely been gone the length of a dart game. "Right," I said disdainfully.

Epona picked up a short, straight pipe from among the debris and pulled a stick from the fire to light it. She took a deep draw, leaned back and sent a stream of smoke toward the ceiling. She smiled, her eyes closed.

"Honestly, I don't understand why you people don't fuck all the time. What an experience—better than drinking, or smoking, or food, or *anything*. I thought I was prepared, I thought it couldn't compare with what I knew, but *damn*. Your world is full of so many things you can touch, but *that*—touching each other—oh, man, is that the best."

I rubbed my temples. The heat and smoke were giving me a headache, and I saw no reason to endure this crap any longer. "If you'll excuse me, Eppie, I think I'll head back to town."

She looked up at me. Her gown fell off one shoulder, revealing perfect skin and the curve of her bosom. "You don't believe I am what they say I am, do you?"

The sudden entrance of sexuality into the situation hit me with the force of a hammer to the stomach. I kept most of it out of my voice, though. "A goddess, Eppie? No. I don't believe that."

She tossed her head to get a stray lock of hair from her eyes. "But it's true. I am a goddess. I chose to come here, to join you in this reality, to see what flesh felt like, because I love you all. I know all your thoughts, your dreams, your darkest secrets and brightest hopes. But I didn't know what it really felt like to be clothed in flesh like you, until I decided to share it." She nearly dropped the pipe as she brought the bottle back to her mouth. "You're all so *hungry*, you have so many *appetites*."

"Well, we like to keep busy." I was annoyed, but there was an edge of sincerity to her I couldn't explain. And I was thoroughly, almost embarrassingly aroused. To change the subject I asked, "So did you like your package?"

"Package? Oh, the trinket Cathy brought." She looked around on the floor until she found it. "I knew it was coming. I wish it didn't have to. But the world unfolds as it should."

She handed it to me. It was a small, worn iron horseshoe, the kind you could find on any pony. Dirt and rust coated it. "Wow," I said. "Lot of trouble for something so ordinary."

"Yeah, Eddie," she said distantly, sadly. "Andrew Reese has finally found me. Do you know who he is?"

I shook my head.

"Andrew Reese is broken to pieces," she sang, and then repeated it over and over so that the rhyme, and the man's name, were forever imprinted in my brain. Devils must sing it in hell.

Then she blinked, shook her head and looked up at me. "What were we talking about?"

I undid the top button of my sweat-soaked shirt. With the fire at my back and Epona before me, I felt like I might burn to a cinder. "Who's Andrew Reese?"

She bent forward and rested her elbows on her knees. She held the bottle in one hand, the pipe in the other. "That's why I wanted to see you. Let me tell you a little story, Eddie. Once before, I decided to walk among you. Not like this, not as one of you. But simply to let myself be seen and heard *as* a human being. I formed an island safely off the trade routes but near enough I might be visited. I made it a paradise, with plenty to eat and drink, but completely uninhabited. And then I waited. I had plenty of time, you understand."

"I imagine you would," I agreed.

"And so my first visitor arrived. Andrew Reese, a handsome young sailor who'd been washed overboard by a storm and managed to survive long enough to reach my island. I let him wander around for a while, get used to the place, until I finally decided to let him find me. I chose a form that he would like, that of a young woman beautiful by his standards."

She grinned mischievously. "You should've seen me, Eddie. I was tall and willowy, delightfully fragile-looking, and yet I allowed my strength to shine through. I made my hair golden, because I knew he liked blondes. My birds attended me, always nearby but never landing. My horses awaited my command. *I* was such a sight, though, I don't think he ever noticed them." She took another puff on the pipe. "He only had eyes for me."

"How'd it go?"

"I brought him to a cottage a lot like this one. I even put out a lavish dinner, with some of this." She held up the wine bottle. "That turned out to be a mistake."

"Now how can a goddess make a mistake?" I asked, convinced I'd finally caught her in a contradiction.

She was too tipsy to notice my mocking tone. "Okay, not a mistake, exactly. See, I decided not to allow myself full access to my knowledge of things. I wanted to feel surprise, to understand truly what it must be like to *not know*. So, because of that, I did something that, had I been at full oneness with everything, I would not have done. I gave wine to a man who should never, ever drink."

"What happened?"

She snorted. "A drunken sailor, a pretty girl, what do you think happened? He didn't try to rape me, exactly, but he wasn't in the mood to take no for an answer. I finally had to subdue him, which he later put down to too much wine. After all, no mere *girl* could overpower him. But I did warn him not to ever again try to compel any living thing on the island to act against its wishes. My little experiment was important to me, I'd grown fond of what I'd created, and wanted to really see what this man was about."

The gown had slipped further down. I wanted above all to kiss the line of her collarbone over to her neck. I couldn't believe I was so monumentally, thoroughly horny; I hadn't felt this much single-minded lust since . . . ever.

"When he sobered up the next day, I watched him in secret as he wandered around the island," she continued. "My animals were gifted with a higher awareness than those you know, so when he spoke to them, he could tell they understood. I didn't let them talk back to him, because I didn't want to send him screaming for the hills. But I did want him to get an inkling of the gentleness and goodness existing beyond his normal perceptions."

She paused for another draw on the pipe. "He understood," she said in a cloud of smoke. "He felt it. Andrew was a decent man, with a kind heart and the ability to feel love. Until he started drinking again. This time he did attempt to force himself on me, and I let him know

I was no ordinary woman. I broke his thumbs like that."
She snapped her fingers to illustrate the ease. "I told him
that I'd forgive his bad manners once, but only once,
and if he did it again, I'd show him just what I could do.
Then I healed him. Of course it didn't occur to him I
was a real goddess, he just thought I was some well-
studied magician or witch. Again, if I'd let myself know
all I could know, I would've seen this wasn't the best approach."

She tossed the pipe casually into the fireplace, where
it fell between two burning logs. She stood and walked
to the door. "He stomped off, furious and embarrassed.
He found a squirrel, who'd become his special companion over the time he'd spent with me, but he was in no
mood for its compassion."

She paused, looked outside, and when she turned
back tears glittered in her eyes. "He grabbed it and tore
its head off as easily as I'd hurt him, because in his
drunken rage and humiliation, he had to hurt *something*.
He threw its little corpse aside, discarded like some
piece of garbage. This squirrel had been his friend, you
understand, it had followed him and listened to him and
kept him company so he wouldn't be alone. It brought
him nuts and placed them at his feet. And he killed it
with no more thought than I just gave to that pipe."

She took a drink, followed by a deep breath. "Whew.
Sorry, it's just all so fresh to me. That squirrel was part
of me, just as you are, just as everything is. When I felt
it die, I grew furious, and let my pain lash the island in a
storm. I almost killed Andrew with it, in fact, but I was
not about to let him off that easily. He fell asleep in the
cottage I'd made for him, but he awoke the next morning back on the beach where he'd washed up. I'd wiped

the island clean of everything, so that it was only a bare rock in the water."

She walked back to me as she spoke. "I told him exactly who I was, exactly *what* I was, and that he was to leave. And do you believe it? He had the audacity to say, 'And what happens if I don't?' "

"What did you do?"

She smiled coldly, and for the first time since I arrived at the cottage, I felt a little hint of fear. "Oh, Eddie, I showed him just what a pissed-off goddess was capable of. I snapped every bone in his arms and legs, then pushed them up into his torso. I twisted him into human jetsam, Eddie, and cast him back to the sea." She gestured with the bottle, sloshing wine across the room. "And I cursed him with the worst fate I could imagine; a long, long life."

She nodded to indicate the end of her story, took another drink and fell heavily into the rocker. "He's still alive, too. He wants to die, because the pain never dims for him, but I'm not ready to let him. Not yet." She finished the bottle and flung it vaguely toward the kitchen, where it shattered against the wall. "But as you can probably understand, he's still pretty mad at me."

"Yeah," I said.

She looked at me with narrowed eyes, as if she'd just noticed the effect she'd had on me. "Uh-oh," she said, her voice slurred, "I got so wrapped up in my story I forgot about yours." She jumped up, nearly fell backward and, giggling, extended her hand to me. "Come on, Eddie. Time for your reward."

She pulled me to my feet and over to her bed. I put up no resistance. When she pulled the sheer gown over her head, I noticed for the first time that she was deathly pale and emaciated; as ill, in fact, as Nicole had said. Not that anything, at that point, was a turn-off. She was still the most sexually arousing woman I'd ever met.

I gently lifted one of her arms. Great scabbed welts ran along the inside, almost from her wrist to her elbow. Some were red and oozy from infection. "Damn, Eppie, what happened?"

"Hm? Oh. This." She pulled her arm free, held it up and dug her fingernails into the soft flesh. She ripped down to the inside of her elbow, and gasped at the sensation. I grabbed her before she could repeat it on the other arm. She struggled weakly in my grasp.

"Don't stop me, Eddie, I *crave* this. Ripping myself open reminds me, in any weird, twisted, perverted way you want to call it, that there *is* life and a world to embrace."

The blood ran in thin trickles down her arm. There should've been more; her illness was serious. But she sighed with almost sexual satisfaction as the pain faded. "I have visions of poking a stiletto through my cheek," she said breathlessly. "Imagine the tear. It's tough, the cheek. But it can be broken."

"You need help," I said.

She shook her head. "I need to be *fucked*. I need to feel it the way you do, while I can. I've indulged every human impulse. I've opened this body to everything, to every*one*. And it's killing me. I don't have long, Eddie. Neither do you."

I should've pursued that comment. It was right there, the bit of information I needed to understand the imminent danger. But when she blatantly grabbed me between my legs, my baser instincts took over, and I no longer cared about anything else.

She pulled me onto the bed. I disrobed as quickly as I could, and she spread herself for me without delay. She wrapped her legs around me and pulled me close, her hands in my hair. Her body was hot with fever, yet amazingly strong. I looked down at her face, drawn tight with something more like pain than desire, and felt emotions I could barely remember gush through me like a river. "Please, Epona," I asked seriously. "Tell me how you know about Janet."

She kissed me with a tenderness that, to this day, can bring tears to my eyes. It was a kiss of such compassion, such unconditional love, that it melted every wall I'd built around my heart and opened me to her. She held me while I cried and said, "I know about Janet, Eddie, because I welcomed her when she crossed through the veil. I felt her pain, the horror at what happened, her utter terror at both dying and leaving you."

I rose and looked into her face again. I saw every woman I'd ever loved, in any sense, in those dark eyes. My mom, my grandmother, Phil's mom, Janet of course, and even Cathy. "I really tried," I sobbed. "I would've died, too. I wanted to. But I didn't. And they made me *watch....*"

She caressed my cheek. "Shhh, Eddie. Janet's safe in the Summerlands now. She'll wait there for you. But she also knows you have more time in this world, and wants you to be happy here."

"With Cathy," I said as I wiped my eyes.

Epona shook her head. Her voice grew harder, sadder. "It's too late for Cathy. And it never would've worked, anyway. She's close to what you need, closer than you can imagine. But she's not the right one." She kissed me lightly. "It's not too late to learn from it, though. Don't be a jackass next time, LaCrosse." She arched her back. "And for now, don't be anywhere but with me."

Like I had a choice. I don't know how long we made love, but I couldn't get enough of her, and before we were done we'd explored every inch of each other with hands and mouths. I rolled her onto her stomach at one point, and as I took her from behind she hissed, "Lick my neck, Eddie. I love that." I obliged.

During one intimate passage, I felt a rough patch of skin on the inside of her thigh. I touched the horseshoe-shaped, puckered design. "Is that a scar?"

She rose on her elbows and looked down between strands of tousled hair. "I do believe it is."

I rose and met her eyes. "Now how would a *goddess* get a *scar?*" I asked dubiously, and kissed it.

She laughed. "A goddess can get anything she wants, Eddie." She ran her fingers through my hair as I continued to lick the crescent-shaped imperfection. "I wanted to mark this intoxicating flesh with something to remind me where I came from. It's so easy to forget among all this . . . *sensation.*" Then she grabbed my hair and pulled my head up to look at her. "And I am, after all, the Queen of Horses."

"Uh-huh," I agreed with a doubtful smile. I was too intoxicated with her flesh myself to really pursue my skepticism, though. When we finished—or rather, when I finished—we lay together, her atop me, and I wondered if Cathy had actually occupied this same spot. It certainly explained her behavior when she returned to the village.

Finally Epona bent over the edge of the bed and retrieved a fresh bottle of wine. She pulled the cork with her teeth and said, "So did I finish telling you about Andrew Reese?"

"You said he finally found you, and that he was broken to pieces," I said. "And he sent you an old horseshoe that meant something important."

"It means the end. Of all this. It has to be this way, and even though I know it, I can't help feeling sad. People see so little of the universe." She held her thumb and forefinger slightly apart to indicate our narrow vision. "There's always so much pain, so much fear before you realize how vast existence really is. I wish I could spare you that."

"Can't you? Aren't you a goddess?"

She nodded, and to be honest, at the time I was ready to believe her. "But I tell ya, Eddie. It's hard being a goddess *and* a woman. Maybe I should've picked one or the other." She took a drink. "Next time, baby. Next time."

I didn't know what she meant, but I sure caught the ominous undertone. Suddenly I recognized that slight tang that permeated beneath all the other odors in the place, especially on Epona's breath. I picked up the cork from the wine she'd just opened and sniffed it.

I sat up. "Eppie, this wine is *poisoned*."

She sighed. "I know."

When she turned up the bottle, I knocked it from her hands. It shattered on the floor. I grabbed her by her shoulders. She felt paper-thin, sandcastle-fragile. "Eppie, everyone in the village is drinking this!"

Again she sighed. "I *know*."

I jumped off the bed and scrambled for my clothes. Eppie rolled onto her stomach and watched me. Her words rang in my ears: *It's too late for Cathy. It means the end of all this.*

"You can't help anybody," she said. She sounded groggy now. "They're all dead. I will be soon, too. We'll pass through the veil together, my folk and I."

The last thing I heard her say as I ran out the door was, "Such plans, Eddie. I had *such plans!*"

TWENTY

I ran as hard as I could back down the trail. I heard neither horses nor birds over Epona's words rolling around in my head.

A bright orange glow appeared above the treetops, far brighter than the torches had been. At last, so winded I could barely see, I reached the edge of the forest and beheld what was left of the village.

It looked like an efficient, brutal army had been at work. All the cottages were burning. Bodies lay on the ground, most unmarked, but some decapitated. There was no discrimination: women and children had been butchered as thoroughly as men.

I knelt beside the closest body and turned it over. It was a man of about forty, with short hair and a paunch. His face was contorted in pain, and black foam collected at the corners of his mouth. The poisoned wine had taken him.

The roof of Betty's little not-a-tavern collapsed in a big puff of sparks. My chest was on fire, too, from all that running, and from the agony of realizing Cathy had to be among the dead.

Unless. . . .

I had to know. I ran through the village, heedless of the heat and danger. "Cathy!" I yelled. I dodged chickens and goats, free of their pens and frantically seeking shelter or escape. I did not look at the other corpses except to make sure they weren't her. I saw familiar faces—the red-haired girl who owed me a kiss had also died from poison—but sought only one. "Cathy!"

"Give it up, hoss," a voice called.

I turned. Stan Carnahan, bare-chested and blood-spattered, stood between two burning buildings like he'd been molded from the flames. If he'd been intimidating before, now he was downright terrifying. He looked capable of ripping a bull in half with only his hands. He carried a sword—*my* sword—also stained with blood. And he was *smiling*.

"The ones the poison didn't get, I've already seen to," he continued casually. "There's nobody left alive here."

Despite the pain in my chest from running, I managed to say, "You couldn't have killed everyone."

"Yes, I could," he said, propping the sword on his shoulder. Blood dripped from the blade and hissed when it hit a fallen burning crossbeam. "I've been planning this for months. Even made a list so I wouldn't forget anyone. Every person in the village is accounted for."

We looked at each other for a long moment. I couldn't just ask him about Cathy, so I chose the next obvious question. "Why?"

"Same as you. Andrew Reese paid me."

That name, and the insidious rhyme, whirled through my head.

"He told me a year ago to come here, become part

of the community and wait for delivery messengers to show up. When that happened, kill everyone in town. Simple job, really. And the pay was unbelievable."

He'd poisoned the wine, and on a night of celebration only the children and a few teetotalers would have been spared. They evidently posed no challenge, for Carnahan wasn't even breathing hard. "Simple job," I repeated.

Another building collapsed. Neither of us looked at it. My pulse returned to normal, then continued to slow, as panic and horror dissolved into cold soldierly professionalism. I saw no reason to delay any longer. "Did you kill Cathy, too?"

He nodded, almost contritely. "She was asleep in the bathtub. It was quick."

Now I was on territory I knew well. He was bigger, and stronger, and better armed, with my own sword no less. But I'd taken on worse odds before.

I let my jacket fall to the ground. After Eppie's hut, and my mad run, and the heat from the burning village, I was drenched in sweat. Yet inside I was solid ice.

Carnahan lowered the sword into a casual defensive stance. I wouldn't catch him on overconfidence. "No reason you can't walk away from here," he said. "I told you being with Epona was the safest place. You weren't in the village, so I got no beef with you. My job is done."

I knelt and drew the knife from the side of my boot. It was only about seven inches long, but it would be enough. I flipped it casually in my hand. "Mine's not."

I threw the knife accurately at his heart. I was good, as our dart game would've warned him, so he was ready and batted it easily aside with the sword. But he never saw the second knife, a mere three inches long, that I had secretly slipped out of a second hidden sheath and threw a moment after the first.

He almost avoided it, though. I misjudged the strength of his parry, so he moved more than I thought. The second knife went right by his head, ineffectually I thought at first.

Then I saw the first jet of blood from the big vein in the side of his neck. He had no idea he'd even been hit at first, until he felt the hot fresh blood spray down onto his shoulder and arm. By the time he put his hand to the wound, a quarter of his blood had shot into the darkness in ever-weakening arcs.

He fell to his knees and dropped my sword. I did not approach him. Blood shot through the fingers pressed against his neck. He said nothing, but I never saw any hatred in his eyes. He was a pro to the end.

When he finally collapsed, I sat and waited until I saw no fresh blood shining in the firelight. It took a while. By then most of the fires had burned down to glowing ruins, and their pops and hisses filled the night.

Finally I stood, retrieved my sword and neatly beheaded Stan's corpse. Always pay the insurance.

The only person I buried was Cathy, in a shallow grave with no marker. I found her charred—boiled, really—body still in the metal tub inside one of the ruined buildings. Her unburned head lay on the ground outside. I put the rest of the corpses on the most active fire, and kept it going until they'd been consumed. The smell was as appalling as it sounds.

At dawn, I returned to Epona's cottage. No horses followed me through the forest. No weird birds sang overhead. The house was exactly as I'd left it, but the woman—whoever she'd been—was gone. Perhaps the poisoned wine had driven her into the forest to die. I didn't know, and didn't really care. I considered torching the place, but I'd seen enough destruction to do me for a while.

Now I sat in the silent ruins of the cottage, the odor of burning flesh once more in the air. The dark-haired woman who once faced me here, who had become my lover and burrowed so far into my head that even now my skin tingled at the memory of her touch, had claimed to be a goddess. Her blond, blue-eyed twin now claimed to be a victim. I didn't believe either of them, but the only way to get at the truth seemed to be buying into those delusions. Someone once hated Epona Gray enough to commit a massacre. If Epona really was Rhiannon, could this someone also be behind the disappearance of her son?

Andrew Reese is broken to pieces.

"Eppie," I said to the air, "I sure wish you were here right now. I could use the advice of a goddess."

A tiny bird sat atop one pile of debris and, just as I registered its presence in the corner of my eye, flew off into the woods. It seemed to leave the same sparkling trail as the birds I'd glimpsed in Rhiannon's cell, but I couldn't swear to it. Its departure dislodged the deer antler it had perched on, which now slid with a soft clatter down the side of the pile. It stopped when it dislodged something else, a small wooden box that traveled the rest of the way to land at the bottom with a thump that dislodged the lid. An object fell out with a solid, heavy thud.

I stared at the box, weathered and decayed but still obviously the one Cathy had carried, and the tarnished, rusted horseshoe that fell from it. "You have *got* to be kidding," I said aloud.

I picked up the box. Still folded in the bottom was a neat piece of vellum that had evidently been treated with something to protect it from the rain, winters and other elements that might cause it to decay over time. I unfolded it slowly and took it to the door so I could examine it in the light.

The language was familiar Boscobelian, although the handwriting was atrocious. The text was obvious and, for the moment, inconsequential. But the name at the bottom gave me what I most needed at that moment.

The signature read, ANDREW REESE.

Andrew Reese is broken to pieces.

And my pieces were now falling into place. Cathy told me she'd been hired in Boscobel, and this was written in its language. I now knew my next step.

I got sudden chills. The chances of finding such a blatant clue after all this time were almost enough to make me buy into divine intervention. Perhaps another goddess heard my prayer and answered it out of professional courtesy.

I jumped as something moved within the pile of bones and sent several clattering to the ground. A big rat poked its head into the light, squeaked at me and withdrew. The disturbance had revealed a human skull, split along the top by a jagged crack. It seemed to laugh silently at me.

I carefully placed the note in my pocket; I'd have plenty of time to think it over on my way to Cape Querna. It wasn't a short voyage.

I glanced up in time to see another bird flit away from a windowsill. Once again I might have imagined it, but it seemed, for a moment, to leave a glittering trail through the air.

TWENTY-ONE

"Andrew Reese?" Bernie Teller repeated thought-fully. "Reese, Reese . . . no, don't know the name."

Two weeks after I found the note in Epona's ruined hut, I sat in Commander Bernard Teller's Cape Querna office on a bright summer day. City noises filled the air outside, but since Bernie's digs were on the sixth floor, we were literally above it all. He reclined with his feet on his desk, his long official sword propped against the end. He was as lean and alert as I remembered. "What sort of guy is he?" he asked.

"Never met him," I said. "Right now he's just a name related to a case I'm working on. Don't know his age, his nationality, anything. But I know he was here thirteen years ago. And he might be . . . deformed."

"Deformed," Bernie repeated.

"Or handicapped from an injury."

"Hm. And you said wealthy?"

"Wealthy enough that he paid a hired killer to spend eleven months in the Ogachic Mountains waiting for his victim to show up."

Bernie idly pulled on his left earlobe, a gesture that

meant he was thinking. After a moment he said, "Hang on. I want somebody else to hear this."

While he was gone, I looked around his immaculate office, only slightly less austere than my own. In one corner stood a shelf with a few legal scrolls. A small painting of Boscobel's Queen Dorothea hung next to it; on the wall behind me was a detailed canvas map of Cape Querna. Through the window I saw, over the intervening roofs, the mast tops of ships anchored in the harbor. This high, the breeze was brisk and clean, with only a hint of salty tang. The harbor city was Bernie's domain now, and he seemed to have it well in hand. At the very least, he'd forced the panhandlers, beggars and other entrepreneurial refuse off the street, and that had made a huge quality-of-life difference.

I first served under Bernie for three months during the trapper skirmishes fifteen years earlier, between the time I left Arentia and the day I met Cathy Dumont. He had the career soldier's typical disdain for mercenaries like me, but once we got past that we discovered similar views on women, money, politics and our jobs. The next time we fought together, a couple of years after Cathy's death, we were both captains, and staged an elaborate ambush for which I let him take the credit. Since going solo I'd dropped into Cape Querna whenever I could, and he'd occasionally sent business my way, as he'd done with the missing Princess Lila. We had not spoken in three years, and the last time I saw him he'd still been a stubbly, rough-edged army major who did not play the political games that gained you higher rank. So either he'd changed, which seemed unlikely, or he'd been sponsored by someone who recognized his integrity as something sorely needed in the notoriously corrupt Civil Security Force. Either way, I was certain that beneath the clean-shaven, smoothed-out and well-groomed exterior the same relentless scruples still thrived.

When he returned, he preceded a uniformed officer with unruly white hair and the unmistakable build of a man used to physical confrontation. "Eddie LaCrosse, this is Leonard Saye."

I shook hands with the newcomer. "Nice to meet you."

"He's been a street officer here for twenty years," Bernie said, "and he knows everybody."

"I know *of* everybody," Saye corrected. He sized me up in a glance. "You're from Arentia, aren't you? You still have a hint of the accent."

"Long time ago," I said flippantly. "Sheer accident of birth."

"So I guess you've been following their big scandal?"

I shook my head. "Don't pay much attention to gossip."

"Well, your King Philip sentenced Queen Rhiannon to life in prison for killing their son. Said she deserved to die, but he wouldn't change the law just for her."

Attaboy, Phil, I thought. "Reckon she deserved it, then."

"But get this," Leonard continued. "She's not in prison, or even in that big tower. She's locked up in a public cell, right at the main city gate. Every day she has to sit outside and let people call her names, spit on her, anything as long as they don't hurt her. She's like an animal in a cage." He shook his head. "Can you beat that?"

"They say revenge is the sport of kings," I said with a

blasé shrug. Inside, though, I was both glad and apprehensive. He'd done what I wanted—punished the queen
publicly, so that word would get back to whomever had
framed her—but I also knew he must be in agony, losing
both his wife and child while simultaneously knowing
she was innocent and his son might be alive.

One of my most vivid memories of Phil was of the
time when he was nine years old and had to put down his
favorite old hunting dog, Rosie. As the crown prince, he
knew all the other kids would be watching, so Phil put
on the bravest face possible. He said a properly dignified
goodbye to the crippled old girl before he dispatched her
with one quick, lethal arrow. Later, though, he cried privately for hours. He told me that if he'd just been able to
explain to Rosie what was about to happen, he would've
been fine. But seeing the love and trust in the dog's eyes,
and that instant of betrayal when the arrow hit home,
was too much. What he endured now must make that
childhood trauma feel like a mosquito bite.

"What can I do for you?" Saye asked, bringing me
back to the moment.

"Ever heard of Andrew Reese?" I asked. Inwardly I
gritted my teeth against that damned rhyme.

Saye thought for a moment. "No. Who is he?"

"I have no idea. Thirteen years ago he was rich
enough to hire a real top-of-the-line sword jockey to
kill someone."

"Who? The killer, I mean."

"Stan Carnahan."

Saye's eyes widened and he let out a long, low whistle. "Wow. That name takes me back."

"Told you he'd know," Bernie said.

"Stan was the top dog in hired swords before he

disappeared. In his own way, he was the most honest guy I ever met. We used to swap shots between drinks or drinks between shots, whichever you like." Saye shook his head in admiration. "Always wondered what happened to him."

"He was a pro to the end," I said, all the explanation Saye needed. "Who would've hired him back then?"

Saye thought for a moment. "Big Joe Vincenzo was around. The Soberlin brothers. Kee Kee Vantassel was on the rise. Nobody else could've afforded him."

"Any of them deformed?"

Saye frowned in surprise. "Deformed how?"

I wondered how to paraphrase Epona's words so they didn't sound goofy. "His arms and legs would've been kind of . . . pushed up into his body. It would make him short, and it'd be hard for him to move around, I'm guessing."

"Oh, hell," Bernie muttered, the way you do when you know a tiresome story is coming. At almost the same instant Saye exclaimed, "The *Dwarf?*"

"Who's the Dwarf?" I asked, looking from one to the other.

Before Saye could reply Bernie said disdainfully, "He's this guy who supposedly runs the whole 'criminal underworld' here in C.Q. Except nobody's ever actually *seen* him. It's always a friend who met him, or an old acquaintance or somebody's brother. They've talked about him since I was a kid. The 'Big Little Man.' "

"So he doesn't exist?" I asked.

"I think somebody made him up hoping we'd waste all our time looking for him instead of chasing the real crooks," Bernie said. Then he looked at Saye, as if daring the older man to contradict him.

"I used to believe the same thing," Saye said carefully. "But I have to tell you, over the years I've reconsidered. I won't bore you with local politics, but it seems whenever someone looks likely to make a real difference cleaning up organized crime in the waterfront area, something happens. A hit, a timely accident, a fire with no apparent cause. All different except in timing. After a while, you see the pattern."

"*You* see the pattern," Bernie said. "There's plenty of people who want to keep the docks dirty without resorting to phantom midget masterminds."

Saye shrugged. "And you're probably right. The stories have been around for so long, he'd have to be an old man by now. But I can't think of anyone else who fits your description. Not now, and not back then."

"Yeah, the trail is pretty cold," I agreed. "Thanks for your help."

"Anytime."

They'd mentioned the docks; Andrew Reese had been a sailor. What was one more razor-thin clue, after all? After Saye left, I asked Bernie, "So your docks have a lot of rackets going?"

"The usual. Girls, drugs, illegal booze. Gambling if you know the right people."

Gambling. People gambled on horses; Epona was the Queen of Horses. Was that a clue, too? Hell, what wasn't? As if it were the least important thing in the world, I asked, "How dirty is the horse racing here?"

THE DAY AT the races, in Cape Querna or anywhere else, was a collection of the saddest, most pathetic people you'd ever see. At night the place was all torch-lit glamour, but the harsh sun revealed all the manure piles, equine and symbolic, hidden by the evening's forgiving shadows.

Drink could get a strong hold on its victims, but a drunk had no delusions that the next bottle would be the one to set him up for life. Gamblers—the ones who were terrible at it but just couldn't stop—believed that the Big Score was always one roll of the dice, deal of the cards or run of the horses away. These were the poor bastards who lurked at the track during the day, betting on the training races to raise stakes for the evening's real thing, hoping for that gambling alchemy that turned dreams into gold.

I wandered around the track area, pretended to inspect the animals and their riders while I really evaluated the rest of the sparse crowd. Trainers lined up the horses at the starting line, their jockeys sharing gossip and pipe puffs over to one side. There was none of the prestigious pre-race ceremony preferred by royals and the moneyed folk; this was a business, and these guys knew there'd be another ride in an hour.

I was working off a chain of "ifs." *If* Andrew Reese was this Dwarf, and *if* he really was a criminal kingpin with a hand in every pie, and *if* he really was behind the slaughter thirteen years earlier, then *perhaps* he would have a perverse interest in horses, *therefore* the local horse racing scene *might* be a place to find a lead. It was such a small hunch it could hide beneath a good-sized flake of dandruff, but it was all I had.

I sought a certain kind of racetrack regular. I wanted a guy who'd once been wealthy and successful, but who had, for whatever reason, fallen on hard times. He'd

wear tattered finery, place small bets with all the ceremony of a major player, and lose with a tinny, pathetic
equanimity. He would also always be on the lookout for
more money, and thus could be bribed to sell his left nut
for gambling funds.

I spotted my guy after the first two races. He looked
about sixty, with unwashed hair stuffed beneath a cap
that was trendy ten years ago. Judging from his expression he wasn't having a good day, and as he shuffled
back to the concourse I fell into step behind him.

"How they running for you?" I asked.

He snorted without looking at me. "As they always
do, sir. My bets must weigh a hundred pounds, because
whichever horse I place them on runs like he's carrying
a whole extra person."

I stepped in front of him and offered my hand. "Eddie
Johnson, sir. What's your name?"

"Lonnie Ratchett," he said with great dignity, accent-
ing the second syllable of his surname. He tilted his
head back so he could actually look down his nose at
me. "Of the LeBatre Ratchetts."

"Well, Lonnie—do you mind if I call you Lonnie?—
I need some help, and I'm willing to pay for it." I put my
hand on his shoulder and steered him into the shadow of
an empty pavilion. In the evening this would be the can-
dlelit wonderland of Cape Querna's society, but now the
chairs had been upended onto tables, the bar was un-
tended and its liquor bottles removed to a safer place. I
picked a table in the middle, so the stacked chairs would
shield us from view. I figured a guy like Lonnie would
appreciate the discretion.

I took down two chairs and gestured for Mr. Ratchett
to have a seat. He inspected the cushion minutely before

deigning to grace it with his posterior. I turned mine around and straddled it, all nonchalance.

"There's somebody in town I'd like very much to meet," I said. "Now, I know you're probably not directly involved with such people. In fact, I can't imagine you even speaking to them in passing. But a man of your experience, I just bet, *does* know where such people can be found."

"I do indeed have the acquaintance of many," he said with fragile pride.

I felt like a jerk for manipulating the poor bastard. Teasing him with my fake respect was like seducing a spinster—his desperation, to be what I treated him as, was pitiful. But I had a job to do nonetheless. "Then I bet you could point me toward the man known as . . . " I leaned closer and whispered for effect. "The Dwarf."

Lonnie leaned back as if scalded. "I know of no such gentleman," he said quickly.

I smiled. "Lonnie, that's just what they *call* him. You know who I mean."

Lonnie had turned ash-pale. "Sir, I am afraid I cannot help you," he said, and started to rise.

Dammit. Nothing for it now but to be a hard-ass. I grabbed his shoulder and slammed him down in his chair. Beneath his faded suit he felt no more tangible than a scarecrow. "That's not the right answer, Lonnie."

His eyes welled up with tears of fright, but I didn't flatter myself that he was scared of me. The Dwarf clearly carried some weight, at least among desperate elderly gamblers. I'd put the old guy in a real damned-if-you-do-or-don't position.

"Lonnie," I began again, "you're a terrible liar. Really. Now take a deep breath, calm down, and let's start over. I'm going to purchase this information from someone; it might as well be you." I jerked my thumb toward the track. "And think about it—people out there who saw us together will assume it's you whether it is or not. So why not make a profit on it?"

He wiped his sweaty face with a ragged, monogrammed handkerchief. Clearly, Lonnie hadn't thought this hard in a long time. Finally he said, "Well, sir, you seem to have the advantage."

"No, Lonnie, it's all yours. I'm just appealing to your good sense."

Lonnie nodded and sighed. "I do not know the whereabouts of the gentleman in question. However, I have often heard that the Dragonfly Club is a place where much of his business is conducted. It is a private tavern in the waterfront district." He gave me the street address, and directions. "And that, sir, is all I know."

"That's more than enough, Mr. Ratchett." I paid him, counting out each gold piece so he could savor the individual clacks on the tabletop. "I hope this helps you get back on your feet."

He pocketed the gold and stood, his petal-thin dignity restored by the money's weight in his pocket. "As long as the gods and goddesses of chance share your wishes, sir, I shall manage quite nicely."

"Light a candle to Epona," I said impulsively. "She's got a thing for horses."

"Is she a lady or a goddess?"

I almost laughed aloud. "When I find out, I'll let you know."

TWENTY-TWO

You needed a password to get into the Dragonfly Club, something Lonnie conveniently forgot to tell me. I resolved, when this was over, to hit him up for a refund.

I left the racetrack and went straight to the waterfront. If the Dragonfly Club followed the pattern of similar establishments, it would operate twenty-four hours a day, so there was no need to dally. I also didn't want to give Lonnie time to warn anyone.

All along the two-mile stretch of low, crudely built storage warehouses, the suntanned denizens of shipping offices and other ocean-based industries scurried about doing purposeful, nautical things. Sailors of all classes, from uniformed officers to likely pirates, filled the streets, alleys and docks. The smell of salt, mildew and dead fish overpowered all other odors. Seagull droppings left white streaks from the edge of every roof. A stranger could easily tell the prevailing wind came from the northeast by the way the northern walls were either weather-beaten within an inch of their structural integrity, or recently repaired.

Lonnie's directions were clear enough. I followed a series of discreet dragonfly graffiti down a labyrinth of alleys, which of course gave me plenty of chances to be seen, evaluated and dealt with before I reached my destination. The first dragonfly, nearly hidden beneath a fresh coat of whitewash, led me between the offices of a cargo company and an out-of-business produce warehouse. The only people I saw were two old rummies passed out in their own urine. By the time I found the next emblem, plainly marked on an old rain barrel, there was no one else in sight. This was the part of Cape Querna that Bernie and his boys would *never* clean up, unless it was with torches and oil.

I passed a stumbling, evidently drunken young man in disheveled clothes far too classy for the neighborhood. He didn't notice me as he went around a corner muttering, "Rigged, it all had to be rigged. . . . " The gambler's lament. The Dragonfly must be close.

At last I reached the weathered, slightly warped warehouse door that, according to Lonnie, was the tavern's secret entrance. The building itself looked too decrepit to survive a good sneeze, let alone one of Boscobel's notorious winter gales. I pulled back one bent plank enough to peer inside, and saw boxes packed for shipping stacked in a neat pile. They were covered with dust, though, and I'd have bet money they were all empty, just part of the building's disguise.

A seagull dropped a rat carcass near my feet. The bird landed, got a better grip and flew away. I was glad I didn't believe in omens.

The same hand-sized dragonfly emblem I'd been following marked the door. I knocked firmly.

A section of wood slid aside enough for two mean eyes to peer out at me. I wasn't dressed up, but I'd gotten a haircut, beard trim and new jacket so I didn't look my usual scruffy self. I wanted to intrigue, rather than impress or intimidate. "Yeah?" the mouth beneath the eyes said in a ragged but unmistakably feminine voice.

I put on my weary sophisticate act. "Can the tough stuff, okay? Let me in."

"Beat it," she said, and shut the peephole. Perhaps my act needed work.

I sighed, counted to ten, then knocked again. No response. I kicked the door as hard as I could several times. Still no response. I did learn that it was more solid than it looked.

I waited until I caught my breath, then leaned close. "Sweetie, either talk to me or send somebody out here to kick my ass, otherwise I'm just gonna embarrass us both."

It took a moment, but the slot opened again and there was a hint of humor in the way she said, "I told you to beat it."

"You need a password, is that it?"

"I need you to take a hike."

"How about . . . 'the Dwarf.'"

I heard a hollow, ripping sound like the wind tearing a sail. It took a moment to realize it was her laughter. Finally she said, "Keep being that funny, you'll make me pee on myself."

I really didn't want to tip my hand this soon, on the off chance that I was right. But I saw no other way to get past this harpy. "Okay, then, how about . . . 'Andrew Reese.'" I leaned close and softly chanted, "Andrew Reese is broken to pieces."

Again I got the harsh laughter, only it was abruptly cut off. I heard her whisper with someone. Then the locks clicked, and the door swung open to allow a man to peer out and look me over.

He had neat blond hair, blue eyes and a smooth, boyish face. He wore an expensive cream-colored suit tailored to his lithe body. He looked me up and down, evaluating me just as I did him. I was faster; I knew he was serious trouble the instant I saw him.

"Come in," he said simply in a flat, quiet way.

I stepped inside a small antechamber, with two doors on the wall opposite the entrance. I imagined one led into the club, and the other to a convenient place for disposing of bodies.

I turned as the rough-voiced girl locked the door behind us. And to my surprise, she *was* a girl—no older than thirteen or fourteen, in a simple dress and with two long braids. I couldn't imagine that voice coming out of her until I noticed a shiny gold ball seemingly arbitrarily stuck to her neck; a matching one decorated the opposite side. She rolled her eyes when she saw me looking.

"Arrow shaft through my neck," she growled. She twisted one of the finials off to show the wooden stub protruding from her skin. "Doctor says it'll kill me if I take it out. So I at least try to make it look nice."

"Isn't it uncomfortable?"

"Not as uncomfortable as being dead."

"That's enough chitchat, Spike, you'll annoy the customers," the blond guy said firmly. "This way, sir." The girl he called Spike smiled at me like she was watching a steer on its way to become a steak.

I followed blondy through the door on the right. It

opened onto a steep, dark stairwell with a single lantern at the landing far below. Like the building facade, the steps were warped with age and humidity. It worked fine as a discreet entrance, but there had to be additional exits. I couldn't imagine negotiating those stairs drunk.

The blond guy took the steps two at a time, his feet barely making a sound. "Didn't catch your name," I called to him.

He reached the bottom, turned and looked up at me. "I didn't toss it."

The stairs ended at another door. The unmistakable sounds of revelry bled through its reinforced surface. Blondy met my gaze with steady, fathomless eyes. The lantern's light reflected from his pupils so he seemed to have a tiny spark inside each eye.

"Welcome to the Dragonfly," he said. "We have simple rules. No fighting, no accosting the waitresses. If one of the floor girls turns you down twice, leave her alone. No drinking to excess. When you run out of money, go home."

"You give this speech to everyone?"

He ignored me. "Present this at the bar. One free drink of your choice, on the house." He pressed a coin marked with the dragonfly emblem into my palm. "I hope you enjoy the evening, Mr. Johnson."

So Lonnie was faster than he looked. "Thank you, Mr. . . . ?"

Again he ignored me. He turned on his heel, opened the door and gestured that I should precede him.

The warehouse floor above formed the club's low ceiling and gave it a cramped, false intimacy. The place was actually huge, and a central carpeted walkway ran its considerable length. Every kind of gambling seemed to be available, from roulette to cards to a tubular track for betting on rabbit races. It had a dance floor with a band, a small café, and of course a gigantic bar that ran along one entire wall.

The heat and noise in the place was exhilarating. As I predicted, the club was packed with both suckers and those who lived off them. Girls wearing little more than scarves and money belts served drinks to the gamblers at the tables. Most of the poor bastards were too enthralled in their games to even notice all the bare flesh. Probably a million tiny candles provided light, and their flames reflected off the gold and crystal surfaces. The dragonfly motif was everywhere, from the goblets and decks of cards to tattoos on some of the girls.

By the time I took all this in, blondy had vanished. With no clear plan, I made my way to the bar. After a moment a staggeringly attractive brunette bartender, with a dress so tight you could count her freckles, leaned over the counter and said, "What'll it be?"

I put down the coin. "What'll this get me?"

She picked it up, eyes wide. "Wow. You're a friend of Canino's. This'll get you anything you want."

The blond guy's name was Canino, then. Seemed a good idea to remember it. With a wink I said, "Anything? Even you?"

"Hell, yeah," she quickly agreed. "If you can wait until the end of my shift."

I knew I was being watched, and wasn't about to let this girl get me alone somewhere, despite her obvious charms. It didn't take much strength to cut someone's throat when their guard was down, and with her knockout figure, I imagined most guys dropped their guard pretty fast.

"I'm actually here looking for another pal," I said. "Short guy. Name's Andrew Reese. He used to hang out with Canino and me. Know him?"

She shook her head. "I've been on my feet since the lunch rush, I'm lucky to remember my *own* name. But didn't you ask Canino?"

"Sure. He said to ask you."

Her eyes narrowed and her smile grew devious. "Who are you, mister? Did you find that coin on the floor somewhere? Canino finds out you're tossing his name around, he'll hand you your liver."

"I promise, Canino himself gave it to me."

"Huh." She stood back and thoughtfully crossed her arms. It almost boosted her charms right out of her dress. "So I got work to do. Do you want to cash that in for a drink, or an hour with me?"

I dropped the coin on the bar with a clack. "A drink's probably safer. I'm not as young as I used to be."

"You have to die from something," she said, smiled with what might've fooled lesser men into thinking was genuine regret, and turned to pour my drink.

I scanned the crowd for Canino's blond head even though I knew he was probably off consulting his superiors about me. He worried me more than anything in the place. Clearly he was on a leash, and I didn't want to find out how tight it was. I might have to, though, to discover who held it.

The girl placed the drink before me, and I took a long swallow. I could do little at the moment but wait and see, unless I decided to lead the crowd in a chorus of "Andrew Reese is broken to pieces." That seemed unwise.

I took another swallow of the really top-flight ale. In all honesty, I doubted I would have enjoyed the girl nearly as much, which was a sad comment on my priorities. She watched me, still smiling, and I raised my goblet to her in appreciation.

I tried to organize my thoughts into some semblance of a plan, but by the time I realized I wasn't thinking straight, no plan would help me. The poisoned drink slipped through my fingers, and I followed it to the floor a moment later.

I AWOKE IN a small windowless room. A single candle flickering in its sconce provided the only light. I lay on a bed that smelled of sweat and sex. This would be one of the chambers where girls like the bartender took their clients. Or victims.

I sat up. My brain expanded to three times the size of my skull, and I immediately lay back down. I probably whimpered.

Sometime later I awoke again. My mouth felt like someone had scoured it with sand. Even the candlelight hurt my eyes. My brain only went up half a size this time, though, and I managed to stay seated on the edge of the bed.

I was shirtless and barefoot. I saw no sign of my belongings, which was kind of annoying since my jacket was brand new. The candle, a chamber pot and a water jug were my only companions. I desperately wanted a drink, but there was no way I was taking a chance on anything else provided by the management.

It took four tries, but eventually I got to my feet. The room showed its appreciation by trying to turn inside out. In retaliation, I banged my head against the wall until my skull's thickness scared the room into behaving.

I put my back to the wall beside the bed and locked my knees so I wouldn't collapse. Whatever they'd slipped me was burning off, and moving around would make it happen faster. I stumbled from one wall to another for what felt like hours before I heard a key clank into the door. I stopped, drenched in sweat, and waited for my visitor.

It was no surprise: Canino. Behind him I saw a long corridor with many identical doors, and heard the faint sounds of the club. He closed the door and pocketed the key. It might as well have been in another country.

He picked up the water jug and held it toward me. "I know you must be thirsty."

I shook my head.

He chuckled. "I don't blame you." He took a drink from the jug, then offered it to me again. I still declined.

"Suit yourself. Well, Mr. Johnson, judging from your scars, this isn't the first time you've found yourself in a tough spot. I assume you know the etiquette. I ask, you answer." He paused for effect. "You visit the Civil Security Force, you accost a total stranger at the racetrack, then you show up here. And always you're asking for Andrew Reese. Why?"

"I'll tell him when I see him," I said, and sat back down on the bed. My voice sounded like two rocks scraping together.

"You won't see him. And you won't see anything but the inside of this room until you're more cooperative. You're not a young man, Mr. Johnson. You couldn't take me on your best day, let alone now."

I had to smile. He was probably right, but he'd also revealed the limits of his connections. His sources at Civil Security weren't high enough to have gotten my real name. "You're that good, huh?"

"Yes," he said. I believed him.

The room began to spin again, and I lay down on my side. Canino didn't move. "I just want to ask your boss a couple of questions," I said half into the mattress. "This doesn't have to get any more complicated than that."

"What makes you think I have a boss?"

I rolled onto my back and draped an arm over my eyes. "Because you're muscle, not brains. A smart guy would've sent someone to pretend they were Andrew Reese, and then I would've left without a fuss." I gestured at the room. "*This* sort of thing happens when a legbreaker has to suddenly work from the neck up."

"You're trying to hurt my feelings," he said, amused.

"I'm trying to make the room hold still."

Someone knocked. I raised my arm to see the girl bartender who'd suckered me open the door and peek in. "You wanted to see me?"

"Yeah, please, come in," Canino said genially.

She slipped in and kissed Canino on the cheek. "How's it going?" she murmured.

"He's being obtuse," Canino said. To me he said, "Isn't she beautiful? She was a student in a private all-girls school before I met her. She had no idea of the effect she had on men. Gretchen, show him how effective you are."

With a smile as vicious as any carnivore, Gretchen stepped away from Canino, turned her back to me and let her dress slide languorously to the floor. A lesser man would've applauded or cried at the sheer beauty she presented. Every muscle was perfect, every inch of delectable skin flawless. In the candlelight she seemed golden, and her dark hair shimmered. She had a multi-colored dragonfly tattooed across the small of her back.

She looked over her shoulder at me. "I think he's too old and fat to appreciate it," she said.

Canino handed her the water jug. "He's a thirsty man. Maybe you should give him a drink."

She turned to face me. This angle was even more magnificent. She raised one bare foot and placed it on the edge of the bed in front of my face. Her toenails gleamed with dark polish. She rested the jug on her knee, then tipped it forward until water trickled down her shin. It sparkled in the candlelight as it ran off her toes and soaked into the mattress.

I met her eyes. I saw no compassion in them at all.

She straightened, poured some water into her palm and sprinkled it on her breasts. Then she handed the jug to Canino. "I think he must prefer boys," she said mockingly. She bent to collect her dress.

As she reached down, Canino swung the half-full jug in a vicious uppercut right into her face. It shattered with a noise that made my teeth shudder. Water sprayed everywhere.

The blow knocked Gretchen upright, and she stumbled back into the door. Her hands flew to her face, and her breath came in little gasps. Blood seeped between her fingers and ran down her arms.

It took all my restraint not to jump up and do . . . something. But in my battered shape, Canino would have easily taken me apart. My heart thundered in my chest, but except for a slight start at the noise, I didn't visibly react.

Gretchen began to whimper as her fingertips gingerly explored her face. The damage she found made her sobs grow louder and louder.

Canino's expression remained impassive. "Think about this, Mr. Johnson. I'm actually very fond of Gretchen. You, I don't even like." He picked up her dress, then dragged her out into the hallway. I heard her first scream just as the door slammed shut.

TWENTY-THREE

I went back to sleep. What the hell else could I do? I had vivid dreams of both Cathy and Janet berating me for my idiocy.

I had no sense of time, but I awoke at the sound of another key in the lock. This one was furtive, though, and the door only opened enough for someone to peer in. I didn't recognize the eyes, but I knew the distinctive voice. "Hello?" Spike whispered.

"Yeah?" I answered softly.

She stepped into the room. "Canino's on his way back down. You don't want to be here anymore."

I nodded. I got to my feet, shook my head to clear the last of the cobwebs, and followed her into the hall. "In here," she said, and gestured at the open door to the next room.

She locked the door behind us. It was dark except for the hallway's flickering lamplight around the edge. We both put our ears to the wooden surface.

Canino's measured steps approached down the hall and he stopped just outside my cell's open door. He stood silently for a long time, and we did likewise. I just knew my every breath sounded like a bellowing ox and would give us away at any moment.

I did not hear a footstep, but the doorknob directly across the hall outside rattled. Then I heard a key, and the slight creak of hinges. After a moment the door closed again, and the lock slid back into place.

Again he moved so lightly I couldn't hear it. He rattled the door beside the one he'd just checked, unlocked it, closed it. I listened so hard for his movement that I nearly yelled when the doorknob right beside me rattled.

In the dark, Spike clutched my hand.

The key slid into the lock. There was no place to hide, and nothing to be used as a weapon. I felt so weak that if he blinked hard at me, I'd fall over.

The key began to turn.

"Boss!" a muffled voice called, and rapid footsteps approached. "We've got a situation upstairs. That naval attaché won what he's supposed to win, but he's drunk and won't stop playing."

Canino did not respond, but the key slid from the lock and two sets of footsteps receded.

Spike sighed. She struck a match and the flame rippled in her shaky hand. She lit the room's single candle. Its furnishings and ambiance were identical to the one I'd just left.

I grabbed the water jug in the corner. It was only about a third full, and warm, but to me it tasted like damn ambrosia. I poured the last bit on my face and rubbed it into my eyes.

"You smell pretty bad," Spike observed.

"Yeah," was the only comeback I could manage.

"He'll figure out where you went. But not for a few

minutes. The only thing he likes more than pain is money. Here."

She gestured at the bed. My boots and shirt were there, but not, I noticed with annoyance, my brand new jacket. "Why are you helping me?" I asked as I dressed.

"You saw what he did to Gretchen."

"Friend of yours?"

She shrugged. "Not really. She's just the latest member of the club." She turned, having to twist her whole upper body to compensate for her immobile neck, and tapped one of the finials. "Who do you think stuck this in me, anyway? And do you know why? 'Just to make a point,' he said." She snorted. "He made his point, all right."

I laced up my boots. "I guess I owe you one, then. Do you want to get out of here?"

"Nah. Except for the neck thing, I've got it pretty good. Nobody bothers me, the money's great, and I don't have to put out unless I want to. It's not bad." Her eyes bore a hopelessness far beyond her years. "Canino thinks I'm his lucky charm."

"Where are your folks?"

"Hmph. I have no idea who screwed my mom at the wrong time of the month. And she's dead. And you can save the pity for someone who needs it. If you get the chance, kill that towheaded bastard and we'll call it even. If not, well, messing with him is its own reward."

I stood and tucked my shirt into my pants. I felt mostly human again. "Won't he be pissed off when he finds out you helped me?"

She laughed. Again I was reminded of cloth ripping. "Like I care, old man. Like I care."

Spike led me to a service entrance that opened onto the club's private dock. It was sometime after midnight, judging from the stars and the moon, and the pier was dark and deserted. Launches, from two big pleasure schooners anchored far out in the harbor, bobbed next to smaller vessels.

"Take that rowboat," Spike said, pointing. "Go left and follow the waterfront until you reach the main public pier."

I patted my empty pockets. "I'd give you a tip, but I've been cleaned out."

"Don't worry about it."

I looked up at the apparently lifeless warehouse that hid the club. It was gray against the dark sky. "So does the Dwarf really run this place?"

"Canino runs it. The Dwarf just pays the bills."

"So is the Dwarf here?"

"No. I've never seen him. But Canino goes up to one of the estates on Brillion Hill a lot."

"Which one?"

"I don't know. I'm not one of the girls who gets invited to those sorts of parties. But he always brings back fresh flowers for the rest of us, if that helps any."

I bent and kissed the top of her head. "What's your real name?"

"Allison," she said with no inflection.

"Thanks, Allison."

I climbed into the rowboat, untied it and pulled away from the dock. The last I saw of her was a silhouette against the warehouse, moonlight reflecting like tiny stars off the golden balls at her neck.

I STAGGERED INTO my boarding house at dawn. Luckily the tavern on the ground floor was empty. I slept for about three hours, cleaned up as best I could, then went down to Bernie's office. I got there before he did, so I was asleep in his chair when he arrived and knocked my boots off his desk.

"You look like you spent the night in a barrel with a bobcat," he said as I moved to the guest chair. "I'm surprised the desk sergeant let you in. What happened?"

"I got snarked at the Dragonfly Club."

He paused in arranging the parchments and papers on his desk. "You didn't tell me you were going to the Dragonfly."

"If I'd known I was going to get snarked, I would have."

He closed his office door. "We've been trying to get undercover people in there for months. If anybody connects you up with me, they'll shut the place up tighter than a convent on May Day. Thanks."

"They didn't know me," I said. "Canino dug up my alias, but not my real name."

"Canino," he repeated as he sat down. "Did you take him out like you did Saye's friend?"

"I wish. No, basically I curled into a ball and whimpered." I gave him the short version of the previous night's events. Spike had confirmed the Dwarf's existence, and considerably narrowed my search area. If I'd only thought to press her about Andrew Reese, I might know for sure that I was on the right track. Still, it was a lot more than I had any right to expect, and it sure beat a stint as Canino's punching bag. "Any idea which estate on Brillion Hill might be the right one?"

Bernie walked to the big map of Cape Querna on the wall. "This is Brillion Hill. You can see how the streets all wind around almost like it was designed to confuse people. There's probably twenty mansions up there, and this time of year they've all got flowers. They even have a big garden tour to show 'em off."

I joined him to gaze at the map. He was right, the roads resembled some sailor's arcane knot. "It would be somewhere they could discreetly have wild parties with the girls from the Dragonfly."

He made an inclusive gesture. "You could do that at any of 'em. These are the cream of C.Q. society. They invented decadence, and they're able to pay to keep it quiet."

I pondered as much as my still-fogged brain allowed. It could take weeks to check each house; there had to be a way to narrow the search. "How old are these houses?"

"Varies."

"Any of them built in, say, the last twenty years?"

"I don't think so. That hill had the defensive high ground over the harbor, so it was the first place settled. It has some of the oldest buildings in town. Big stone things, like castles that never grew all the way up."

"But they've changed hands over the years, right? They're not still owned by the founding families."

"Some are. Most aren't."

"So if you were rich and powerful enough to buy one of these, but also, let's say, deformed, you might have your mansion modified to suit your disability."

He sighed. "Enough with the damn Dwarf, Eddie. Your little girlfriend might've been feeding you a line, you know."

"*Somebody* yanks Canino's chain."

"Yeah, and you're yanking mine."

I ignored his skepticism; I'd just had an idea. "Who's the best mason in town?"

"Like I'd know," Bernie said. But I knew he'd find out.

CAPE QUERNA'S TOP household design man, who'd turned his masonry skills to making sure rich people always felt rich at home, had a shop right on the edge of the Brillion Hill district, in a refurbished home that had probably once been as grand as those he now served. It was surrounded by a small landscaped yard and trees pruned to perfection. It advertised, without actually advertising, that gracious living was its prime commodity. Bernie and I tied our horses next to an expensive covered buggy with a liveryman and driver lounging beside it.

A tasteful sign by the road identified the business as *Tanko Interiors*. Beneath it was the slogan: *The best homes for the best people*. A tall young man in ruffled cuffs opened the door before we could knock. He disdainfully regarded our attire. "Yes?"

Bernie held up his identification pendant. "Civil Security. We need to speak with Mr. Tanko."

"He's with an *important* client right now," the ruffled guy said snottily. "Perhaps if you made an appointm—"

I could've told him that wasn't the attitude to take with my pal. Bernie punched him right in the center of his chest, so fast I barely saw his hand move. Ruffles made a tiny *"oof!"* sound, his eyes popped wide and he started to fall. Bernie stepped forward and caught him.

"Hey! You got a fella in distress here!" Bernie yelled. He lowered the red-faced young man to the floor, where he wheezed as he tried to catch his breath. "Sorry, friend," Bernie muttered as he undid the florid collar. "Next time try manners."

The foyer was huge, with well-chosen paintings on the salmon-colored walls. Luxurious chairs and couches were provided for waiting clients, and a decanter of wine stood open beside a tray of classy, jewel-crusted mugs. Overhead a huge chandelier hung like a diamond rose. At night, with all the candles lit, it would've been bright enough for ships to navigate by.

A door slammed at the far end of the room, and a man walked rapidly toward us. He seemed to be enveloped in a swirl of colors, with a bright blue puff-sleeved shirt offset by a yellow scarf and his own frightfully red hair. "Oh, my God!" he cried in a high, twittering voice. "What's happened to Cecil?"

"Looks like some kind of seizure," Bernie said. He stood to greet this newcomer. "Happens sometimes when folks don't cooperate. You the owner?"

"Good heavens, did you do this?" the yellow-scarfed man exclaimed. If possible, his voice grew even more shrill. "You rude wolverine, you! This man is an artist, he has a delicate constitution!"

Again Bernie held out his identification. "He'll be fine, and so will you if you just calm down. We're looking for Robert Tanko. Is that you?"

"Yes, yes, that's me," he said as he fell to his knees beside Cecil. "My little dove, can you hear me?"

A woman with an enormous plumed hat appeared from the same door that had disgorged Tanko. She had a body that curved in all the right ways, and her clothes were cut to show it off. "Bobby," she called impatiently, "they're walk-ins, and I had an *appointment*."

"Reschedule it," Bernie told her. "Civil Security business."

The woman's eyes first opened in surprise, then contemptuously narrowed. She started to speak, but Bernie cut her off. "And don't ask me if I 'know who you are,' because then I'd have to say I do. And yes, I know who your husband is. *And* I know about your little jaunts down to Lewis Beach with your herbalist, something I bet your husband *doesn't* know."

Her mouth snapped shut, and she turned red even through her considerable make-up. She flounced past us out the door, stepping over Cecil as if he were something her dog left on the rug.

Tanko glared at Bernie. "How *dare* you—"

"The more you keep acting like a spoiled brat, the longer this'll take," Bernie said. "Your friend here will be good as new once he catches his breath, and we only have a couple of questions. Where can we talk?"

Tanko started to protest further, then thought better of it. He helped Cecil, still woozy, into a padded chair, then we followed him into his private office. Like the foyer, it was classy and stylish, dominated by a huge table piled with drawings and designs. A floor-to-ceiling archway behind the desk opened onto a garden.

Tanko shut the door and whirled on us. All traces of swish vanished. "Who the hell do you think you are?" he demanded, his voice a full octave lower. "You can't just come in here and start beating on people, I don't care what your badge says."

"We're the guys with the questions," Bernie said as he looked around, unruffled by Tanko's complete change in demeanor. "My friend here," he said with a nod at me, "will do the asking." Bernie then leaned against the wall by the door, stuck his hands in his coat pockets and left me the floor.

Unlike Bernie, I didn't hide my surprise at Tanko's personality reversal. Tanko saw my expression and laughed. "Oh, come on, *nobody's* that much of a hummingbird. It's what people expect from a man in this profession. Rich old men have to be able to trust me alone with their trophy wives; you think I'd get any business if I didn't flutter around in this kind of get-up?"

"Must be tough on your wife," I said, noting the band on his finger.

"I never said I liked girls. Just that I wasn't a hummingbird." He winked at me, sat on the edge of his desk and folded his arms. "So what's so important that Cape Querna's finest have to hassle someone like me? Are you finally going to redo those hideous uniforms?"

"Somebody on Brillion Hill has modified a house to accommodate their handicap," I said. "A guy with arms and legs that don't work right, that look like they've been pushed up into his body. He'd have money, so he'd come to you, the top man in your field. And even if he went to someone else, I'm betting you know about it. All I need is an address."

Tanko's eyes narrowed. "And just who are you again? I haven't seen your badge."

"Mine's big enough for us both," Bernie said.

"Not from where I'm sitting, tough stuff. What happens if I say I have no idea what you're talking about?"

I looked around until I spotted a large wooden cabinet. "Bet you keep very neat records. Be a shame if they got all mixed up from us looking through 'em."

"That's illegal," Tanko protested, but clearly he knew such niceties weren't a consideration.

"Then tell me the address," I said.

He sighed and undid the scarf as if it choked him. "Some of my clients won't take it too well that I'm giving out that kind of information. They like to think their dealings with me are confidential. I've been known to make changes for them that facilitate certain, ah . . . illegal intimate activities."

"Oh, come *on*, Tanko," Bernie snapped impatiently. "Otherwise I get a dozen of my clumsiest and least aesthetic officers down here and we turn your tidy little business into a rummage sale."

Tanko swallowed hard. He looked at me for sympathy, but I kept my expression neutral. He paced to the arch that overlooked the garden. "Okay, fellows, we'll play your game. How much," he asked quietly, "to make you two go away?"

"I can't hear you," Bernie said; he'd heard him just fine.

Resigned, Tanko nodded. "Yeah," he said softly. "I'm sorry, then, gentlemen. I'm not telling you a thing."

Before either of us could respond, he held up a hand. "That's right. You came in here with threats and scare tactics." He found a quill, dipped it into an inkwell on his desk and began to write. "But I didn't *tell* you anything. If you're honorable men, you'll pass that information along. Bob Tanko told you nothing."

He handed the parchment to me. On it was a street address. "If you tell anyone any different, I won't see the next sunrise," Tanko added with fatalistic calm. "I've always liked the dawn. I'd hate to miss it."

I blew on the ink to dry it, then put the parchment in

my pocket. "He's too tough for us, Bernie. He won't crack."

Bernie nodded and dislodged himself from the wall. "Yeah. Damn near wore myself out trying to shake him loose."

Tanko nodded gratefully. As we left his office, Bernie paused and kicked over a large potted plant. The dirt and water spilled onto the carpet. When he saw Tanko's aghast expression he said, "Just to make it look authentic."

TWENTY-FOUR

B ernie didn't take it very well when I told him he couldn't tag along. He took it even less well when I wouldn't share the address with him. If Canino was involved, he pointed out, then likely some major illegalities took place in and around my destination. I sympathized, but I also knew I had to do this alone. Bernie was both my friend and the long arm of the law in Cape Querna, and I might have to break a few statutes to resolve things for Phil, Rhiannon and myself. I couldn't risk either implicating or confronting Bernie in a pinch.

Back in the boarding house I tried to catch up on some lost sleep, but I was too anxious to relax. I risked a drink, not knowing how it might mix with the dregs of the Dragonfly's joy juice still in my system. It had no effect of any kind.

I stood on the balcony and watched night approach over the ocean as the sun set. From dark blue to purple to black, the sky darkened like a bruise forming over Cape Querna. Beneath it roamed the people who hated the light, whose furtive acts needed to be hidden from decent, daytime eyes. Tonight, I would be one of them.

My strategy was simple. Go to the address Tanko gave me, sneak into the place and see if, as I suspected, the Dwarf was also Andrew Reese. After that, I'd have to improvise.

My sad little plan was based entirely on my only real clue, the note I'd found at Epona's old hut. I lit one of the balcony's torches, unfolded the faded piece of parchment and looked it over one final time. Translated, it read:

> *I KNEW YOU WOULD COME BACK. AND YOU KNEW I'D FIND YOU.*

I read no hidden meaning, no inside joke or inadvertent irony that might give something away. I saw only the bitter cackle of triumph from an old enemy. The rest of my chain of reasoning was so insubstantial it might have been made from fairies' hair.

It wouldn't have been so bad if people hadn't been counting on me to be brilliant. I imagined Queen Rhiannon, now scruffy and despondent in her cage beside the city gate. Each morning the same work traffic would pass her, and she would endure their jeers and stares knowing she was innocent. Was she allowed to speak to any of them? Would she eventually form relationships with her tormentors the way all prisoners do? Or was she kept silent, in public isolation, overhearing but not participating in the city life around her? Would her guards abuse or coddle her? Would Phil demand daily reports, or try to pretend she wasn't there? And would all this finally convince her to admit she *did* know who she was, and why someone hated her so much? Or had she told the truth all along?

Completely out of the blue, I had a vivid flash of my hand on Epona Gray's inner thigh, sliding toward the horseshoe scar. A cushion of sweat smoothed my palm's progress along her fever-cooked skin. She had been real, I was absolutely sure. She had been a genuine, tangible woman. But I'd never touched Rhiannon; she told me about the scar, but I never saw it. So how could I know if she truly was Epona Gray with blond hair and blue eyes?

That was my basic dilemma. I just wasn't *sure* of anything. I couldn't believe Epona Gray had been a goddess; that was just goofy. And I didn't believe Rhiannon was an amnesiac. Yet I *was* sure that, somehow, they were the same person. How could that be true? Rhiannon could not still be so young and unchanged after ten years unless she really was supernatural. Epona had been deathly ill, so she *couldn't* have been supernatural. One, or both, had lied. Because nothing made sense if both had told the truth.

I packed all my belongings and left the bag on the bed. If I returned to claim it, I wouldn't be staying long, and if I didn't, the housekeeper shouldn't have to bother on my account. I wore dark clothes that, I hoped, would seem like formal evening wear at a distance, but would allow me to hide in the shadows if needed.

I slipped through the crowded, smoky tavern without being noticed and went into the stables. The boys had finished feeding and grooming the guests' horses for the evening and gone off to do whatever stable hands do after work.

My stolen ride stood patiently in her stall. The dim light from scattered oil lamps turned her a deep chocolate color. She tossed her head slightly when I put the saddle on her back, but made no protest when I cinched it tight. I pulled the bridle over her head, and she accepted the bit without complaint.

I looked into her eyes. For the first time with any horse, I didn't get that *frisson* of alien, vaguely malicious intelligence. "You're a pretty good girl, aren't you?" I said as I stroked her face. "Hope you like being with me, because I don't think you'll ever find your way back to those border raiders in Pema. I guess if we're going to keep working together, I really should give you a name."

She gently tossed her head in what truly seemed like agreement.

"I've never named a horse before. Let's see . . . I guess I should base it on some quality you have. You're patient, you're smart, you're loyal . . . hm, 'Loyola'?"

The horse just looked at me as if I was an idiot.

"You're right. What if we shortened it to 'Lola'?"

I swear the animal cocked her head as if thinking about it, then whinnied and stepped forward to rub her snout against my cheek.

"Lola it is, then," I said as I swung my leg over her back. "Hope I'm still around tomorrow to introduce you to people."

I'd memorized the route from the map in Bernie's office. I rode Lola though the dark streets toward Brillion Hill, doubling back several times to make sure I wasn't trailed by either Bernie or someone connected with Canino. Foot traffic thinned out as I neared the mansion district, and once I reached it I passed only closed buggies delivering the scions of these wealthy families to ritzy galas. I heard music and crowds behind some of the massive privacy walls, while others remained mysterious and silent.

The small castles and newer houses on Brillion Hill reflected the world of my own childhood. I'd been one of those decked-out rich kids living from party to party. I could dance, use the right fork at a lavish dinner, negotiate a wine list and play a passable piano. My partner in crime had been the ultimate cool dude, Crown Prince Phil. And for a while, my girlfriend had been the delectable Princess Janet. At that moment, though, it seemed no more real than some book I'd once read.

I passed numerous huge, ancient gates before I reached the one that bore the number Tanko had written down. Through the heavy iron bars I saw a three-story house, newer but not really new, behind the tall trees. The grounds grew thick with flowering bushes, and I recalled Spike's comment that Canino always brought back fresh flowers from his visits to the boss. Only a single light gleamed in one window; no galas tonight for the Dwarf, apparently. The gate looked solid, and its lock mechanism appeared in good shape. There was a gatehouse, but it was unmanned.

Only after I'd absorbed all this did the gate's design register. The bars were decorated in the shape of a giant horseshoe, upside down so the luck wouldn't spill. I almost laughed.

A buggy approached as I took in the sight. I rode on as if still searching for the right address. Lola's hooves clopped on the cobblestone road as we passed two other homes. When the traffic finally disappeared and I had the street to myself for a moment, I stopped and slid quietly to the ground. I led Lola into the shadows beneath a thick, ancient oak branch that stretched over an estate wall and almost across the entire street. I tied her to the lowest limb, and if she stayed still and quiet, she'd be invisible until dawn.

I pulled the brand-new Edgemaster Series 3 dark-steel sword from the saddle and strapped the scabbard across my back. The trusty Fireblade had served me well, but its blade was far too shiny for night work. I'd picked up the new sword earlier that day, and although taking an untried weapon into combat was a beginner's mistake, there'd been no time to break it in. I waited while more buggies passed. Then, ducking from shadow to shadow, I returned to the gate.

I lingered in the dark beside the gatehouse for a long time, listening for any movement on the grounds behind the wall. Crickets and mosquitoes, uncaring of social status, went about their business here just as they did among the common folk at the bottom of the hill. Two carriages passed on the street, one silent and one full of giggling debutantes. I heard nothing from the house or the surroundings.

There was no reason to prolong this. I crouched by the gatehouse door and picked the lock with more speed and silence than I could've managed on the gate itself. I slipped into the tiny building, then through the opposite door and onto the estate grounds. I ducked behind a tree near the wall and again waited for any sign I'd been spotted.

I could see the layout better from here as well. The driveway led in a graceful arc to a carriage house where guests could disembark with no fear of the weather. The main building's first story boasted towering windows that opened directly onto the front porch, but were now closed and draped into darkness. Up-stairs that single dim light still burned in one window, but I couldn't see its source. A buggy passed on the street just over the wall behind me, and the noise echoed in the silence.

It certainly didn't seem like the hideout of a criminal mastermind. No guards, no vicious dogs, barely even a lock. I wondered if, like Lonnie, Tanko had rushed to warn them I was coming. More likely he'd given me the wrong address just to get us out of his office.

I moved from tree to tree, each time closer to the house. There was a small, narrow moat around it that was likely a holdover from its pioneer days. Anyone not weighed down by armor could easily leap it, and small foot bridges crossed it at several places. The water in it was dark, and its surface sparkled just enough to tell me it was flowing, however slightly. I crouched in the bushes beside the carriage house and was contemplating forcing a window open, when I heard the distinct sound of splashing in the moat behind the house.

It took several minutes of dodging from one bush to another to reach the rear wall of the estate. Torches lit the back of the house where a patio had been added, but I couldn't see over the rows of damn hedges that formed a small, shoulder-high topiary maze.

At the very back of the yard, a gigantic old black-jack oak towered over the newer trees that had been landscaped in. These oaks usually lived on gnarled rock outcroppings overlooking the ocean, which Brillion Hill had once been before men built things all over it. To have grown this large, this one must've been spared from the original clearing, because I'd never seen one with a trunk this thick. Wincing at every faint crackle of bark and creak of branch, I hoisted myself into the tree and climbed high enough to get a wide, unobstructed view.

A section of the moat had been enlarged to form a kind of swimming pool. A lone figure traversed it with awkward, uncertain strokes. The swimmer was small like a kid, but lacked a child's pale pudginess. This character seemed lean, tanned and somehow elderly. His exertions reeked of desperate effort, but he wasn't drowning. He methodically reached one side of the moat, turned and started back. At this distance I couldn't make out his face.

A door opened, and my old friend Canino emerged from the dark house. He wore pale slacks and a pink tunic with rolled-up sleeves. He was barefoot and carried a tall tankard. I heard his voice clearly over the swimmer's splashing.

"The ledgers for this month are on your desk. Kandinsky was short again; I'll pay him a visit."

The figure in the moat bobbed up and down, struggling to tread water. "His daughter is around fifteen now, isn't she? Use her virginity as leverage, if she's still got it. I can't ignore that kind of shoddy management."

Canino sipped his drink. "How do you know he's not doing it deliberately?"

The figure in the water swam to the edge of the pool at Canino's feet. "Because he's the latest in a long line of idiots named Kandinsky."

"Then why do you still use him?"

"Because I know him. He completely lacks the

capacity to surprise me. His grandfather tried to cheat me once, and I made sure his child-fathering days were over. His father spent ten years in prison for trying to fix an election against the guy I was backing. I've seen him grow up, and I know fear of me keeps him honest. Too bad it can't make him any smarter. Give me a hand out of here, will you?"

Canino put his drink on a table and reached for the offered hand. He pulled the swimmer from the pool, and I got a rush of alternating terror and excitement.

The naked man was no more than three feet tall. His head and torso were of normal size, and that's all he was: a head with short black hair and a muscular, tanned torso. His hands stuck out directly from his shoulders, the right one up and the left horizontal. His feet dangled from his hips, the left one quite a bit lower than the right. His genitalia, at this distance, appeared normal.

Canino lowered him to the patio. He moved with an understandably odd, jerky grace to the table and retrieved a bright red towel. Somehow he tied it around his chest, and it still dragged on the ground.

"I'm going to get dressed," the Dwarf said. "I'll look over the ledgers and get back to you with any other problems."

Something nearby moved at the periphery of my vision, and I froze. There was no breeze, and I had not changed position. Anything that moved had to be alive.

Close to my hand I both felt and saw motion on the branch. Curled up atop the wood, barely visible in the darkness, was a small furry shape. It could not be a squirrel, because they weren't nocturnal, and it was too small for either a possum or a raccoon.

Now that I'd noticed one, I suddenly realized the tree was full of these same creatures. It was a miracle I hadn't grabbed one as I climbed. They were tiny, no bigger than my two fists put together. I felt a serious case of the creeps rising as I tried to figure out what the hell they were, until one suddenly rolled over, stretched and yawned. Both relieved and excited, I recognized it as a tiny monkey. They weren't native to Cape Querna, yet a monkey had been essential to framing Rhiannon, and its presence on the Dwarf's estate was at least a minor confirmation.

As the Dwarf waddled toward the house, the door opened again and a girl walked out. She wore a skimpy top and a low, long sheer skirt. Her face was hidden behind what I thought at first was a white mask. She stood aside and held the door open.

"Hey, Gretchen," the Dwarf said with malicious cheerfulness. "You look thirsty; would you like a jug of water?"

His laugh echoed in the dark house. Gretchen walked heavily over to stand next to Canino by the moat. He did not look at her as he said, "Care for a swim?"

She shook her head. Her voice had none of its former cockiness. "The doctor said I shouldn't get my bandages wet."

Canino smiled but still didn't look at her. "You'd swim if I asked you to, wouldn't you?"

She nodded, thoroughly defeated. "Of course."

He handed her his drink. "That's okay. I'd rather see you dance."

He picked up a lap drum and settled himself in a chair, the drum between his knees. Gretchen put his drink on the table next to him.

"Please don't make me dance," she said in a voice so small I barely heard it. She pointed to her bandaged face. "It hurts when I move, even a little. The cuts start bleeding again."

Canino said nothing, and began tapping out a slow rhythm.

"Why do you enjoy hurting me?" Gretchen choked out, sounding like a little girl. "All I ever did to you was like you."

Canino remained silent and motionless except for his hands on the drum.

Gretchen slid her feet back and forth, her slippers skitching against the stone patio. She began to sway to the beat, although I heard her sniffle and choke as she did so.

I'd never get a better chance, and carefully plotted my descent. I'd scaled the tree in blissful ignorance, but now I climbed down as a nervous wreck. If I disturbed one sleeping monkey, they'd all go off in a screeching, leaping cacophony. I timed my movements to the rhythm of Canino's drum, and when my feet finally touched the ground, I almost wanted to cheer.

If she'd glanced up at the wrong moment Gretchen might have seen me, but it was dark and I was good at stealth. I used the perimeter of the hedge maze to hide as I scuttled around the yard, until I crouched out of sight fifteen feet behind Canino in the shadow of a silver maple.

I pulled a miniature crossbow with only a foot-wide prod span from a holster strapped to my lower leg. The weapon folded down to a slender tube no bigger around than my thumb. I snapped the prods out and wound the cranequin as tight as it would go.

Gretchen had shed her top and was now dancing in only the sheer skirt. Her bandaged face showed wet stains from both tears and blood. She moved like a doll dangling from a string.

I loaded a short, razor-sharp bolt into the crossbow. I'd get one shot if I was lucky. If this whole dance routine hadn't been some ruse to lure me out. I felt no particular sympathy for Gretchen beyond what I would for any victim of cruelty; after all, she'd slipped me the sleepy-time and helped Canino torture me. But Canino might not comprehend that, and assume I'd react the way most men would at the sight of a half-naked damsel in distress and come to her rescue. If this was a trap.

It was time to stop thinking. I stood, leveled the crossbow and shot Canino through the back of his neck.

I don't know what sort of reaction I expected, really. But I was surprised when he did nothing at all except stop drumming. Gretchen froze in mid-spin, eyes wide inside the holes cut in her bandages, then quickly crossed her arms to cover her bare breasts. Given our previous encounter, I thought her modesty misplaced.

I waited, but Canino still didn't move. Had I gotten lucky and sliced his spinal cord? I wondered if I dared take my eyes off him long enough to recock and reload the crossbow. I decided that would be foolish, so I dropped the weapon and drew my sword. I really didn't want to get within blade-range, but I also couldn't just stand there and wait for something to happen.

I took a step forward, and Canino stood up and turned to face me. The movement was so quick and graceful I barely held back a yell.

The bolt tip protruded from the front of his neck, to one side of his Adam's apple. Blood stained the collar of his pink shirt, but not as much as I expected, because the bolt itself blocked the bleeding. He breathed with difficulty, but his demeanor was so calm it was terrifying.

"Now this is ironic," he said with a smile. His voice was suddenly rough and husky, with a raggedness identical to Spike's.

I didn't say anything.

His knees wobbled, and he grabbed the chair for support. "You didn't even give me a chance," he rasped.

"Had a feeling you were too good to give a chance to," I replied.

Suddenly Gretchen stepped forward and yanked the bolt from the back of his neck. It popped free with a wet smacking sound. He spun to face her as blood gushed from both holes. She stood with the bolt in her hand, fresh tears soaking the bandage around her blazing eyes.

Canino lunged toward her and she made no move to evade him. I never saw him draw the knife, but he drove it into her belly and then ripped it upward with all his fading strength until the bone of her sternum blocked it. He pulled her close and worked the blade deep into her, probing for her heart. He found it.

They stayed motionless for a long moment, two lifeless bodies propped together like tent poles. Their mingled blood pooled at their feet. At last they collapsed, smacking into the wet patio stone beneath them. Droplets of red splashed into the moat and vanished into the night-black water.

This whole lethal encounter had taken less than three minutes, and occurred in almost total silence. I sheathed my sword, slipped the crossbow back in its tube and quietly stepped into the shadows. The door through which the Dwarf had entered the house remained open, and no light showed anywhere inside. I listened intently, unable to believe the little freak was really alone inside the huge dark house. Where were the other guards, or the additional strong-arm thugs like Canino? Did he really feel so secure?

I wouldn't learn anything standing on the patio like some kid selling cookies. No one appeared to check on Canino, and no one moved about inside. I slipped through the open door into the main room, and waited until my eyes adjusted enough so that I wouldn't trip over the furniture. The light from the patio torches reflected from an enormous chandelier over a long, elegant dinner table that ran lengthwise toward the door. Along the walls were overstuffed sofas, and beside each a little footstool to allow the Dwarf access.

Huge paintings covered the walls, all with an identical motif: horses in agony. Some were drowning, some being burned alive, some simply ridden to the point of exhaustion. The styles were as varied as the subjects were similar. I recognized some of the artists, masters from across the world, and was impressed with the Dwarf's resources, if not his taste. An original Finkelman must cost a damn fortune.

Near the front of the room, a huge staircase swept upward in a graceful arc around the foyer's entire perimeter. This puzzled me, until I saw that a smooth ramp ran alongside the steps, and explained the need for such a gradual slope. The Dwarf, unable to use steps, would need something like this to reach the upper floors.

I took the steps silently, listening for any movement around me. The house was deathly quiet; I could even hear the pool rippling outside, and the occasional crackle of the torches. The staircase did not creak, but I felt it shift under my weight, and knew it might give me away. It made me, if possible, even tenser.

I reached the second floor landing. To my right, the hallway stretched away into darkness, but down the opposite hall I saw the same faint glow I'd observed from outside. It came from under a door halfway down the corridor. No other goal presented itself, so I crept toward it. I passed several other closed, silent rooms before I reached the lit one.

I paused. I had no idea what to expect, so I could really prepare for nothing. I could only hope that the clues and hints that led me here would see me through whatever happened, for the sake of my best friend and his wife. I put my hand on the knob, opened the door and stepped into the room.

TWENTY-FIVE

⁓

The smell of incense surged over me the moment the door opened. I slipped in and closed it behind me, wincing at the hinges' faint protest in the silence. Then I looked around.

The dim light came from a dozen small candles on a tiny altar. It reminded me of the little girl praying in the mines below Poy Sippi. The place was filled with bizarre objects, some displayed on tables and shelves, some propped against the walls. Each had a vaguely equine theme, although there were as many winged stallions and unicorns as there were depictions of everyday horses. Some, I suspected, were parts of actual animals, preserved in all the arcane ways people use to hang on to the dead.

I methodically scanned the room. The Dwarf was so small he could have found a dozen easy hiding places in the flickering shadows. I saw no sign of him, so I walked over to the altar. I wondered what sort of things he would offer to his apparent horse deity.

I should've known. The central icon was a horse skull impaled by a golden spike. Vicious spur wheels covered in dried horse blood marked the four cardinal directions.

A riding crop lay where a ceremonial knife normally rested. The Dwarf's hatred of horses extended even to his religion. Hell, apparently it *was* his religion.

As I stood by the altar, the door creaked open behind me. I froze. The polished side of a ceremonial bowl reflected a squat, furry shape about waist high. It had a peaked head, wide shoulders and long arms.

I had a knife up my sleeve, probably my easiest weapon to draw in a hurry. But I didn't. I slowly turned, careful not to make any abrupt motions. Whatever this creature was, I didn't want to startle it.

The light was too dim to make out any details, but the general shape was unmistakable. It was an ape, standing very still just outside the door. I could hear its breathing in the silence. I didn't know much about these animals, so I had no idea whether I should be quiet, make noise, bluff an attack or fall to the ground and cover my head. So I just stood there.

A long moment passed. Then the ape shuffled forward into the room. I may not have been an expert on gorillas and such, but I'd seen a lot of animals move, and this was all wrong. I crossed my arms and said, "Very funny."

The Dwarf laughed. The costume allowed most of his face to peek through, so I saw his big smile. "I couldn't help it, I love wearing this thing. People never worry about what the monkey might hear." He pulled back the furry hood and bent his head far to the side so his hands could smooth down his hair.

In the candlelight, he looked younger than he had from a distance. His features seemed normal, even friendly. I knew better. He said, "Tried having a suit like this built to give me normal human proportions, but the technology just isn't there yet. I have to settle for a chimp. It's actually more useful than you might think."

"So you wear it around the house a lot?"

"Nah. I just put it on to light the candles. My hands aren't really good with fire." I heard the slight squeak of wires and cables as the fake hands closed around a taper, lit it from one of the burning candles and then touched the flame to some others that had gone out.

"So, here you are in my house," he continued. "You trespassed onto my property and, if you got this far, killed two of my friends outside. I'm guessing that you're not here collecting for charity."

"I only killed one of your friends. And I can really only take half the credit for that."

He waved one of the monkey-suit arms dismissively. "It doesn't matter. Canino was useful, but they all go quick eventually. There'll be another one along." Apparently satisfied with the number of lit candles, he snuffed the taper and wriggled out of the costume. Its framework kept it upright, so he resembled a molting insect. He wore a tunic cut to his odd proportions. I recalled Epona Gray's description of the damage she'd wrought on the unfortunate sailor Andrew Reese: *I snapped every bone in his arms and legs, then pushed them up into his torso. I twisted him into human jetsam, Eddie, and cast him back to the sea.* This man certainly looked as if such a thing had happened to him. "Who knows? Maybe even you. Need a job?"

"I prefer being self-employed."

He shrugged. The gesture made his whole body wobble. "Then I can assume you're here on business?"

"Yeah."

I watched his every move. I sensed he was dangerous far out of proportion to his appearance. "Buying or selling?" he asked.

"Neither."

"What else is there?"

"Insurance. I'm taking out a policy on a friend's life."

He narrowed his eyes at me. "You're a smart guy to get this far. Don't turn stupid by threatening me. You think I'd be able to live here all alone if I didn't know how to protect myself?"

"I'm sure you can. I'm no slouch myself. I took out Stan Carnahan once, too."

It was small, but I saw the muscles in his cheek tremble as he clenched his teeth. "Who?"

"Let's move this along. Once upon a time, you washed up on an island and, like most sailors, behaved very badly to the lady who lived there. Bad luck for you that she turned out to be a goddess. She made you into what you are now, and I'm betting you've been waiting for your chance to get her back for it ever since. You knew she'd reappear somehow, somewhere, so you kept your eyes and ears open. Maybe that was the whole reason you developed this underground criminal network of yours. You eventually caught wind of her little experiment in the Ogachic Mountains, and paid a bad man a lot of money to insinuate himself into the group. Then you sent a nice girl named Cathy to deliver your little 'gotcha' present. And you did get them, all of them, including the goddess who let herself be human enough to die."

In the candlelight, his expression changed from amusement through anger until, at last, he seemed about to cry. "How do you know all this?" he asked, his voice raspy with emotion.

"Because I was there, too, on the night it happened. And I made sure your bad man didn't walk away."

"But she died, didn't she?" he whispered. "She did die?"

I nodded.

He sighed with relief. "For a minute I thought . . . well, it doesn't matter. She died."

I shook my head a little. "You're a freak in more ways than one. One lethal revenge wasn't enough for you. Because the lady really *was* a goddess, she showed up again, as the queen of Arentia. You weren't going to trust proxies like Stan Carnahan this time, so you wangled an invitation to a state function in Arentia City. I know how it works, with enough money and a couple of connections it wouldn't have been too hard. Canino was the actual guest, though; he took you along in your monkey suit." *Blond man with the ugly chimpanzee*, Vogel had written in his report. "When the queen left the banquet, you slipped away after her. You confronted her somewhere between the main hall and the nursery." *You're right, though, it couldn't possibly take that long*, Rhiannon had said. "But after all that time, all that effort, she didn't even remember you, did she? She saw the same thing I do right now: some little, pathetic monster. That must have pissed you off no end."

I could imagine his rage, confronting the woman he believed had done this to him and having his grand moment of revenge spoiled by her amnesiac blankness. He swallowed hard, and his eyes grew shiny. "I just wanted her to kill me," he said softly. "I thought that when she died before, I would, too. But I didn't."

"Sure. You had a 'plan B,' though," I continued. "You drugged her and got her loopy enough to let you into the nursery. You took her baby out hidden in the suit; you probably doped him up a little as well, just to keep him quiet. You took advantage of what was at hand in the castle to set up the murder scene, and used the meat and bones of one of your pet monkeys as the final touch. Then you disposed of the baby until Rhiannon decided she remembered you. But that never happened, and never will."

He shook his head, and it dislodged one tear down his cheek. "I'm no baby killer," he said.

"I never said you killed him." *Andrew was a decent man, with a kind heart and the ability to feel love*, Epona had said. "I know exactly where you left him. You see, I can count to six, even when someone says it's five."

"Then why haven't you told the bitch?" he snapped petulantly. He sounded for all the world like a teenager caught out past curfew. "I'm sure she'd be just delighted to know her brat wasn't really murdered."

"I will. Once I take out that insurance."

He laughed chillingly, shook his head, then suddenly his eyes opened wide. He snapped his fingers and stared at me. "Wait. I know who you are. Yeah. King Philip's childhood friend, let me think . . . LaCrosse. Edward, the current Baron LaCrosse."

This bothered me a lot more than I let on. How the hell could he know that?

His demeanor changed almost at once, and his smile grew vicious. "I know a fair bit about you, too. Golden boy gone bad, as I recall. You let a bunch of trail raiders rape and murder the princess of Arentia."

I tried to minimize it. "Old news."

"To some, maybe. But a fellow like you doesn't get over something like that, ever." He waddled toward me, and the candlelight illuminated his cold, malevolent grin. All trace of the hurt victim had vanished. "When you're built like me, you learn pretty quickly that the only thing stronger than muscle or steel is information. And I know something about that day I just bet you never told anyone."

I barely got out the words, "Nothing to do with this."

He continued as if I hadn't spoken. "You're more responsible for the death of the late Princess Janet than you ever let on. See, there were over a dozen thugs involved that day, and by the time they were finally chased down, a couple of them had left and been replaced by new men. One of those veterans ended up working for me, and he told me a very interesting story."

This couldn't be true. The Arentian army had hunted down and slaughtered all of the ones I hadn't killed. It was in the news broadsheets. I'd read about it myself. I even identified some of the bodies.

"He said they were riding down the road minding their own business, on their way to a job in Hefron and not even out to cause any trouble, when they passed the spot where you and the princess were picnicking by a lake. One of his buddies made a pretty rude comment about the young lady."

Like black bile boiling through a thin crust, that afternoon came back to me. I felt the glorious sunshine, smelled the flowers, saw Janet's tears of happiness when she accepted my proposal of marriage. Then *they* rode past.

I'd do her from behind, the big bearded guy said loud enough for me to hear, and the rest of them laughed.

"You got all irate about it and acted like you were some hotshot," the Dwarf continued.

I'd jumped to my feet and yelled, *Hey! You apologize to the lady!*

"They intended to ride on, assuming you were some local farm boy showing off for his girlfriend. But you wouldn't let it go."

Eddie, forget about it, Janet had said. *It's no big deal. Don't let it ruin the whole day.*

"You hopped the fence and drew your sword."

Eddie! she'd yelled, more annoyed than frightened. *Stop acting like an idiot!*

"You challenged the guy who'd made the remark to a duel, right there on the spot."

Fancy sword you got, the bearded guy said, and took a lazy swipe at me with his own weapon, intending to just smack me with the flat of his blade. But I parried it, and stabbed him in the heart. The entire fight took seconds.

"And when you killed him, that's when the rest of them got pissed off."

Holy shit, he's dead! a greasy little guy had exclaimed, bending over the fallen man. Then he looked at me. *You son of a bitch, he was just goofin' around!*

"You were tougher than they thought, and you took down a bunch of them before they finally got you under control. By then everyone was freaking out, and they took it all out on your girlfriend. They made you watch, too, then thought they'd killed you. But they were wrong."

Shit, she's dead, one of them had said, rising from Janet's body, his groin covered in her blood. *Then so's this asshole*, another one replied, and drove his sword into me. He missed my heart but got my lung, and I felt like I was burning alive inside my chest. Janet's eyes were open, and one of the men nudged her head with his boot so that it lolled to the side and stared at me. I gagged on my own blood and felt it run down my chin.

"When they found you, they called you a hero, didn't they? But you always knew better."

The Dwarf's words grew distant, even though he was three feet away. My heart was so loud I could barely think.

He was *right*, and I'd spent the intervening years rewriting the story in my own head just so I could make it through each day. We'd both been victims, I'd fought heroically, and I left Arentia from my own deep-seated nobility, not . . . not my utter shame at the truth. This was the darkest thing in my soul, and this minute monster had just dragged it into the candlelight of his own little sanctuary.

"And you think solving this great crime will make it up to her brother, don't you? That's the whole reason you've done this." He laughed. "And you called *me* a freak."

I'd been prepared for anything, I thought, but not this. The room seemed impossibly small and hot now, and my breath came in shallow, rapid bursts. My chest tightened painfully, especially around the old sword scar. I'd spent so long holding all this inside, keeping it hidden, that I had no idea how to let it out. It logjammed in my throat, choking me.

But luckily, my professional reflexes weren't emotionally involved. When the Dwarf aimed his tiny, probably poisoned stiletto at me, my arm reacted before I even knew it. I palmed the knife in my sleeve and stepped aside, avoiding his blow and striking my own right in the little bozo's heart. As I spun, I drew my sword and slammed my back into the door, ready to defend myself, although I knew I'd dealt him a lethal blow.

The Dwarf wobbled a little, then regained his balance. He looked down curiously at the knife stuck in his chest. A trickle of blood oozed out around it. "Hmph," he said, wincing. "You are quicker than you look."

I stared and didn't move. My *knife* was stuck in his *heart*. I'd felt it strike home; no bone or hidden armor had deflected it. He should be dead, or at least seriously inconvenienced. But it seemed no more urgent than a mosquito bite.

He looked up at me, amused by my shock. "Come on, you know what she did to me. She wouldn't let me die. That means no one can kill me. That's why I went to see her in Arentia."

Then something occurred to him. With a grin of comprehension, he said, "My God, you never really *believed* her until this moment, did you?" He threw back his head and positively cackled. "That's great!"

"What the fuck *are* you?" I said. My voice sounded weak and raw.

He sang, "I'm Andrew Reese, and I'm broken to pieces." He laughed again. "You think *that's* hard to believe? How's this: that time I spent on her island?"

He stepped closer and looked into my eyes. "That was *five hundred years ago*."

TWENTY-SIX

The sky grew lighter in the east by the time I left the Dwarf's estate. As I crossed the yard toward the gate, the monkeys in the trees stirred and hooted at me. The noise was both loud and somehow arrogant. I bet the neighbors loved this guy.

I was numb in every imaginable way. I walked out in a true daze, not caring if anyone saw me. Since I was splattered with dirt and blood, and carried something that would have been impossible to explain, only dumb luck or divine guidance got me out of the house and down the street unseen. I even left the gate open, out of some perverse desire to show off my gory handiwork.

I shambled along the curb toward my horse. If anyone saw me, they must have assumed I was some drunken reveler returning home. Lola still waited patiently under the tree branch, although a ticket stuck over my saddle horn warned me against leaving my horse on the street in the future. She snorted and pawed nervously as I approached, overpowered by the smell of blood and violence around me.

"Shh, girl, I know, just take it easy," I murmured. She quieted down but still watched me closely, especially the package I carried wrapped in part of a fancy table-cloth. If animals are as sensitive as some people say, this object must have well and truly terrified her.

I climbed onto her back and nudged her into the street. It was bright enough to see the city below us as we descended toward it, and the sails of ships in the harbor glowed pink with the dawn. I passed a milk wagon laboring its way toward the mansions; I hoped it wasn't the day the milkman collected his bills.

In my room, I undressed and stuffed all my bloody clothes, even my boots, into the fireplace. There wasn't much kindling available, since most travelers didn't use fires in the summer, but the owner accepted my story that I needed to sweat out a case of the sniffles and scrounged up some extra wood for me.

The intense heat and perspiration helped me reconnect to the world outside my addled head. I lay naked on the floor in front of the hearth, shivering despite the fire, and let my mind go back over the night. It wasn't pleasant, but I knew if I tried to deny it, or rewrite it as I had Janet's death, it too would blindside me in the future. I was through lying to myself, about anything.

Eventually I fell asleep. At first my dreams mingled Janet's awful death with what I had done at the Dwarf's mansion, but suddenly all that fell away and I found myself, surprisingly, standing outside Epona Gray's cottage. The sun was bright, and multicolored birds flitted through the air leaving trails of shimmering sparks. The little building was neat and intact.

The door opened, and Epona emerged. She was staggeringly beautiful, her dark hair loose and shiny and her skin radiant. She was barefoot and wore a flowing, low-cut gown. Her eyes twinkled with amusement. She crossed her arms and leaned against the lintel. "So you figured it out."

"Yeah," I said.

"Neither of us lied."

"I know."

"And you believe it?"

An emotion I couldn't identify swelled in me. My vision blurred with tears. "I believe it. I believe you. I believe *in* you."

She laughed, but gently. "Please, Eddie, don't get maudlin on me now. You still have a lot of work to do. But you fought down the darkest things within you, and you deserve a rest. So take this as a gift."

Three of the shimmering birds flew down and hovered, like hummingbirds, before me. I held out my hand, and one of them tentatively came forward, nudged me with his tiny beak and then settled into my palm. At the instant of contact, I felt lighter, younger and happier than I could ever remember. All the weight of guilt, self-doubt and regret left me. I think I cried out.

But whatever happened, it woke me up. The position of the sun through the window told me it was well past noon. My muscles ached, and my joints popped as I uncurled from my fetal position. The fire had done its job and consumed all my incriminating belongings, and was now reduced to smoldering coals. I spread the ashes so they would extinguish on their own, and poured water in the basin so I could clean up.

I looked at myself in the mirror, pale and still shaky, and accepted that the person I saw there had indeed done the things I had done. The weight of a lifetime of deceit was gone, and I recalled Epona's magical bird from the dream. Had it been a genuine vision, or just my own mind rationalizing me out of my despair? At this point, I could accept anything as real.

I washed up, put on some clean clothes and my extra pair of boots, packed the rest of my stuff and prepared to leave. I took special care with my souvenir from the Dwarf's house; an awful lot depended on it reaching its destination. Just as I tossed the bag over my shoulder, someone knocked at my door. I knew it was Bernie before I opened it.

He wore a neat, pressed official uniform and was freshly shaved. His eyes were cold and professional. "Leaving town?" he said without even glancing at my bag.

"Good morning to you, too," I said as I stepped aside to let him enter.

"It's afternoon," he snapped, and closed the door behind him. "You know where I've been for the last five hours? Up on Brillion Hill investigating the murders of Clarence Canino and Gretchen Paltrow. Some delivery man found 'em dead on a back porch, and the folks in that part of town like to feel safe. So they expect an arrest to happen quickly." His eyes swept the room, taking in the fresh ashes. "Know anything about it?"

"Nah. Tanko gave me a bogus address. The number didn't even exist."

He held out his hand. "Let me see it."

I looked him in the eye. "I threw it away."

He walked to the window and opened it. "It's hot as my fat wife's armpit in here," he muttered. The salty wind lifted the curtains and stirred the ash in the fire as it made a breeze up the chimney. Bernie knelt by the hearth. "Buttons in with the coals," he said. "Somebody burning clothes?"

"Not much firewood this time of year."

He looked up at me. "Did you kill 'em, Eddie?"

I shook my head. "I shot Canino, but the girl killed him. He gutted her before he died."

"What about the Dwarf?'

I shrugged. "Apparently he doesn't exist."

"You mean anymore."

I smiled. "Bernie, if I'd killed the guy, I'd tell you. You know that."

"We found a whole house laid out for special access. We found clothes cut to fit a dwarf. We found an awful lot of blood in the wine cellar, and what looked for all the world like a fresh grave. But when we dug it up, no one was in it."

"And you think I did all that?"

"Somebody did."

I went to the window and looked out at the clean, twinkling ocean far below. "Bernie, I swear to you, I didn't kill anybody. Not Canino, not the girl, not the Dwarf. I'm not saying I wouldn't have, just that I didn't. And that'll have to do you. I'm still working for my client, so I can't tell you any more than that." I turned to face him. "I'm going to leave now, unless you plan to arrest me."

He nodded at the window. "Lean out a little and look to the north."

I did, and saw a dark plume of smoke rising into the sky. It came from one of the warehouses along the docks. "The Dragonfly?"

"Yep," he nodded. "Already burning down. The fire crew is down there trying to save the other warehouses, the legitimate ones. No telling how many bodies we'll find in there."

I felt a brief pang for spike-necked Allison, but her fate was out of my hands. "Hm. Quite a coincidence."

"And you had nothing to do with that, either?"

"Not a thing."

Bernie ran his hand along the mantel above the fireplace. "I got no reason to doubt you, I suppose. And nothing to really hold you on. In a few months, I may decide you've done me, the city and the common good a big favor." His eyes snapped up to meet mine. "But for right now, I'd just as soon you left town. Quietly. And don't come back for a visit before winter. By then, I should be your pal again."

I nodded. I didn't offer my hand, and neither did he. I left without another word.

I RETURNED QUIETLY and quickly to Arentia. I took a room above a pub in one of the far-flung suburbs of Arentia City. I wasn't yet ready to approach Phil; at least one major task remained to be accomplished. But I needed reliable, discrete assistance.

I didn't know how to reach Sir Michael Anders directly without giving myself away to the rest of Arentia's officialdom. But he'd been quite free with the details about his young lady friend Rachel, and I recalled her highborn family from my own youth. I sent a messenger boy to her requesting she forward my confidential request to Anders. It took several days, but eventually he showed up at the pub, dressed like any other tradesman on a day off.

He sat down next to me at the bar without a glance, and when the bartender moved out of earshot said softly, "You look awful."

"That's because I work for a living," I murmured back. "We need to talk; meet me out in the barn in ten minutes." His nod of assent was so slight I barely caught it.

I paid for my drink and went behind the building to the stable, where Lola stood patiently in her stall. I picked up a brush and stroked her neck and mane while I waited for Anders. He arrived casually, although I knew he'd verified that no one followed him. If I hadn't been alone, he would have feigned confusion and asked for directions back to the main road.

He leaned against the door of the stall. "Hey, that's the same horse you stole in Pema."

"Yeah."

"I thought you would've made horse stew of her by now."

"She's not so bad. Better than some people I know. Excluding present company."

"Thanks. So what's so urgent you had to worry my girlfriend to reach me?"

I stopped brushing Lola and looked at him seriously. "I need a huge, possibly career-ending favor from you."

He didn't blink. "Like what?"

"I need to get in and see Rhiannon alone."

He chewed his lip for a moment before saying, "I guess you know about her sentence."

"Just what I've heard second-hand."

"The king imprisoned her for life at the main city gate. Her cell is built into the actual wall itself. During the day she has to come out into a cage, sit on a stool and basically take any shit anyone wants to throw at her, symbolic or literal. At night, she's locked into her chamber. The guards are forbidden to let anyone else near her; even they can't speak to her except to give instructions. I know them; they won't bribe, and I'd hate to take them on in a fight."

"Can we trick them?"

He shook his head. "If it were any other prisoner, maybe. Not this one. She's all they have to worry about."

"I *have* to see her alone, Mike. I can't tell you any more than that right now, but it's the only way to get Phil back his son."

It took a moment for this to register. He only reacted with his eyes. "The prince is alive?" he whispered.

I nodded.

"And you know where he is?"

I nodded again.

"Then why aren't we going to get him?"

"Because he's safe where he is. If we bring him back here, I have to be sure there won't be another try on his life. And to *be* sure, I need to be alone with the queen."

Anders nodded. He climbed onto the stall gate and idly swung back and forth, like a thoughtful adolescent. Finally he said, "I outrank them. I can order them to leave their post. It won't stay secret for long, though."

"I don't need long. Twenty minutes will be enough."

He stepped back to the ground. "You're right, I'd be risking my career to trust you. If you let me down, my new job will be kicking your ass."

I grinned. After the sleazy folk I'd met in Cape Querna, working with Anders was like rain on a hot afternoon. "Fair enough."

We scheduled our jailhouse visit for the following evening. The next day I entered Arentia City on foot with the rest of the proletariat during the morning rush.

I wanted to see Rhiannon's public punishment for myself.

The walls around Arentia City dated from a time when their strength meant the very survival of the culture. Fifteen feet thick and thirty feet high, they now served mainly as traffic control, funneling pedestrians and wagons onto the four main thoroughfares. Every few years a city commissioner or busybody noble would suggest either tearing down the old wall or knocking extra gates in it, but nothing ever happened. For one thing, it would mean redesigning all the money, which prominently featured Arentia City's walled skyline.

The wall, though, wasn't a solid barrier. It housed a network of passageways and rooms designed to shelter soldiers under battle conditions. One of these rooms had been remodeled and secured to function as Queen Rhiannon's permanent prison cell. It contained a cot, a small table and the basics of toiletry, but nothing else was allowed. She could have no comforts or personal belongings at all. Food was delivered through a slot, and dishes passed out the same way. She was issued one candle a month.

Her cell opened straight out of the wall on the city side. A metal cage bolted to the stone enclosed the doorway and the space in front of it, where a crude stool became her new throne. The exposed sides allowed the citizens an unobstructed view of their fallen queen when, every day, she emerged at dawn to take her place in the cage and endure her public punishment.

In the time I'd been gone, a cottage industry had sprung up around the queen and her crime. Two books had been rushed through scribing, and there was talk of a major theatrical production. A singer named Stephanie something was packing them in with her song about Rhiannon. An enterprising artist had produced a line-drawing parody of the queen's official portrait, modified to show a tiny foot hanging from her mouth. He sold this image on flags, tunics and ale mugs.

Folks working the early shift had made the queen's morning humiliation part of their breakfast routine. A hundred people had already gathered around the cage by the time I reached it. Some sipped tea and nibbled on toast, others exchanged gossip or greeted old friends. It felt more like a temple social than a public shaming.

Then a hush spread through the crowd. The metal door inside the cage opened, and Rhiannon emerged from her cell. She was now gaunt and pale, with dark circles under her eyes and hair frayed and ragged with neglect. She wore a dress made entirely of old muslin rags haphazardly sewn together. Her bare feet and legs were dirty. She shuffled to the stool without looking up at the crowd.

I stayed far enough back that I doubted she'd either spot me, or recognize me if she did. I saw an awful lot of sympathy on the faces of the folks watching, who'd witnessed the gradual breakdown of the once-proud beauty. As far as they knew, she'd committed one of the worst crimes imaginable, but that had happened out of sight, in the great castle that looked down on them. Her slow decay in the cage was front and center every morning, and I doubted anyone could see it day after day and not feel something.

Rhiannon settled onto the stool. The frayed dress revealed generous amounts of skin, but there was nothing erotic about it. She was too drained and insubstantial. Finally she looked around at the faces, some of which must have grown familiar. Her eyes shone with either fever or tears. She lowered her head and her posture collapsed as she prepared for the day's abuse.

No one spoke at first. Some folks muttered "bitch" and "murderer," but not loudly enough to be identified. A few walked away in disgust. Had the novelty of tormenting the queen worn off so quickly?

Then four teenagers, two well-dressed rich boys and their adoring, giggly girlfriends, wormed their way to the front of the crowd and pressed their faces against the bars. They hooted and laughed at the despondent queen. Rhiannon glanced at them for a moment, then cast her eyes back down.

"Hey, do you know how a baby is like a grape?" one of the boys loudly asked.

"They both give a little whiiiiine when you stomp them!" the other boy cackled.

The girls laughed as well. A few onlookers tittered or glared at the kids, but most of them simply looked elsewhere. No one spoke up for the queen.

"Hey, you know what's pink and spits?" one of the girls asked. "A baby in a frying pan!"

Again they laughed. And still no one chastised them or defended Rhiannon. She sat, head down, hands limp in her lap. My own temper raged at these amoral punks, but I reminded myself that, for them, Rhiannon *was* guilty of a truly ghastly crime. This was part of her legal punishment. Still, the cruel enjoyment they got from it turned my stomach, and I saw from other faces in the crowd that they felt the same way. But no one stepped forward to do anything. Including me.

"Come on, this is booooring," one of the girls said, and pulled at her boyfriend's arm.

"No, wait, I got one more," he said. "Why do you stick a baby in a boiling cauldron feet first? So you can see the look on its face!"

Satisfied that they'd asserted their moral superiority, they pushed their way through the crowd to the main road and disappeared in the traffic. A ripple of relief passed through the spectators. "Goddam spoiled brats," one man muttered. "Assholes," snarled another.

Rhiannon hadn't moved. She remained hunched over, small and weak and broken, a shadow of the glamorous prisoner I'd seen only weeks earlier. Her filthy hair hung stringy and loose, where previously it had shimmered like gold.

Murmuring conversation resumed around her, and the watchers drifted away to their respective jobs. Finally there were too few people for me to hide very well, and I turned to depart. Although we'd only met once, I couldn't count on her not recognizing me. I couldn't count on anything about her.

Movement caught my eye. A tiny bird dropped from its perch on the bars across the top of the cage and hovered for just a moment beside Rhiannon's slumped form. I couldn't see if it touched her or not. Then it skittered away back into the sky.

Rhiannon took a deep breath, and suddenly sat upright. She tossed her unkempt, dirty hair from her face and looked out at the watchers. It was as if somehow the bird had given her a shot of energy, or as the one in my dream had done, taken away a big chunk of her anguish.

I recalled the birds on her windowsill in the prison tower the day I met her. Had they been the same kind? The same birds that lurked around Epona Gray's cottage?

I discreetly hung around the area for the rest of the morning and watched the other watchers. Most people simply ignored Rhiannon, and she paid them no mind. She occasionally looked around or changed position, but most of the time she just sat, head down, immobile.

The resemblance to Epona Gray had been strong before, but now it was uncanny. Rhiannon had lost so much weight that her once-show-stopping curves had straightened into angular lines, and the occasional ragged cough spoke of potential illness. Like Epona, she was dying. Unlike Epona, I might be in time to help.

When a summer storm hit shortly after lunch she sought no shelter, but remained on her stool as the rain beat down. I gathered it was the closest thing to a bath she got. As I watched from beneath a shop awning, she cupped her hands and drank the collected water. She raised her face to the sky, eyes closed, and let the rain pummel her. In the gray light she looked blood-drained and colorless.

My thoughts turned to Phil, ensconced in his luxurious castle. I didn't have to see him to know his condition. He was in agony as well, knowing his wife and child were suffering and unable to do anything to help them, except trust me. Trust the guy who'd caused his sister's death.

I had a theory that explained how the woman in the cage could be both Epona Gray and Rhiannon. If I was right, I was a goddamned genius. If not, then it was a cold, heartless universe and I didn't want to live in it anymore.

Thunder boomed overhead. Rhiannon flinched.

I would know soon.

TWENTY-SEVEN

〜

"Fifteen minutes," Anders said.

"We talked about twenty."

"Yeah, well, it's an imperfect world."

He pressed the key to Rhiannon's cell into my hand. Then he went to wait at the guard station where, moments earlier, he'd dismissed the two men on duty. They had not been happy about it, and left with promises to go straight to their division commander. Those lost five minutes were probably a measure of how upset they were.

The room inside the wall had originally been a siege armory, and the old weapon racks remained, rusted and empty. A bunk allowed one guard to sleep while the other remained on duty. A table bore evidence of a recent card game. And at one end of the room, a new wall closed off what was now the queen's chamber.

Except for the narrow meal slot, the inner cell door had not been opened since Rhiannon was first incarcerated. The key took some real effort to turn in the lock, and the bolt mechanism scraped like a frying cat. The lamp from the antechamber threw a shaft of yellow light through the opening.

Awakened by the noise, Rhiannon sat on the edge of her bed and clutched the blanket around her. Her ragged clothes, still damp from the rain, lay neatly across the table. "Who are you?" she gasped, fear in her voice. "Please, no one's supposed to be in here."

"That's true," I said as I lit a candle. "Not even you." The room smelled of sweat and dirt, a damp odor that invoked the creepy feel of mold and fungus. I held up the light so she could see my face.

"Mr. LaCrosse," she said blankly.

"We don't have a lot of time," I said as I put the candle on the table. I grabbed the blanket and yanked it away from her; the thin fabric ripped as she tried to protect her modesty.

"No, please!" she gasped, pitiful and helpless. She wrapped her arms around her emaciated torso and pressed her legs together. "This isn't right, you shouldn't do this," she said without looking at me.

I pushed her back on the cot, held her down with one hand over her mouth and used my knee to part her legs. She screamed, but it was so thin and muffled no one outside the room could've heard it. She had no strength to fight, but she thrashed and struggled as best she could.

I lifted her left leg to see her inner thigh in the candlelight. And there it was: the same horseshoe scar as Epona Gray. I'd touched her, so I knew she was tangible; and now that I'd confirmed the scar, I knew a lot more. I released her, climbed off the bed and tossed the blanket back at her.

She wrapped herself in it and huddled back against the wall. "Why did you stop?" she spat. "Was I too dirty? Now that I'm just a common prisoner, I don't even rate your brutality? Is that it?"

I couldn't look at her. My voice was very quiet when I said, "I needed to satisfy myself about something. Now I have."

Her fury, though, was just getting started. "You still think I'm lying about my amnesia, don't you? Well, look around you. Would I lie just so I could be kept here for the rest of my life? What secret could be worse than this?" She tied the blanket under her arms and got to her feet. "You said you were Philip's friend. That meant you were supposed to be mine, too, because he *loved* me then! Where were you when he was condemning me?"

I faced her. "You didn't kill your son. I know it, I can prove it, and even more, I know exactly where he is."

She did not react for a long moment. Finally, in a tiny voice, she asked, "Where?"

"I'll get to that. First I need you to do something that's going to seem kind of strange, but if you don't, you and anyone you care about will never be truly safe." I reached into my pocket and brought out the small opaque jar I'd claimed at the Dwarf's house to hold my souvenir. I opened the top. "Hold out your hands. And it's pretty disgusting, so be ready."

I poured the contents into her cupped palms. She jumped, but didn't drop it. She turned slowly toward the candle, as if more light would make it less repulsive. "What is it?"

"It's a heart."

She looked at me, eyes wide inside their dark circles. "A *human* heart?" she whispered.

I shrugged. "Maybe."

At least it had been once, when a rough-hewn sailor washed ashore on a beach five centuries earlier. And when I'd attacked the Dwarf in his little sanctuary, pinned him with my weight and used my knife to carve the organ from his chest, deep down I truly thought it would turn out to be a normal human heart. Certainly the hot blood that spewed from him seemed mortal, as did his terrified screams for help. Thanks to his over-confidence, though, there was no one in the house to hear them.

But it wasn't until I held the bloody thing in my hand and stood up that I realized the full extent of Epona's curse. Five hundred years earlier she'd doomed him to a life of unending pain and torment; that meant that even though I'd removed his most essential living organ, he would not *die*. He writhed on the floor, experiencing every moment of the agony that would've long ago killed anyone else. The sounds he made barely qualified as human.

"You *bastard!*" he finally gasped. His hands flopped like the fins of a landlocked bass. "I have . . . all of your life . . . to get you back for this!"

I looked at the heart, then at the man without it. For the first time in this whole nasty business, I was absolutely sure I was right. "Remember what you said about information? You gave out a little too much. You told me how to kill you."

His back arched, and blood poured from the ragged gash in his chest. "You . . . *can't* kill me, you . . . *asshole!*" he spat through clenched teeth.

"You're right." Although I was covered in blood, in my head I was somewhere very calm, completely clear about what I needed to do. "And I won't."

Then I'd gagged him, wrapped him in a blanket, tied him with rope and buried him in the center of his own hedge maze. His struggles and curses grew weaker but never stopped entirely, and I imagined that when I'd pounded the last spadeful of dirt on top of him, I could still faintly hear his muffled voice. I carefully put the sod in place and hid all evidence of my tampering. Then I dug a fake grave in the wine cellar to throw off anyone who came looking for him. As far as I knew he was still buried, still in agony, and would probably, eventually, worm his way out like a blood-drained grub. And I had no doubt he would make good on his promised revenge if I turned out to be wrong.

Now Rhiannon stared down at the heart of Andrew Reese in her trembling hands. "It's still warm," she whispered.

"Yes. I need you to crush it."

Her eyes popped wide. "What?"

"Crush it, rip it apart, tear it up. Destroy it. Only you can do it, and you won't ever be safe *unless* you do it."

She swallowed hard. "Whose heart is it?"

I shook my head. "I can't tell you. But it was the person behind everything that's happened. You have to trust me, Rhiannon."

After a moment she smiled a little. "I never heard you say my name before."

I heard a distant thud, like a door slamming somewhere within the wall's network of tunnels. "There's not a lot of time," I said.

She nodded, bit her lip and squeezed the organ in her right hand. Blood oozed out between her fingers. Then she twisted it, wrenching the tough muscle tissue until it finally began to tear. She grunted with the effort, the tendons straining on her skinny arms. Her face darkened, and her repressed fury and rage flowed into her hands. The heart slipped and popped as she thrust her fingers into the holes and tore ventricle from auricle with all her strength, at long last literally breaking Andrew Reese to pieces.

Finally it lay in ragged chunks on the floor, and they quickly shriveled into hard, blackened blobs. I crushed one beneath my boot; it fell to powder. Hopefully back in his long-overdue grave, the same thing happened to the Dwarf.

Rhiannon's fingers were bloody, and droplets spattered the blanket and her bare shoulders. She breathed in great ragged gasps. Then she looked at me and raised her crimson hands. Her eyes gleamed with tears barely held in check. "Who am I, Mr. LaCrosse?" she asked softly. "*What* am I?"

You're a goddess, I wanted to tell her. You visited this world twice unsuccessfully, once in your real form, and once as an actual human being. Except that the knowledge of your true self tripped you up both times. Your first try created your greatest enemy, and your second one blindsided you with the utter intensity of being human. This time, though, you made yourself forget your divine origin, and so you experienced humanity as one of us, both the noblest and the most base.

But I only said, "You're my best friend's wife."

Anders appeared at the door. "Time's up," he said urgently, then as an afterthought nodded at Rhiannon. "Your Majesty."

"We're taking her out of here," I said.

Anders blinked. "We are."

"We're going to get her son. Then we're bringing them both home."

I heard crisp soldier-shouts down the hall behind Anders. "That could be a little bit of a hassle," he pointed out.

I grinned. "Nah. Just follow me."

Halfway down the hall, a torch burned in a bent and corroded sconce. Beneath it I pressed a single loose stone and a hidden door scraped open. Anders, then Rhiannon, and finally I slipped through, and the door closed behind us just as the reinforcements obliviously ran past.

"How'd you know about this?" Anders whispered in the dark. "I spent half an hour today looking over the diagrams of this place, and it wasn't there."

I didn't answer. The story involved me, Phil and a badger that escaped from us when we tried to sneak it into the castle. Phil still had a tiny scar on his right thumb where the animal expressed its displeasure. I can't recall *why* we wanted a badger—I think we were nine years old—but one side effect of trying to find the little shit was that we learned some secret passages forgotten since the wall was first built. And without asking I knew that was exactly why Rhiannon's cell had been placed here, near an escape tunnel known only to him and me.

A few minutes later, we emerged outside the wall through another hidden and forgotten door into the dense trees of the King Hyde Memorial Park. The oaks and maples grew higher than the wall, and beneath them were many shadowed clearings. Hidden in one of them, we listened to the commotion caused by our escape on the other side of the wall, and I knew we didn't have long.

"Now where are we going?" Anders hissed.

"To the royal hunting preserve," I said.

Rhiannon looked surprised. "That's where Philip found me."

"Yeah." I turned to Anders. "Can you go get the horses?"

He scowled. "Back where the entire Arentian army is mobilizing to find us? Oh, sure. Would you like a cup of tea, too?" Before I could respond, he'd vanished into the darkness with barely a rustle of the thick vegetation.

I took off my jacket and handed it to Rhiannon. She pulled it gratefully over the tattered blanket. Then she tentatively reached out and touched the closest branch of the tree that shadowed us.

"I never thought I'd feel living wood again," she said softly. "And don't make a snide comment." She rubbed one leaf gently between her fingers. "Can you feel when something's alive? Sometimes I think I'm the only one who can. Especially now, after being kept away from living things for so long."

She was only an outline in the darkness. I stepped toward her, put my hand on her shoulder, and felt it small and bony beneath my coat's fabric. I turned her toward me. I couldn't see her face, but she gasped.

My hand slid down to her waist and I pulled her close. She was so small and weak it was easy, and I felt her hands on my shoulders. She didn't push me away, though. She did turn her face up, so that the moonlight filtering through the trees glinted off her eyes. "I won't stop you," she said, a whisper so quiet the crickets almost drowned it out.

I held her like that for a long moment as the night flowed around us. If she'd done or said anything, I would have released her. But she didn't. I held my best friend's wife, my own old lover, and an actual goddess in my arms, and I knew she loved me. Not the way she loved Phil, or Pridiri; something reserved only for me, something for which even she didn't know the source. Then I pulled her against me, and held her tight. I needed one last chance to know she was truly real.

Her fragility made me ache in sympathy, as Epona's had thirteen years earlier. I was careful as I wrapped my arms around her. Her unwashed body and oily hair should have been revolting, but they weren't. I felt as if I held a treasure, all the more valuable because even she didn't know what she was.

She shuddered, and for a moment I thought I'd squeezed her too hard. Then she sniffled, "Thank you," into my shoulder. She put her arms around my neck and shook with quiet sobs. I let her cry herself out, until I heard someone approach through the trees. I pushed her into the shadows and drew my sword.

The brush rustled, and Anders stepped into the clearing. "We should go. I've got your horse and mine, but it wasn't feasible to get one for Her Majesty. I'm sorry, ma'am, but you'll have to catch a ride with one of us."

We followed him to the spot he'd left my horse and his own. Lola tossed her head in greeting to me, and I scratched her cheek in return.

Rhiannon stepped up to Lola. Her eyes were as big as the horse's. "This is a strange question, but . . . have I met your horse before?"

"Not in this life," I said, the irony all my own.

She stroked Lola's cheek. "I feel close to all horses, but somehow especially this one," she said, almost a sigh. "She's so smart, and strong, and loyal to you. This mare would die for you, you know, because you've treated her with kindness, and more importantly, respect. She's been your partner, not your property."

Anders looked at me, his eyes wide and skeptical. He clearly thought the queen had gone a bit stir crazy after all that time in her cell, and even I was a little uncomfortable, but for a whole different reason. "She'll do," I agreed.

Suddenly Rhiannon realized how she sounded, and nervously laughed. "I'm sorry, I can't explain any of that. I must've been a horsewoman in my earlier life. Too bad I can't remember it." She smiled sheepishly and handed me Lola's reins.

"Yeah, too bad," Anders agreed. "Can we go now?"

I helped Rhiannon onto the saddle in front of me, both her legs hanging off the right side. She snuggled against my chest as we trotted off toward the road that connected Hyde Park with the royal forest.

It was late enough that the traffic was thin, and the alarm from the queen's escape did not overtake us. I knew that once we reclaimed Pridiri, we could return to the city by the main gate and march right up to the castle door.

When we got within sight of Prince Pridiri's hiding place, we hid off the trail in a thick grove of trees. Mosquitoes, drawn by our sweat and the blood splattered on Rhiannon, swarmed us. I pointed up the path ahead. "He's in there."

Rhiannon gasped. "*That's* who took him?"

"No. But that's where he is."

Anders looked skeptical. "You're sure? I mean . . . "

"I'm sure."

"*Why?*" Rhiannon said, packing outrage and incomprehension into her whispered query.

I dismounted and handed the reins to Rhiannon. "Give me five minutes. Mike, if I haven't signaled you by then, use your best judgment."

I walked out of the woods and down the path to the cottage door. No lights showed behind any of the curtains. I knocked like I really meant business. "Hey! Open up!"

A lamp blazed in a window, and somewhere a baby started crying. I knocked again, and used the same voice that once sent tough mercenaries into battle. "No bullshit, open up! I mean it!"

The door opened, and royal game warden Terry Vint appeared. He held up the lamp to verify my identity. "Eddie?" he said sleepily. "What the hell—"

"I'm here for Pridiri, Terry," I said. "His mom's down the road, and she'll be here in about five minutes. I don't want any trouble."

Shana Vint appeared behind him, holding a fidgety baby. Two other small children clung to her nightgown skirt. "Terry? What's going on?"

"I don't know," Terry said, but I saw the flash of genuine terror in his eyes. "What are you talking about?"

"Just tell me if I've got this right. The night Queen Rhiannon supposedly murdered her son, a scary blond guy showed up here with a baby. He figured one more face in this brood wouldn't be noticed. He wouldn't tell you who the baby was, but he told you to keep him, and threatened your own kids if you let anybody know. You're a good judge of people, Terry, and you could tell he was for real. Once word got out of what happened at the castle, though, you knew who he'd given

you. Hiding him right under the king's nose was brilliant. When the crisis started, Phil had no spare time
for hunting, so nobody came out here. And you kept
quiet, just like you promised."

Terry swallowed hard. "I couldn't risk my family,
Eddie," he finally choked out.

"I know. And you were right, the guy would've
killed any of your kids without blinking. But not anymore."

"How do you know?"

"I was there."

He absorbed this for a moment. Then he sighed,
with both relief and apprehension, and motioned Shana
forward.

She disengaged from her own brood and stepped to
the door, holding the same fat, dark-haired baby I'd
seen in her arms weeks before. Tears ran down her
face. "He already feels like one of mine."

"Eddie, man, damn. How'd you *know*?" Terry asked.

"When I visited you, you told me you had five kids.
Mentioned it a couple of times. I counted six, and
since the baby doesn't look a thing like either one of
you, I could guess who he was." Oh, if only I were so
bright. It took weeks for that nagging detail to finally
announce itself. But nobody else needed to know that.

Shana held Pridiri out to me. I shook my head, and
whistled sharply to signal Anders. To Shana I said,
"You can give him back to his mother."

Rhiannon emerged from the woods like a ghost ma-
terializing from the darkness. Her pale skin and flaxen
hair glowed bone-white in the moonlight. Shana gasped,
for a moment actually convinced this was some ghoul-
ish banshee. Then Anders appeared behind her, leading

the horses. I stepped aside so Rhiannon could see her son.

With a cry she ran forward, practically knocked me over and took the baby from Shana. She swayed as she clutched him, murmuring, "Pridiri, Pridiri, my baby." Terry and Shana slowly knelt, and gestured at the rest of their now-awakened clan to do the same.

Rhiannon spun in place, laughing and crying. Finally she stopped, saw the Vints on their knees and wiped at her tears. "I don't know why you hid him from me, Terry," she said, torn between relief and anger, "but thank you for at least keeping him safe."

"They're not the bad guys," I said. "They're victims just like you."

Rhiannon and Shana exchanged a significant, probably mother-exclusive look. Then the queen smiled. "Then I thank you even more for caring enough to protect him. Please, stand up. Under the circumstances it seems silly to be formal."

"Would you like to come in?" Shana said, reflexively polite before she could stop herself. The thought that the queen might accept the invitation visibly terrified her.

Rhiannon looked at me over Pridiri's fuzzy head. "I'd really just like to go home now."

"Yeah," I agreed.

TWENTY-EIGHT

⟨ornament⟩

The city gates were guarded and blocked by the time we returned, but of course they let us through when they saw Rhiannon and Pridiri. After conferring with Anders, the royal guard sent a messenger to the king and cleared a path all the way through town from the gate straight to the castle door. Some of the big, burly soldiers even visibly cried as the queen and crown prince passed them.

Word spread through Arentia City like the spring flood through Neceda, and the streets filled with citizens anxious to witness Rhiannon's triumphal return. By the time we reached the steps that led up to the king's great hall, the cheering had grown so loud it blocked out all other sound, like storm waves crashing on a beach.

Phil, Wentrobe and a dozen castle guards waited at the top of the stairs as our horses stopped at the bottom. The doors to the great hall stood open behind them, and I saw pages frantically lighting the chandeliers. Phil wore his crown and royal cape, and as I dismounted and helped Rhiannon to the ground, he swept down to meet her. I took Lola's reins and pulled her aside so nothing impeded this reunion. But when Phil at last stood before her, neither of them made any move. They faced each other in grim silence.

The cheers gradually faded as it dawned on the crowd that their king had imprisoned an innocent woman, who now stood ragged and filthy before him with the proof of her innocence squirming in her arms. Her feet were planted wide in a fighting stance, and I was near enough to see the fury blazing in her eyes.

Anders stood nearby, his hand casually on his sword hilt. We exchanged a guarded, uncertain look. Like everyone else, we wondered what Phil would do.

The king removed his crown and handed it to Anders. He draped his cape around Rhiannon's shoulders. Formally, he knelt before her.

A gasp went through the crowd; the king of Arentia fell to his knees for *no one*.

Then Phil lowered himself all the way to the ground and publicly kissed his wife's dirty feet.

I swear my hair blew back from the approving scream that erupted from the crowd. Phil stood and wrapped his family in a tight embrace. Our eyes met over the top of Rhiannon's head and I saw the depths of his gratitude.

He retrieved his crown from Anders and placed it on Rhiannon's head. It was too big, and so rode askew on her greasy locks. All of Arentia City laughed.

The rest of the evening—the entire night, in fact— was given over to a spontaneous celebration. It started after Phil and Rhiannon adjourned to their private quarters, where I'm sure the first thing she did was bathe. At least I hope it was. Wentrobe woke the kitchen staff and had them fire up the ovens, then led a raid on the wine cellar. I never saw the old guy move so purposefully. By the time the king, his clean and slightly breathless queen, and their son returned to the great hall the party was in full swing. Someone dragged a band from a tavern and they played ragged, bawdy dancing songs that ordinarily would never have echoed in the palace, especially on Wentrobe's watch.

I drank a little, thanked Anders for all his help, but really didn't feel like joining the party. I was too tired, and too many things had happened that didn't really merit celebrating. Ideally I would've just left, but Phil was no ordinary client and I really did want to see him one last time. So I slipped out and returned to the secret spot on the castle roof until the party died down.

I hadn't noticed how clear the night was until I settled in against the chimney. The stars shone like frozen sparks thrown from lightning, and I easily picked out all the constellations I'd learned in school. The waning moon still provided plenty of illumination.

My attention stayed on the stars. Some believed that each one was the soul of the dead, and they shone more brightly when someone they loved thought of them. Were the two brightest stars that night the souls of Janet and Cathy? I hoped so, because in that glorious sky, I knew they'd found peace.

This high, even in the summer, the night wind grew chilly. Rhiannon still had my jacket, so I shifted to the chimney's opposite side. Here I had a view across the moonlit city, fully alive at the news of the queen's return. A soft rushing sound I attributed to wind at first grew louder until I recognized it as cheering. The *whole town* was still cheering. Wow.

I didn't quite fall asleep, but my mind drifted until

I completely lost track of time. When I snapped back to the moment, I tried to quickly reorient myself by the changed position of the stars. Before I could, though, the rooftop door opened. I thought I'd have to explain that I wasn't some burglar trying to get into the royal treasury, but when I peeked around the chimney, I saw Phil emerge and make his way across the slanted roof. He dropped wearily onto the shingles beside me and leaned back against the brick. "I'm exhausted," he said.

"I bet."

"There'll be another big soiree tonight to officially welcome back the queen. We'd both really like you to stay."

"Can't say no to a king."

He handed me a small flask from inside his jacket. I took a drink and passed it back. "I owe you one," he said.

"Nah. Friends do this stuff."

We sat silently for a while. Then he said, "Is there anything you need to tell me privately? About Ree?"

I slowly shook my head.

"So you didn't find out anything about her past?" he pressed.

"That wasn't what you asked me."

"Come *on*, Eddie, I need to know."

I turned to face him. "Phil, suppose I told you I found out the most horrible, repulsive thing about her? Something that would make you never want to be near her, let alone touch her, ever again. Would you want to know?"

He nodded.

"Now suppose I said I found out the most amazing, transcendent, beautiful thing imaginable about her? And that knowing it would make you feel unworthy to even be in her presence. Would you want to know that?"

"What does *that* mean?"

"It means I don't know who or what the hell she really was before, Phil. But now she's your wife, your queen and the mother of your little boy. And man, does she love you. That'll have to be enough."

He scowled in frustration. "What if something like this happens again?"

"Not a chance," I said with absolute certainty. I *wasn't* that sure, of course, but I wanted Phil to be. And the relief in his eyes was payment enough.

We passed the flask and watched the eastern sky grow lighter until neither of us could keep our eyes open. We went inside, and I slept most of the day. If I dreamed, I don't recall.

THE OFFICIAL PARTY celebrating Rhiannon's exoneration and Pridiri's return from the dead was as big an affair as Wentrobe could organize in a little less than twelve hours. Anyone of note who could get to Arentia City was present, and the free food and liquor meant a lot of people came to town. Phil and Rhiannon held court seated on their matching thrones, each in their best official trimmings. I'd never seen either of them in their work clothes before, and the effect was suitably impressive. They passed Pridiri back and forth often, neither wanting anyone but the other to care for him.

For about ten seconds that evening, I'd considered wearing the LaCrosse crest on my dinner coat. One had mysteriously appeared in my closet, no doubt at Phil's instruction. I tried it on and checked myself out in the mirror; my father looked back at me. I returned it to the closet and dressed in nondescript, borrowed finery.

I lurked around the party's sidelines, raiding the bar and buffet but avoiding anyone who looked like they might recognize me. I also couldn't keep myself from scanning the crowd for ugly chimpanzees. Eventually the sound and noise got to me, and I eased out of the banquet hall. People milled about all areas of the castle, and I pretended to be taking in the wonders of the royal family's art collection until, near midnight, I entered the dark Hall of Portraits. I startled one teenage couple necking in a corner, and they scurried away. It made me smile, though.

Again the big room was lit only by moonlight, only this time I wasn't drunk, and the sounds of joy and life from the banquet soaked through the centuries-old stone walls. I looked up at Janet's picture for a long time before I realized I wasn't alone.

Rhiannon drifted from the shadows. Her golden hair shimmered, and her jewels twinkled like trails left by her mysterious birds. Her gown swished across the marble floor. "I hope I'm not intruding," she said.

"It's your castle."

She laughed. "So why aren't you with the rest of us? Dining on ashes?"

I shrugged. "Maybe. Better for you than crow."

She stood beside me and looked up at the portrait. "Philip told me a lot about her. Sometimes when I look at that painting, I feel like I knew her, too. I feel the loss."

"I'm sorry for that," I said. I meant it.

She took my hand. I didn't look at her. "I owe you more than I can ever repay," she said. "All of us do."

I shrugged. "It's my job."

She turned my face toward her. "No. Not what you did. And what you're still doing. I know you could tell me who I really am. Or I should say, who I used to be. No, don't bother to deny it. But you won't. Because it would do too much damage, wouldn't it?"

"I don't know what you're talking about. Really."

She gazed into my eyes for a long moment, then released my chin and looked away. "I suppose you'll be leaving soon," she said sadly.

"Yeah."

"You don't have to, you know. Your castle and lands are still there. Philip rents them out occasionally, but he's never officially confiscated them to the crown. Even if he had, all you'd have to do is ask."

"Arentia ain't my home anymore. *Isn't* my home anymore. See? I can't even speak good no more. I'd just embarrass all of us."

She laughed. "Just so you know the drawbridge is always down for you." She leaned close and gave me a quick kiss, on the lips, which lingered just an instant too long to be fully chaste. She smelled of clover and sunlit meadows. Then she drifted back toward the great hall, leaving me alone once again.

TWENTY-NINE

~~~~~~~

So I went back to Neceda, not much richer but a fair bit wiser. The mud had disappeared during my absence, and the town was back to its mean, rapacious little self. I'd found a small bag of gold, each piece embossed with Phil's stern profile, hidden in my saddlebags. It wasn't enough to be considered a reward, because he knew I'd never accept it, but it did cover my expenses, which was fair enough.

The first thing I did was arrange a meeting with King Felix's elderly emissary. On a bright morning two months after my return, the old man again sat across from me and regarded me with his tired, defeated eyes. He was dusty, and sagged in his chair as if he'd ridden all night. "Dead?" he repeated flatly. "You're absolutely certain?"

I nodded. "I'm sorry. Pass on my condolences to the king." I nodded at the bag of gold on my desk between us. "And make sure he gets my refund."

He looked at the money as if it were snot that needed wiping away. "And where," he asked coldly, "is her body?"

"Cremated," I said sadly. Oh, was I sad. "I arrived

just as the ceremony started. I verified it was her, but I couldn't convince them to let me retrieve the body. You know how they are."

"Convenient," the old man said.

I shrugged. "Unfortunate."

"No, I think it's pretty fortunate. That you arrive just as the moon priestesses are setting the funeral pyre for the poor indigent girl they'd found murdered. And only you knew it was Princess Lila."

"Still, what's done is done. I don't feel right taking King Felix's money under the circumstances."

The old man took the bag, hefted it in his hand and then tucked it into his belt. "You were gone a long time. If your friend Commander Teller hadn't insisted you were honest, I'd have thought you'd simply taken our money and vanished."

"Something came up while I was gone, and took a little while to resolve."

"More successfully than this, I hope."

I nodded. "It all worked out for the best."

His eyes narrowed as he looked me over. "Perhaps that's it."

"What's it?"

"There's something different about you. In your eyes. Something's not there any longer."

I said nothing.

I followed him downstairs into the tavern. Two uni-formed soldiers from the army of Balaton awaited him, and they all rode out of town together. I closed the door, took a seat and nodded to Callie behind the bar.

She put a tankard in front of me. "Did you make a lot of money off that guy, Mr. LaCrosse? He looked rich."

"He was." I took a drink and smiled wryly. "And unfortunately, he still is."

Callie looked at me, her brow wrinkled in thought. "You know, Mr. LaCrosse, I like you and everything, but sometimes I wonder . . . are you any good at your job?"

I was glad I didn't have a mouthful of ale when she asked me that. "I'll let you know as soon as I figure it out myself."

Angelina stuck out her bottom lip, blew a stray black curl from her face and looked at me with disapproval. "So do you ever plan to really work again?"

"My tab's paid up," I replied.

"Sure. But you're starting to settle and spread, if you know what I mean. You need exercise."

"My kind of job isn't on a schedule like yours. I just worked for six weeks straight, I deserve some time off."

"Hmph," she snorted. "You say you'll only be gone for a couple of days, then you travel all over the place and come back with a sack of gold, a fancy horse and no new scars. Nice work if you can get it, I suppose."

The front door creaked open; the hinges were purposefully left ungreased so no one could slip in unannounced. A tall figure stood backlit by the morning sun. She wore boots and trousers, but her shape was definitely feminine. In her right hand she carried a large, vaguely round cloth-covered object.

Angelina put her hands on her hips. "Come on in, you're letting all the flies out."

She stepped into the room and the door slammed shut behind her. The sleeping man made a slurred, startled sound but didn't awaken. The woman reached into her pocket, pulled out a piece of vellum and, after consulting it, said, "Uh . . . I was told I'd find Edward LaCrosse's office here."

Since I sat right in front of her, she clearly didn't know me, and Angelina knew how to handle this sort of thing. "His office, yeah," she told the newcomer. "It's upstairs. But he ain't in it."

"Great," the woman said wearily. She was about thirty-five, with short red hair and freckles. Her crow's feet and tan told of a lifetime spent outdoors, and she had a healthy, lively glow about her. She put the covered object on the far end of the bar and took a seat. "Guess I'll be doing some waiting, then. Give me something strong enough to pass the time but not so strong I fall in love."

Callie put a tankard in front of her. The redhead took a long drink and sighed. "That'll do it, all right. That'll do it. So do you expect this LaCrosse guy back anytime soon?"

I was sure I didn't know this woman, yet there *was* something familiar about her. I tried to look her over without being obvious, but the longer I did, the more I was sure I'd never seen her before. Finally, I signaled Angelina with a little nod.

"I didn't say he left," she told the redhead. "I just said he wasn't in his office." She jerked her head at me. "Eddie LaCrosse, this is . . . ?"

I stood and walked down the bar. She put down her drink, wiped her mouth with the back of her hand, then extended the same hand to me. "Liz Dumont," she said, "Dumont Confidential Courier Service. Man, you folks are a little paranoid, aren't you?"

Her last name hit me like a brick dropped from a

siege tower, and suddenly I knew why she seemed familiar. If Cathy had lived, *this* is how she would have looked, and the coincidence was too astounding. It was also too astounding to keep off my face, because Liz stared at me like I'd suddenly sprouted horns.

"Whoa, there," she said warningly, and pulled her hand away. "Maybe you ain't seen a redhead in a while, but I'd appreciate it if you wouldn't stare."

"I'm sorry," I said, and sat on the stool beside her. "You just . . . you remind me of someone. Do you have a sister somewhere?"

"Ha!" she snorted. "Yeah, I had a sister. A twin. The original Dumont in Dumont CCS. Do you know her?"

I shook my head.

"Figures. She ran off a long time ago. Haven't heard from her since I took over the business."

Even acknowledging all the strange things I'd experienced lately, this was by far the eeriest. "So, what can I do for you?" I managed with a reasonable facsimile of nonchalance.

She reached into her pocket. "First, I'm supposed to give you this."

She handed me a small, expensive envelope, sealed with wax embossed with a stylized letter "R." My first thought was of another message from a man with the initial "R," delivered by another red-haired woman named Dumont. The hair on my neck stood up.

I turned the envelope over. My name was written in an elegant, feminine hand on the front.

"Wow," Angelina said, "I didn't think any of your girlfriends knew how to write."

"You have no idea," Liz said. "I was in Arentia City, and I got summoned by this good-looking kid to meet this lady right there in the castle. I think she must've been somebody important, because she had that air about her, you know? When she told me where I'd find *this* guy, I almost didn't believe she could know someone here." She shrugged. "No offense."

Callie leaned across the bar, oblivious to the view it gave of her cleavage. "Well, open it, Mr. LaCrosse," she said impatiently. "Maybe you're being courted."

I broke the seal and withdrew the note. On scented paper, I read:

I hope this note, and gift, find you well and happy. I can't explain this, but I feel very strongly that the woman delivering this to you is someone you should meet. It's almost like she's somehow meant to right something that was once done wrong. I know this doesn't make any sense, but I trust that, after all we've been through, you can handle one more bit of strangeness. My love always.

It was signed, *Ree.*

I folded the note, put it back in its envelope and placed it on the counter. Liz scooted the big covered object down the bar toward me. "And then I have to give you this," she said.

I removed the cloth to reveal a birdcage. Inside was one of the tiny shimmering birds I'd seen around Epona, and Rhiannon, and in my dreams. It looked plump and healthy, and flitted among the perches as, no longer covered, it began to sing.

"A bird," Angelina said, surprised and a little disappointed. "Somebody sent you a *bird*."

"Oh, he's adorable," Callie said, and began whistling to it.

"I'm kind of fond of him, too," Liz said as she

watched the bird's antics. "So take good care of him. I've had lots worse company."

"Aw," Angelina teased, "is'm got a wittle fwiend now?"

"Apparently," I agreed, and bent to look more closely. Even inside the cage, it moved so quickly I couldn't see any real details, except that whenever it moved, the air seemed to momentarily sparkle in the space it left behind.

"So what're you going to do with him?" Angelina asked. "Because if you expect me to clean up bird shit while you're gone on one of your 'jobs,' you're lickin' up the wrong thigh."

"I'd never lick up your thigh, Angel, you know that. I'd just taste all that other spit."

She clutched her chest as if stabbed, but her eyes twinkled.

I picked up the cage and walked to the door. I propped it open, unlatched the cage and waited. The bird fluttered inside for a moment, then shot through the opening and vanished into the sky. A moment later I saw it hovering near one of the apple trees beside the road.

I shut the door and went back to the bar. The three women looked at me. I shrugged. "If he wants to stay around, he can stay around."

Angelina sighed and shook her head. She asked Liz, "Are all your jobs this strange?"

Liz laughed. "Some are even weirder." She cut her eyes at me, and I felt a jolt deep in my chest. Liz's bangs fell onto her face, and she tucked them behind her ear with a cocky, adorable little grin. Then, just as she turned away, I swear I saw her cheeks flush red.

I smiled.

Liz finished her drink and produced another sheet of vellum from her pocket. She didn't meet my eyes when she handed it to me and said, "So if you'll just sign this receipt, I'll be on my way."

I took it, Angelina produced a quill and ink bottle from behind the bar, and I was about to sign it when I stopped. "Wait. You can't get paid the rest of your money unless I sign this, can you?"

She sighed; I wasn't the first recipient to point this out. "No, but you're *gonna* sign it because it's the right thing to do." She looked at me, her eyes tired and pleading. "Okay?"

"Yeah, of course I'll sign it," I agreed as I folded it. "But not until we've have some lunch."

"Ohhh, no," Liz said instantly; I wasn't the first recipient to try this, either. "If you're gonna give me a hard time, I'll take my chances convincing my client. Besides, if she truly knows you, I bet she won't be surprised."

"Ah, Eddie ain't so bad," Angelina said. "A little lazy, but otherwise, he's a decent guy."

"And he always says nice things to me," Callie added.

I winked and flipped Callie a coin, then returned my attention to Liz. "Come on. Could a guy who gets sent little birds really be dangerous?"

She tilted her head thoughtfully, and looked so much like her late sister it was spooky. I knew she wasn't Cathy, of course; one woman couldn't replace another. But something Epona had said about Cathy came back to me: *She's close to what you need, closer than you can imagine. But she's not the right one.* Who was I to argue with a goddess?

"All right, you've got a point," Liz said. "But *just lunch*. I'm a busy gal, and I can't spend all day in Neceda." Then she laughed. "Damn, I can't believe I'm doing this."

"Ah, all my dates say that," I said.

She laughed again. It was a good laugh, full of promise. A hell of a laugh if you thought about it.

Turn the page for a preview of

Burn Me
Deadly

Alex Bledsoe

Available September 2009
from Tom Doherty Associates

A TOR HARDCOVER   ISBN 0-7653-2221-8

Copyright © 2009 by Alex Bledsoe

ONE

The blonde dashed out of the darkness into the moonlight, right in front of me.

My horse, Lola, tried to bolt in surprise. I yanked on the reins and drew her up short. She reared and nearly threw me, but I held on and turned her away so she wouldn't trample the woman. We spun for a moment like a trick rider in a show, kicking up dust on the dry, deserted road. Then she found her footing; I pulled the reins tight and managed to regain control.

The cloud raised by our near accident momentarily obscured the woman. As it dissipated, I got a good look at her. She was young, with leaves and twigs tangled in her hair. She wore only an oversize man's jacket that hung past her hands and thighs. Scratches laced her slender legs and dirty, bloody feet. She stood with her eyes closed, face screwed up and arms covering her head as she anticipated the impact.

My voice was higher than normal when I demanded, "What the *hell,* lady? You could've killed us both!"

She opened her eyes and stared at my horse for a long, silent moment. Unscrunched, her moonlit features were very attractive. "Wow," she said softly, "that was close."

"No kidding," I snapped, still battling Lola's skittishness. The mare tossed her head and snorted, not convinced that all the danger had passed. If only I'd been as smart.

The woman's dirty face showed marks of recent tears. She grabbed Lola's bridle and said, "Please, sir, I have to get away from here." She looked over her shoulder toward the dark woods from which she'd emerged. "I'm in terrible danger."

"Uh-huh," I said dubiously. I followed her gaze and saw nothing, but unsnapped the catch on my scabbard just in case. Muscodia was still a pretty uncivilized country, and this road ran for miles through the dense, sparsely inhabited woods between Neceda and Tallega. At this time of night a lot of nefarious things could happen with no one the wiser, and I was too old and too experienced to fall for the frightened-damsel-as-bait bit. "How about you tell me what you're doing out here undressed like that?"

She met my skepticism with a well-practiced imitation of a hurt kitten: she dropped her chin, raised her eyes and pulled her mouth into a tiny pout. I think her lower lip even trembled. "I'm in *danger,* sir. Please, I'll explain everything later, but right now, I must get away from here." She turned her head and moonlight fell on the marks of big fingers around her neck. "Please. Look at me."

"Your husband get mad at you?"

"I don't have a husband. The men who did this did other things as well, but those things . . . don't show."

I scowled. I'd made an overnight run to a big manor

house outside Tallega, delivering a sealed parchment
and a bag of gold to some woman on behalf of a com-
promised nobleman. She'd taken the money, laughed
at the note and slammed the door in my face. Her foot-
men made it abundantly clear I shouldn't wait for a
reply. Now it was after midnight, and what I most
wanted was to be home with Liz, in our nice soft bed
with her nice soft body pressed against me. Also, every
instinct screamed that *this* damsel was trouble the same
way a hurricane was rain.

Still, I couldn't just leave her half-naked on a deserted road in the middle of the night. "All right, climb
on," I said wearily. "I can take you into Neceda." Lola
snorted with disapproval as I scooted back to make
room for the girl on the saddle in front of me. She felt
skinny and weak as she settled back, both her legs dangling off the left side, and clutched the saddle horn. I
nudged the horse with my heels and we trotted off
down the road.

The night was clear, and we stood out plainly on the
road whenever the moon shone through the trees. I
suppressed the urge to keep glancing behind us, or to
spur Lola to a gallop. More than likely whoever had
injured the girl was passed out drunk somewhere; if
not, then I doubted they'd push for a confrontation.
The kind of men who beat up women seldom had the
stomach for a fair fight.

I said into my new companion's ear, "Okay, so
what's going on? Who are you?"

"My name is Laura," she replied. "Laura Lesperitt.
And you?"

"Eddie LaCrosse."

"Ah." She turned and looked back over her shoulder

at me. The helpless maiden look had been replaced by something far more calculating. "From one of the minor noble families in Arentia, then. If it's the same LaCrosses."

She was right, but I saw no need to discuss it; I'd burned those drawbridges years ago. "You know a lot."

She nodded modestly. "A little *about* a lot."

When she offered no further information, I prompted, "And someone strangled you because . . . ?"

"Because I wouldn't tell them what they wanted to know."

"And what's that?"

Again she turned and looked up at me. The moon cast dark shadows that hid her eyes. Her smile was weak and sad. "Oh, Mr. LaCrosse, you think you can help me, don't you? You think you can ride up and save me, like a knight in a children's story. But these are bad, bad people. And if I tell you what they wanted to know, they might do the same thing to you to find it out."

"They might try," I said.

My confidence made no impression. She turned away, looked out at the passing trees and pushed the jacket sleeves up past her elbows. A livid, fresh injury that looked like the touch of a heated iron marred the insides of both arms down to her palms. The pain must've been awful. Her wrists were also rubbed raw and bloody from struggling against ropes or manacles. "They carried me to a small house in the woods three days ago. They took my clothes and kept me in chains. But I had to get away before they made me tell, so I picked the lock when they weren't around and fled. I stole this"—she indicated the jacket—"from a farmhouse where everyone was sleeping."

"Why didn't you ask the farmer for help?"

Again the sad, wan smile. "They had children. I didn't want their blood on my head if I was caught again."

"But you don't mind mine."

She shrugged. "I'd prefer not. But I could live with it better."

"And so you're not going to tell me what this is about?"

She shook her head.

I took a deep breath, feeling like an idiot in advance for what I was about to say. "Look, *I'm* not some farmer. I'm a freelance sword jockey with an awful lot of hilt time behind me; maybe I *can* help."

Again her eyes rose to meet mine with slow, dramatic amusement. "A 'freelance sword jockey,'" she repeated. "So what does that entail? Saving damsels in distress for a fee?"

"Ideally, yeah. But since I'm my own boss, sometimes it's just because I feel like it."

"And you feel like saving me," she said. It wasn't a question.

"I don't know about 'saving' you, but I *am* offering to keep people from beating on you any more tonight. What you tell me after that is up to you."

Something changed in her face, and for a moment she looked ancient, with despair deeper than any I'd ever seen. And I'd seen a lot of despair. "The only way you can help me tonight," she said with slow, deliberate words, "is to get me to Neceda alive. Nothing else will truly help me."

We rode in silence for a bit. The trees began to thin out, and just ahead awaited the edge of the forest. Past it the road descended and snaked across miles of open prairie, as vivid in the moonlight as it might be on an overcast day. Scattered across the plain were small camps of travelers, a few with fires still lit. In the far distance glowed the lamps of Neceda, and just beyond that sparkled the Gusay River. The waxing, nearly full moon lit the vista in shades of blue and white.

When she saw the distant town she sat up straight and tightly grasped my arm. "We may make it," she said softly.

"We'll make it," I said with certainty.

I was tense, and alert, and experienced in just about every sort of attack. So when the blow struck the back of my head, damn near hard enough to knock my beard from my face, I was so surprised it took me a moment to realize I was falling from my saddle onto the road. I'd heard no one approach, either on foot or horseback. These guys were *good*.

I landed awkwardly, too stunned to react but not completely unconscious. Sparks danced around the edges of my vision. My body pinned my sword to the ground; the hilt dug painfully into my side. I reached for it, but my limbs would not respond with any speed.

The dust from our pursuers drifted over me. Above the roar of blood and pain in my head, I heard Laura scream. We were too far for any of those camped on the prairie to come to our aid, even if they were so inclined.

A horse stopped beside me, and someone dismounted almost in my face. Expensive black boots, decorated with a silver dragon design that sparkled in the moonlight, hit the ground. Above them a stern, annoyed voice said, "Shut her the hell up. You can make her scream all you want back at the house, at least until she tells us where it is." Laura's screams were suddenly muffled, as if by a gag or a big hand.

"What about this guy?" another voice asked.

"Bring him along, too," dragon boots said. "We don't know what she told him. Oh, hell, he's waking up."

One of the boots rose out of my field of vision and came down hard on the side of my head.

I AWOKE, SORT of.

My whole skull was numb. My fingers tingled, and when I tried to wiggle them I found my wrists were bound tightly behind my back. I tried to move any other body part, but nothing cooperated.

I lay facedown on a rough wooden floor. A fire lit the room, and I felt its heat from my left. Over its homey smell, I caught the tang of blood and the odor of scorched meat. Or flesh. The air hung with the echo of the sound that had awakened me: a woman's scream.

"Uh-oh," a voice said. "I, uh . . . I think she's dead."

"You *killed* her?" another voice demanded. I recognized it as the one associated with the dragon boots.

"No, I didn't kill her," the first voice said with professional annoyance. "I *do* know how to do this, you know. But look how burned she is."

"From *your* irons."

"No," the torturer insisted. "I didn't do this. Not on her arms and hands."

"How do you know?"

"Because I'm a professional. I have a *style*. See here

on her tits? And here? I made these; they're very specific, they have a pattern and everything. These others are . . . arbitrary."

"What the hell does that mean?" a third male voice demanded. "I'm so tired of you and your damn big words, like you're some kind of wizard or something."

"It means I didn't make those other burns," the torturer sighed.

A moment of silence passed. Again I tried to move, but I was still too foggy. It took every ounce of strength not to fade back into that nice padded darkness.

"No, that's not what it means," dragon boots said, his voice cold with fury. "It means she *moved* them. Sometime between her escape and the time we caught her, she hid them somewhere else. *That's* how she got burned."

"Where?" the clueless third man asked.

"How the hell do I know?" dragon boots exploded. He slammed his hand on a table I couldn't see. Rattling metal told me it held the interrogator's special tools. "We didn't know where she hid them in the first place, so how could we know where they are now?"

"The boss won't be happy," the third man said.

"Let me worry about him," dragon boots snapped.

"What about her boyfriend?" the torturer asked, and nudged me in the side with his foot.

Hands grabbed my hair and bent my neck painfully back so they could look at my face. I played dead, which wasn't hard. "This guy? You saw what he had in his saddle bags. He's just some dumb-ass in the wrong place at the wrong time."

"I could still find out what he knows," the torturer said. His eagerness really did scare me.

"He wouldn't last five minutes in this shape. No, we'll dump them both. Have to start from scratch. We know she hid them around here somewhere, so we'll just keep looking the old-fashioned way."

He released my hair, and my head thumped hard against the floor. That was all it took; I dove back into quiet, peaceful nothingness.

WHEN I WOKE up again, I was bathed in moonlight.

The clear sky above was alive with stars, all twinkling happily at me. I blinked, waited for the dizziness generated by that movement to pass, and then blinked again.

I lay on my back on the ground. I was untied, my arms and legs thrown wide like I wanted to embrace the night. A rock dug painfully into my behind, but I lacked the energy to move away from it. With tremendous concentration I turned my head to the right.

Laura Lesperitt lay beside me. Most of her front teeth, one eye and half an ear were gone. She was naked, and her upper torso was a mass of poker burns, cuts and bruises. I saw what the torturer meant: his points of contact were small and precise, but something else had burned the insides of her arms from wrist to elbow. The scabbing told me she'd been alive when most of it happened, but the milky stare of her remaining eye said she was past the agony now. Insects had already collected around the injuries, and a shadowy canine form slipped through the darkness beyond her: a wolf or coyote, cautiously approaching a free meal.

I tried to rise. I managed a feeble finger-wiggle.

We lay in a gully or a dry creek bed, where the light only reached us because the moon was straight overhead. The sides of the ravine rose sharply and seemed to my befuddled brain as if they might snap closed over us, trapping us in darkness like those fly-catching plants.

Suddenly a shadow blocked the moon. A shape in the air above me grew larger and made a high, keening sound. I knew some birds of prey hunted at night, and I recalled childhood stories of giant owls that would swoop down and snatch misbehaving brats from their beds. I'd never seen a bird large enough to lift a human being, but then again, this night seemed to be all about bad surprises.

Then my brain cleared enough for me to comprehend what I was actually seeing, and I used every last bit of available energy to roll twice, just before my horse, Lola, crashed down onto the spot I'd occupied. Her equine screech of terror ended with the sharp, wet sound of impact. Big globs of something splattered over me.

Three men stood silhouetted in the moonlight on the edge of the cliff. Dust glittered in the air from where they'd driven Lola over the edge. I lay very still; did they realize she had missed me?

I heard their murmurs without catching any words. Then they turned and walked away, apparently convinced I was as dead as my horse, and the girl. Boy, were they in for a surprise, I thought grimly. Especially that bastard with the dragon boots. All I needed was time to catch my breath.

Then I coughed, tasted blood and got a fresh jolt of agony from my side. I realized the girl and I had *also* been tossed off that cliff. I tried to rise, knowing if I stayed put I'd be dead by morning. But just breathing exhausted me, and before I knew it the night wrapped me up and again took away the pain. If this was death, I wouldn't protest.